T0146497

The quaint coastal town of South Cove, California, is all abuzz about the opening of a new specialty shop, Tea Hee. But as Coffee, Books, and More owner Jill Gardner is about to find out, there's nothing cozy about murder . . .

Shop owner Kathi Corbin says she came to South Cove to get away from her estranged family. But is she telling the truth? And did a sinister someone from her past follow her to South Cove? When a woman claiming to be Kathi's sister starts making waves and a dead body is found in a local motel, Jill must step in to clear Kathi's name—without getting herself in hot water.

Books by Lynn Cahoon

The Tourist Trap Mysteries
Tea Cups and Carnage
Murder on Wheels
Killer Run
Dressed to Kill
If the Shoe Kills
Mission to Murder
Guidebook to Murder

Published by Kensington Publishing Corporation

Tea Cups and Carnage

A Tourist Trap Mystery

Lynn Cahoon

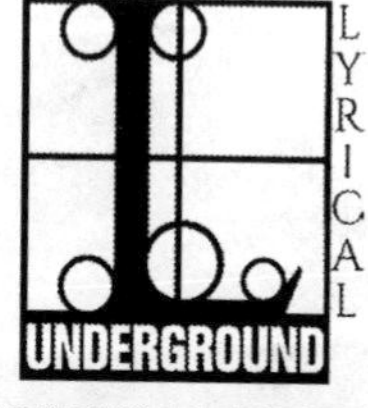

LYRICAL PRESS
Kensington Publishing Corp.
www.kensingtonbooks.com

Lyrical Press books are published by
Kensington Publishing Corp. 119 West 40th Street New York, NY 10018

All Kensington titles, imprints, and distributed lines are available at special quantity discounts for bulk purchases for sales promotion, premiums, fund-raising, and educational or institutional use.

Special book excerpts or customized printings can also be created to fit specific needs. For details, write or phone the office of the Kensington Special Sales Manager:
Kensington Publishing Corp.
119 West 40th Street
New York, NY 10018
Attn. Special Sales Department. Phone: 1-800-221-2647.

First Electronic Edition: June 2016
eISBN-13: 978-1-60183-631-1
eISBN-10: 1-60183-631-7

First Print Edition: April 2016
ISBN-13: 978-1-60183-632-8
ISBN-10: 1-60183-632-5

Printed in the United States of America

To the Florida/Georgia line crew—Thanks for putting up with my murder plotting discussions.

Acknowledgments

Imaginary friends are frowned upon once a child reaches a certain age. As a writer, I spend a lot of time with my imaginary friends. Jill, Aunt Jackie, Greg; they all inhabit my thoughts as I twist around a plot for a new book. Just as important as my imaginary gang is my work gang. These are the people who keep me sane during the day or, sometimes, acknowledge my craziness in a good way. I appreciate the way you see each problem as a challenge and face it with humor and fun.

Much thanks to the writing community. When meeting other authors online or in conferences, I've found out one true fact: We're all the same. In love with storytelling and willing to do anything for a chance to write, one more tale.

As always, thanks to the Kensington crew for making me look good. You all rock.

Chapter 1

Is family defined by blood or is it more than that?

I looked around the table at the June Business-to-Business meeting as attendees started to gather. Aunt Jackie stood with Mary Sullivan, her best friend. I loved hearing them talking about the cruise my aunt and her new boyfriend, Harrold, would be taking in a few months. Bill Sullivan, the committee chair and Mary's husband, stood at the counter, refilling his cup and glancing around the room, as he took stock of the attendance. Typically, these meetings had about ten to fifteen representatives, but summer was the busy season for our tourist town. Even with the busy schedules, we had almost a full house at twenty. I'd had to send Sasha into the back to pull out a couple of boxes of cookies to serve.

They were all here for one reason. Kathi Corbin, the newest member of our community and our committee was holding court over at the couch near the romance section. Kathi's Texas drawl and infectious laugh had the men enthralled. I'd heard rumors the girl had been a Miss San Antonio and had been shortlisted to win Miss Texas, except something had gone awry. She hadn't taken the crown home, ending the competition at the bottom of the top ten.

Having only been in one beauty contest in my entire life and that on a whim, I couldn't imagine where she'd gone wrong. She seemed to play the role well. I walked over to the couch where she was holding court and handed her a cup of coffee. "I'm Jill Gardner, South Cove business liaison to the city council and owner/manager of Coffee, Books, and More." Or at least my aunt lets me think I'm the manager of the shop, even though she makes most of the decisions and then tells me what she's done.

She took the cup from me. “I love your place. I hope we can make some sort of agreement on you guys selling my products over here. If we partner, we’ll both increase our business.”

“Let’s talk next week. I’m sure we can carve out an agreement.” I tried to source locally-made product for the shop. The treats were all made by Pies on the Fly, a local bakery. To me it made good financial sense to help another South Cove business survive. I walked back to the table and surveyed the room.

Sasha paused next to me with a filled carafe of coffee. Sasha’s my newest employee and came to us as an intern through the Work First program last fall. The single mom had quickly fit into our small staff and Aunt Jackie and I decided to hire her after the ten-week program ended.

“She’s quite the charmer,” Sasha whispered. Her happiness made her soft brown skin glow. “Even Josh is offering to get her more coffee.”

I nodded. The room was separated into two groups. The women clustered around the table waiting for the meeting to start, and the men, except Bill, assembled around Kathi. An old Martina McBride song started going in my head about a woman out for fun but before I could answer Sasha, Bill clapped his hands above his head, trying to get everyone’s attention.

“It’s five past starting time, folks. I want to honor your busy schedules as well as our host’s kind offer of her space. I’m pretty sure Jill would rather be serving coffee and this amazing Apple Caramel cheesecake to paying customers.” He smiled at me and waved the group over to the table. “Bring your coffee with you. We’ll pass around the carafes while we’re talking.”

Kathi sat. Josh Thomas and Dustin Austin jostled each other for the chair next to her. As they jockeyed for position, Mayor Baylor slimed into one of the chairs next to Kathi. Austin dodged and dove into the other, leaving Josh holding onto the back and steaming.

“There’s a chair next to Jill,” Bill called out to Josh, the portly owner of Antiques by Thomas and, up until a few months ago, Aunt Jackie’s gentleman caller. I waved at him and pointed to the chair. For my trouble, I got the evil eye as his shoulders slumped and he let go of the chair. Dustin Austin, owner of the bike rental shop, grinned as he tilted his gray dreadlocks toward Kathi’s ear and whispered something that made her laugh.

Bill turned her way and Kathi shook her head. “Sorry, but you all are so entertaining. I can’t believe I didn’t move here years ago.”

“Glad you’re enjoying your first meeting. Now that we’ve all settled in, Mary, do you want to give a summary of the upcoming Summer Beach Blast?” As Bill looked at his wife, I saw the adoration he had for the woman even after so many years.

Mary smoothed her skirt as she stood. "As you know, summer traffic really picks up around the Fourth of July, but June can be a little slow. So we're sponsoring a festival starting tomorrow to bring in tourists and hopefully customers for your shops. Our bed and breakfast is already full for the weekend and we're hearing that the others in town are nearing capacity."

A loud motorcycle roared up Main Street and Mary, along with the rest of the committee members, switched their attention to the window. All I could see was a huge bike with an equally large rider in black leathers. I could see he wore a gang patch on his leather jacket, but couldn't read the lettering in the short time before he disappeared out of my view.

"And that's what worries me about these activities." Pointing to the window and the now-vanished rider, Josh interrupted Mary's presentation. "Are we sure this will bring in the right types? I don't want to see any of those motorcycle gangs taking over South Cove. Let them stay in South Dakota where they can't do any damage."

"Not all motorcycle clubs are gangs." Dustin had started renting scooters in addition to the bikes last month after he'd received a large inheritance from his recently passed wife, Kacey. Well, actually, recently murdered wife. But Austin had been cleared of her death even though I still thought he should be charged with being a royal jerk.

"That's right. My cousin rides a motorcycle and he's not in a gang at all," Kathi added to the discussion. "He just can't afford a real car right now. He's kind of between jobs."

"We bought advertising in upscale local publications, so we're targeting a specific customer." Mary looked around the room, trying to get back to her prepared notes.

"I don't care who comes into town as long as they have money to spend." Harrold held his coffee cup and toasted Mary. "I appreciate you setting up this program. Go ahead, tell us what we can expect."

Mary smiled gratefully at Harrold and I saw my aunt pat his hand. On my left, I could feel the rage coming off Josh like Harrold had just stolen his last dollar. I tried to circumvent the upcoming blowup by diverting the attention back to Mary. "Be sure to mention the beach party on Saturday. That's my favorite part."

"Oh, there's a beach party? I want to help. I've ran a snow cone machine before, do you all have a snow cone specialist?" Kathi clapped her hands together and actually bounced in her chair, gaining the attention of the men at the table. I heard a sharp gasp of air escape Josh's lips.

Mary tapped her empty coffee cup on the table. "If I could have everyone's attention." She waited for the group to turn back toward the front.

Man, those guys must be getting cricks in their necks turning them so much.

"We'll get to the party, Jill." Mary considered Kathi. "I appreciate your enthusiasm for the festival. I'm sure we can find something for you to do to help. Let's just go over the schedule first and maybe something will pop out at you."

She took a breath and dove into the list of events happening starting the next day and running through mid-next week. Mary scheduled the celebration to start on a Wednesday to try to bring in traffic to our normally dead days. We were setting up the new Coffee, Books, and More mobile annex at the beach starting on Thursday. I'd scheduled Sasha and Aunt Jackie to man the main store, but Toby had to be at his real job as one of South Cove's finest. He'd be doing security for the event when he wasn't mixing coffee drinks. I didn't know when the guy slept.

We'd also hired Nick Michaels for the summer. His mom ran Sadie's Pies on the Fly and was one of my BFFs. This would be the kid's first full-time week since he came home from Stanford for the summer. I hoped he was up to the challenge.

As I considered our staffing for the Summer Beach Blast, I noticed the table had gone quiet. Mary had sat down and Bill, and the rest of the table, was looking at me. "Sorry, what?"

"Way to pay attention," Josh muttered. "He asked you if you wanted to attend the city council session next time to present our results."

"Oh, yeah, I could do that." I looked at Mary. "Aren't you going to be there?"

"Our daughter is expecting our first grandchild this month, so I'm heading to Idaho as soon as labor starts." Mary smiled at Bill. "I know I'm leaving at a bad time, but you can't plan babies."

"As long as you leave me talking points, I'd love to step in for you." Okay, so love wasn't quite the emotion I was feeling. I wrote a note so I'd remember to attend. I tended to file my liaison reports electronically and hadn't been present at a council meeting for months. Both Mayor Baylor and I liked it that way. He didn't have to pretend he liked me and I didn't have to be around the guy.

We finished off the rest of the agenda in record time. I looked at Bill, hoping he'd close the meeting early rather than opening the agenda up for new business. Josh fumbled with a list from the pocket of his black suit and ran his hand over the wrinkles in the page that had been folded and unfolded several times. I snuck a peek at the list and groaned. All the items he tried to get onto the committee's agenda month after month were on the list. He must have read my thoughts because he narrowed his eyes and moved the paper out of my line of sight.

"Now, since we have a little time," Bill said, and I watched Josh sit forward in his chair, waiting to pounce on the opening. Bill didn't even look Josh's way as he continued. "I'd love to learn more about our newest member. Kathi, can you tell us a little about you, your new store, and why you came to South Cove?"

The men around the table broke into applause as Kathi stood, blushing. "Why, aren't you all the sweetest things?"

I looked at Aunt Jackie across the table, who shrugged. I guess I just didn't get why Kathi was a big deal. Yes, she had a southern drawl, and, I'll admit she was beautiful, but the men in the room were treating her like some Hollywood starlet had arrived in our little town. I realized Kathi had started talking and I was still zoned out.

"So, I decided to take my love for china into a specialty shop that only sells tea-related items. Tea Hee will sell specialty teas, tea cups, saucers, and tea pots. The idea came to me one day when I was in my grandmother's china cabinet and noticed how many different sets of good china we'd collected over the years. Of course, many of the sets were missing pieces, but they all had enough cups and saucers to put on a good tea party with the girls. And who doesn't like a good tea party on a sunny afternoon?" Kathi paused, looking around the room, focusing her attention at me. "I'm sure Jill and her friends often get together in the afternoons for tea and gossip. Am I right?"

I froze as every member of the table turned their attention to me, shook their heads, and went back to watching Kathi. That just ticked me off. "Actually, no, most of my friends have jobs during the day so afternoon get-togethers are kind of hard to plan. We do like to do girls' night at Darla's winery every week or so."

A flicker of anger or disappointment passed behind Kathi's eyes and then her mask was back on and I questioned even seeing it. "Well, that's just sad. Women need more time to bond. There's nothing like girlfriends to keep your life settled. Men come and go, but a good girlfriend is gold." She shook a finger at me. "That was what my mama always told me when I was a child. You'd be happier if you followed Mama's advice."

I wanted to tell her I had plenty of strong friendships with women, but Amy and I had just gone through a rough patch and I had made Sadie mad a few months ago by not telling her that Greg was going to question her kid. Okay, maybe my female relationships weren't as strong as they needed to be. However, I didn't think that an afternoon of serving tea and cookies at the house was going to make my friendships stronger. Besides, with Kathi's description of her new business, I was sure she'd be back on the train to Texas in less than three months. Teacups were too specialized a niche to generate business for a new shop.

So I smiled and nodded. "Your mother sounds like a smart woman."

"Oh, she was a bit of a drunk and had the worst taste in men, but she did have a good point once in a while." Kathi turned and looked at Mayor Baylor. "Even a blind dog can find a bone once in a while, am I right?"

Our creepy mayor laughed and smirked at me. "Go on Kathi, tell us more about the tea shop. It sounds fascinating."

I tried not to gag, but I must have made some noise in the back of my throat as Bill looked at me. Leaning over the table, he whispered, "Are you all right?"

I was far from all right, but before I could do more than nod, Sherry King pushed open the door to the shop, letting it slam into a table that was sitting a little too close. Pat Williams, her sidekick, rolled her eyes and gently shut the door.

"I'm so sorry I'm late. We had such awful traffic on Highway One from Bakerstown today. Pat and I had our weekly mani-pedi appointment this morning. Frighteningly early, but you all know how hard finding personal time is when you run a successful shop." Sherry pulled a chair up next to Mayor Baylor but twisted her head when she saw Kathi. "Who is she?"

Now, this was getting entertaining. I leaned back in my chair and waved a hand toward Bill, encouraging him to answer Sherry's question.

He coughed into his hand, then made the introductions. "Sherry, this is our newest member, Kathi Corbin. She's opening the shop next to The Glass Slipper." Bill looked at Kathi. "Sherry and Pat run Vintage Duds. Go ahead Kathi, you were saying?"

And with that, he turned the floor back to Kathi, who spoke for over twenty minutes on the subject of Tea Hee, her time in the pageant world, and how she'd made the decision to move because Texas was just so freaking hot.

Sherry's face turned pink five minutes into Kathi's discourse, red at ten, and by the time Bill closed the meeting, I would say Sherry's face was a lovely shade of royal purple. The girl didn't like anyone stealing her limelight and especially not someone who, to be frank, was prettier.

I thought I might just give Sherry a mirror and tell her it was magic. She was acting more like the evil queen than I'd ever seen her reveal in public. And I loved it.

Sue me, I'm shallow. Especially when it comes to my boyfriend's ex-wife. Yep. Greg King, South Cove police detective, and also my boyfriend, had once been married to the woman.

Of course, I knew she didn't see me as competition. How? She'd told me so on more than one occasion.

A smile still curved my lips as I cleaned up after the business meeting. I shoved a chair back under a table and wiped the top of the table clean.

"That was some show." Sasha put two more chairs under the table.

I put the last chair in place and looked around the room. The shop was back in order in a total of eight minutes. We were getting better at this cleanup process. "I wasn't sure you were watching. I saw you over on the couch reading."

"Trying to read. The circus was just too entertaining." Sasha stretched. "I'll watch the shop until Toby gets here. Don't you have a class with Amy this morning?"

"Yeah." I glanced at the clock. I still had ten minutes before I was supposed to meet Amy Newman at the city gym. I retrieved my gym bag from the back office and strolled down Main Street to the building that housed the rec center along with a small daycare. Sasha had Olivia on the waiting list for the next open slot.

South Cove sat smack dab in the center of the coast line. We got our traffic from tourists wandering down Highway One and looking for a quick bite to eat or a break away from the road. The town had one diner, one coffee shop – mine, one bookstore – mine, and a ton of artists' shops including The Glass Slipper, across the street from my coffee shop. Tourists could choose from a variety of lodging options, from one of our upscale bed and breakfasts, to a lower-priced hotel on the main highway, to a luxury villa at The Castle. Oh, and we had South Cove Winery. Now, isn't that the perfect tourist town?

The morning air was cool and helped me get the meeting out of my head. The only good thing that had happened was how mad Sherry had been when she stomped out. Someday that woman would realize the world didn't revolve around her. And with Kathi around, someday could be sooner than Sherry knew.

I opened the door to the gym and went straight to the women's locker room. Greg had convinced Mayor Baylor to sponsor a martial arts class at the gym, mostly so his deputies could fit it into their schedule. Greg, Tim, and Toby were already playing a quick game of hoops to pass the time. The men were already dressed in shorts and t-shirts by the time I walked into the gym. Greg looked over at me and his eyes crinkled and he winked at me. Then he threw a three-pointer and gave me a full-on smile. The boy was a showoff, but he was my showoff.

Amy waved me over to the mat where she was stretching out. She patted the place next to her. "I didn't think you were going to make it. Long meeting?"

I sank down to the floor and stretched over my legs. "Don't ask. It was brutal, and, since Mary's going to Idaho, I have to go to the next city council meeting to do the report. Can't I just give it to you? You have to go anyway."

"No way. Mayor Baylor has made it perfectly clear I'm there in an administrative role only. He'd crap if he saw my first draft of notes. I'm always planning tomorrow's to-do list or writing my shopping list." She nudged me. "Look at that fine piece of man. Who is he?"

Two men had just strolled into the gym. Matt, one of the newest South Cove residents who worked at the winery and was also Darla's boyfriend, and another guy, tall, dark, and handsome, with a touch of scruff on his face. Bad boy incarnate. I recognized the guy as one of the band members who were playing the winery this week. He'd come over to the table where Darla and Matt sat with Greg and I.

"One of Matt's friends, Blake something. He sings lead for Atomic Power, the band playing at the winery." I stretched over my straight legs, watching as the newcomer was introduced to the group. "Are we the only women in this class?"

Amy grinned and stood as the instructor called the group over toward the middle of the gym floor. "Isn't it amazing?"

Chapter 2

Ninety minutes later, Amy and I were in our favorite booth at Diamond Lille's eating lunch. I watched as my friend inhaled her burger and I went back to my fish fry basket. The food made me forget about the stiffness and pain my body was going to feel just as soon as I stood up. "I think your exercise class is going to kill me."

"It's a great workout. You have to be on a waiting list for months to get into Tony's classes. I can't believe Greg convinced him to come here." Amy took a sip of her vanilla milkshake. "What's up with that?"

"I have no clue." I looked thoughtfully at the French fry in my hand. "I think they were college friends or something."

After one class, I was already rethinking my decision to sign up for the class so I decided to change the subject. Amy and I had gone through a rough patch a few months ago and we were still being careful of each other's feelings. Maybe a little too careful. I missed the ease our friendship had before the fight. Greg kept telling me to just be patient, that it would regain its temperament, but I wondered, not for the first time, if Amy and I could be who we had been. "Have you met Kathi Corbin yet?"

Amy served as the city receptionist, Mayor Baylor's secretary, the city council's scribe, and the city planner. She had a degree in the planning stuff, but it took all the jobs cobbled together to make a full-time position. She liked the freedom working for South Cove gave her. Especially since she got to surf most evenings and weekends. "Kathi's been in the offices a lot lately. She's definitely a looker. I swear, Marvin can be downstairs in the staff kitchen but as soon as she walks in the door, he's right there. It's kind of creepy."

"I bet if Tina was there he wouldn't be so quick to fawn over Kathi." The mayor's wife Tina had an iron fist when it came to her husband and their marriage. What Tina wanted, Tina got. And she didn't take kindly to him even looking at other women.

"Tina's out of town with the girls. They went to LA for a spa week." Amy grinned. "They're probably eating seaweed and doing who knows what to their bodies."

"Our honorable mayor better watch his actions. Tina may be out of town, but that doesn't mean she doesn't have spies watching out for her interests." Carrie, our waitress, stood next to our table. She'd worked at Diamond Lille's since before I'd moved to South Cove. She refilled my iced tea glass and Amy's water. "Tina won't take kindly to him sniffing around the new shop owner."

"Seriously? You really think Tina has someone watching him?" I stared at Carrie as she paused, perching the two pitchers on the edge of the table.

"I know she does. You girls are both naïve. Tina Baylor didn't get to be the mayor's wife by letting things fall to chance." A man yelled her name out from the kitchen. "Tiny's in a mood today. I better run. You almost ready for your checks?"

"Sure." I waited until Carrie was out of earshot before turning toward Amy. I'd lived in South Cove for almost six years now but the ins and outs of life in a small town still surprised me. "Did you know about Tina's spies?"

"No, but I wouldn't put it past her. The woman reviews our phone records monthly. She says she's looking for any potential campaign contributor so she can reach out when he's running for office. But Carrie's explanation makes more sense." Amy picked up her milkshake, looked at the creamy concoction, and set it aside. "I'd dump Justin before I'd put myself through all that to make sure he was faithful."

"You don't need to worry. Justin adores you."

Amy picked up her milkshake and drained it. "He does, doesn't he?"

"Darn right. Hey, I wanted to thank you for pushing the council to support the library fundraiser. I know you were the driving force behind their covering the room cost." Aunt Jackie and Sasha had gone to the last council meeting to ask for the funds.

"I didn't do much. The grant funding was a no-brainer. The high school library has been out of date since before I went to school there." Amy polished off her French fries. "I'm surprised you're not heading up this project. Literacy is kind of your hot button."

"I wanted to give Sasha the opportunity to put this one together, especially since it's for the age group of her book clubs. She said she could use it for a project next fall in one of her classes. The woman's a dynamo." I glanced at my watch. "I better get home. Emma's probably dancing in the kitchen waiting for me to let her out."

I waved goodbye to my friend and headed toward the end of town and my house. I'd inherited the place from Miss Emily. She'd been the catalyst to my giving up a corporate law associate position and moving to South Cove. The woman had been a friend, mentor, and even surrogate mother to me before she died. I found out that not only had she willed me the house, she'd also given me her substantial fortune. I call the money the Miss Emily Fund and so far, the money has sponsored a couple scholarships as well as funded an anonymous donation to the South Cove Elementary library when the school board cut their book-buying budget to almost nothing last year. Sure, it was in my best interest for them to be able to order books from my store, but mostly, it drove me crazy thinking they'd prioritized sports over books.

Books should always win. I guess that's why when I designed my perfect small business I made it part bookstore, part coffee shop. The idea was genius and I've never regretted it.

Strolling towards home, I thought how lucky I was to be able to walk to work. No fighting traffic, no crazy drivers, and no paying for parking. When I worked in the city, my monthly parking bill was as large as some people's daycare budget. Here, my new Jeep didn't even leave the garage most days. I watched as a tour bus unloaded passengers in front of The Train Station. Good thing we'd eaten early; Diamond Lille's would be packed in about ten minutes. As the last of the group crossed the street, a motorcycle weaved through the pack, gunning his engine and zooming too close to a woman wielding a walker. Glancing up the road as I ran over to her to make sure she was all right, I thought it might be the same bike I'd seen that morning. When I reached the woman, she waved me away.

"I'm fine. The jerk just scared me, that's all." Then the gray-haired woman lifted up one hand and flipped off the disappearing back of the motorcycle dude. I smiled as she finished crossing the street and hoped I was as feisty when I got to that age.

Returning to the sidewalk, Harrold stood in his open doorway watching me. "That was almost a train wreck there." His eyes sparkled at his joke.

"The speed signs are clearly posted. I don't know why those types even get off the highway. They can't see anything as fast as they go through town anyway." I leaned down and petted Levi, Harrold's new rescue dog. "How are you today, buddy?"

"He's getting fat. Your aunt keeps feeding him from the table when we eat at home." Harrold absently reached down and petted the dog's neck. "I don't know what I'm going to do with her."

I held up my hands. "Don't look to me for advice, I've never been able to stop her from doing something she'd put her mind to."

"I hear you're doing a fundraiser for the library. Jackie's all excited."

Harrold and my Aunt Jackie had been dating for a few months. They had the same interests, enjoyed each other's company, and seemed like the perfect match. Of course, before Harrold, Aunt Jackie had been spending time with Josh Thomas. What that couple lacked in common interests, Josh made up for in his earnest adoration for my aunt. In the end, the one-sided love hadn't been enough for her, and now Harrold was part of our group.

"The library needs so much updating, it's not funny. We donate a lot of books, but those kids deserve a well-rounded experience. I think the fundraiser might become an annual event." I realized I hadn't checked in with Sasha about the last-minute planning before I left the shop. I made a mental note to talk to her tomorrow before the Summer Beach Blast took up our attention for the week. Which gave me exactly five minutes first thing in the morning.

Waving goodbye to Harrold and Levi, I ambled my way back home. Since the spring rains had just ended, the lawns were green and the flowers blooming. Everyone was edgy about water still, since one good rainy season didn't mean the drought was over, but it was a good start. And I enjoyed the green landscape much more than the brown it had been during most of the winter months.

Emma sniffed my hand when I reached down to greet her after unlocking the front door. "Yep, I've been visiting Levi."

She woofed at me and ran to the kitchen door. Apparently I'd been forgiven for visiting her buddy without her, or she just really had to go outside and she would pout later. Emma was my golden retriever and a gift from Greg. She was also my running buddy. I took a mental inventory of my energy level after the workout with Amy and decided I had enough juice to take a quick run. I went upstairs and changed and when I got back downstairs, we headed to the beach.

The parking lot was filled with cars and I remembered too late that Mary and Darla were setting up for the start of the Summer Beach Blast. Toby was supposed to drive the food truck down this afternoon right after his shift. Sasha and Nick were charged with stocking the insides.

The truck had been parked in our back lot since I'd had it repainted at Bakerstown Auto Detail. Now, instead of the deep green sixties theme, the truck was tan with black letters. A large cartoon coffee bean sat relaxing in a lawn chair and reading a book. The truck was cute and I thought branded our store well. This was our first outing since we'd bought the truck from Dustin Austin a few months ago. Lille was still giving me the evil eye when I ate at her restaurant. She'd been in the running to buy the truck originally, but had banned the first seller from her establishment once he revealed he'd sold it to Austin.

Her loss, my win. Besides, Austin had promised not to sell the truck to Lille. Homer Bell, the truck's first owner, had a long memory. And he had liked the food at Diamond Lille's so his banishment still irked the man.

Emma looked up at me as we crossed the parking lot. Typically, I let her off her leash here and we'd run together down to the shoreline. Today, there were too many people for me to take a chance on her mowing down someone in her excitement to greet them. "Sorry girl, you're just going to have to stick with me today. I'll fill up your swimming pool when we get home."

Greg had brought home the kiddie pool in late May and Emma loved splashing in the water. She even had pool toys. Yes, we were that kind of dog parents. Of course, Greg was only in our lives part time, but I was hoping he'd come on full time sooner than later.

As if I'd wished him by rubbing a magic lamp, Greg crossed the beach and met me halfway to the ocean. Squatting, he rubbed the dog's ruff. "Hey Emma, I didn't think you'd get a run today." He looked up at me. "Are you feeling okay? That workout was brutal."

The workout was a specialized martial arts program. Most of the time today had been on exercises that focused on the core muscles. I had a feeling that my stomach was going to be screaming in the morning when I awoke, just from the sheer number of crunches we'd done. Attending twice a week, the class would either get me in amazing shape or kill me. I wasn't sure which would happen first.

Greg didn't have to know that. I smiled. "I thought it was great."

He laughed. "You're lying. But I love you anyway. How come you picked that specific class to attend anyway? Bruce is doing a self-defense for women class that goes in the evening. Matt said Darla's excited about going."

"You think I need to be in an all-female class? What, I can't keep up with the guys?" I tried to keep my tone even, but depending on Greg's answer, I knew I might go all postal on the guy.

"Oh, no. You're not getting me to fall for that. I was just wondering why you joined the class. I'm not saying what class you should take. Momma didn't raise no fool." He stood, giving Emma a quick pat, and then kissed me. "I've got to get back to checking out the setup for the festival. Should

I stop by later? Maybe we could head out to Sally's Deck down the road for dinner and a couple beers?"

"I'd love to not have to cook. And if we go to the winery tomorrow night, Blake's band will be playing and we can dance." Emma nudged me with her nose on my leg. "Looks like I've got to get going too. See you tonight."

I started jogging down the beach and whispered the words I still hadn't been able to say directly to Greg but I was practicing. "Love you."

As I ran, I thought about my relationship with the handsome Greg King. We'd been a couple for over a year now and even though we'd moved past the making out stage, we both still hung on to our own homes and routines. My last boyfriend had moved in with me after we'd been dating a month. One morning, I realized he hadn't gone home for over a week. That's how I knew he'd moved in. We'd never talked about it.

Luckily the guy moved out just as silently. We'd had another fight, the third one that week, and when I'd come home from work, his stuff was gone and I never saw him again.

Greg stayed over sometimes and we'd had weekends together in various locations, but neither of us had brought up the subject of the next step. Maybe it was time to stop practicing those words and actually tell the guy.

As I circled back around to the parking lot and the road to my house, I'd made up my mind. I was going to tell Greg I loved him.

Just not tonight.

My cell rang as soon as I got inside the house. I stood at the sink and after pouring a glass from a pitcher I kept in the fridge, I took a big gulp of water as I checked the display. Aunt Jackie.

"Hey, what's going on? Don't tell me there are issues with the food truck." I brought my glass of water over to the table and sank into one of the chairs.

"Why are you always looking for trouble, nothing's wrong." My aunt's theatrical sigh told me she was on her last nerve and the festival hadn't even really started.

"So why are you calling me on a Tuesday afternoon? You never call. What's so important that it couldn't have waited until tomorrow?" I flipped through the mail and sorted out the junk, piling it so I could run it through the shredder in my office later today. Shredding envelopes was surprisingly satisfying. I wish I could do the same thing with the bills that I piled in the other stack.

"Well, shoot me if I thought something might be worth knowing." My aunt could actually make her voice ooze disapproval over the phone and when she did, I knew I was crossing from being annoying to being out of order.

"Sorry, I'm grumpy." I rubbed my forehead, wishing away the migraine I felt coming on. "Please tell me what's going on."

I could almost hear the shrug my aunt had perfected over the years. "I guess so." Her voice dropped. "I had a woman come in and ask about a job. Don't worry, I told her no, that we were full up at least until after school starts. We're growing so fast, we might need to hire then. But I'm getting off subject. Like I said, I told the woman we weren't hiring."

I still didn't know the direction this discussion was heading. I sipped my water, waiting her out.

"The woman's name is Ivy Corbin. She swears she's Kathi's sister." Aunt Jackie paused, letting the news settle in.

Now my aunt had my attention. "I don't understand. Kathi should have tons of openings soon, and could probably use her now to start planning the storefront. Why would she be looking for a job with us?" I put the glass down on the table.

"I wondered the same thing, so I asked her why she wasn't working for her sister." My aunt greeted a customer, then came back to the phone conversation. "She said that the two of them didn't work well together. I guess she's in town trying to mend their relationship."

"Does Kathi even know she's here?" I looked at the cabinet where I kept my chips. I had fresh salsa in the fridge. Deciding I was more bored than hungry, I walked the stack of mail into my home office and turned on the shredder.

"I don't think so. Hold on a second." I could hear my aunt ringing up an order, so I shredded some of the credit card offers I'd gotten that week. I could probably open a packing shop with all the shredded paper I created just from junk mail.

Finally, I heard my aunt back on the line. "Anyway, I called for something else. I wanted to talk to you about the finances for the library event. Can you come down and we'll go over the plans?"

"Can't I look at them tomorrow morning?" I glanced at the wall clock: two o'clock. Greg would be here at six, which left me time to walk back into town, but honestly, I wasn't feeling it.

"No, I need to send out deposits today. It won't take long and you need to be more involved in the planning." The unspoken rebuke was clear in her tone. She'd seen through my plan to leave this event to her and Sasha, mostly because I didn't like the whole event-planning part.

I knew my aunt wasn't going to give in, so I turned off the shredder. "I'll be there in ten minutes." I let Emma outside. She loved spending afternoons on the back porch, guarding her domain from the rabbits and any other little creatures that happened to visit. Typically, I'd be curled on the swing, reading and sipping a glass of iced tea. I know, rough life. Emma did three circles, then plopped down hard on her bed when I let her back in, showing her disappointment in our change of plans. Glancing at the shed-turned-Toby's apartment, I didn't see his truck and figured he was still at the shop. I didn't spy or keep track of his comings or goings, but sometimes, I did feel a little safer knowing that the part-time deputy, part-time barista was only a few steps away if he was home.

I headed into town again. Traffic was busy, but most of the cars had the South Cove resident sticker on the bumper. The mayor, or probably Amy, had come up with the sticker as a way to keep the police from ticketing local cars for parking too long on the street. Of course, when festivals occurred, the sticker could also keep you from parking in visitor spots without getting a ticket. It was a double-edged sword, but I figured the mayor was making money off selling the stickers and ticketing the town folk. Mayor Baylor always had the bottom line in mind with his best ideas.

The tour bus had already loaded their charges and left town. The city council had bought advertising in the local tourist agency monthly, which got us quite a bit of bus stop visits. I'd seen an uptick in sales on days the tour bus came through. Or I guess I should say Aunt Jackie had noticed and shown me the increase. Starting in the fall, I was taking two classes in a Masters of Business degree. I had finally decided I needed to understand what my aunt was talking about when she went over the state of the business on a monthly basis.

Toby was at the counter when I entered the shop. He jerked his thumb behind him. "Her majesty is in the office. And boy, she's in a mood today."

"I got that feeling when I got my command performance notice." I grinned at Toby Killian. He'd been Aunt Jackie's first hire at a time I didn't think we needed any employees. The good thing about hiring Toby was he brought in a lot of customers. I was considering doing a photo shoot with him for a Coffee, Books, and More calendar that we'd sell at the shop. I had all the months planned out. Toby fake-skiing for January. Holding a heart-shaped cake for February. It would at least sell to all of Toby's girls, as we called the students from the cosmetology school who drove the ten miles into town for their coffee, lunch, and study breaks.

"Good luck," he called out as I walked through the doorway into the back.

Aunt Jackie sat at what I still pretended was my desk and looked up at me when I came in. Her face was ashen. When she saw me come into the room, she sighed. "We're in trouble."

Chapter 3

My mind went first to her health. She wasn't a spring chicken even though she acted like one. "Are you okay?" I stepped around the desk and put my hand on her forehead.

She slapped my hand away. "I'm not sick. I thought we'd go over the entire project, but then…" She pointed to the chair. "Sit down, we need to talk."

"What's going on?" Now I *was* worried. My aunt was typically in control of everything, but now, looking at her, a chill ran down my back.

"It's about the check the city sent us to cover the space rental for the library event," Aunt Jackie said, her gaze still focused on the empty desktop.

"Yeah, Amy told me the council voted down Mayor Baylor and we got the sponsorship. Are you telling me they backed out? Did he get the money blocked? Crap, I just talked to her." I sat up in the chair. If this was true, I was going to march down to the jerk's office and turn in my council liaison badge. He could find someone else to herd the cats, I mean, business owners in town. I'd done a good job. The least he could do was support a library event. It's not like the money was going directly into my pocket. But then wouldn't Amy have known about the problem at lunch?

"Calm down. The payment came through. I saw the envelope come from City Hall last week." My aunt still wasn't meeting my gaze.

"So what happened? Why are we in trouble?" I didn't understand, but I saw the beads of sweat on her forehead. Seriously, she was going to the hospital if she didn't perk up in the next few minutes.

"I can't find the check." My aunt finally met my eyes. "The day it came in the mail, Harrold and I had plans in the city so I slipped it into the desk and planned to deposit it the next day. But I forgot about it until today when I was finalizing the event details. I've looked everywhere, the check is gone."

"Maybe you deposited it." I started rummaging through the piles on the desk.

Aunt Jackie slapped my hand and I sat back. "You don't think I checked there? Or that I'd forget a three-thousand-dollar deposit?"

"Amy will just issue us a new check, no worries. Have you called her?" I didn't understand why my aunt was so upset. We'd figure it out. The event was over two weeks away, plenty of time for Amy to cut a second check.

This time my aunt sank back into the chair. "I called her. The check's been cashed. She asked the bank for a copy but it takes a few days since their record department is in Omaha."

"The city uses a Nebraska bank?" Now that didn't make a bit of sense as we had a branch of Rotary Bank just down the street. The new manager, Claire LaRue, was a frequent customer, not just for her coffee fix, but she also was a little obsessed with the New Adult books we sold. The last time she was in and bought a stack, I told her I was going to have to start putting an upper age limit on buying the books as I had to keep reordering once she visited.

"I can't help myself," she'd giggled. "I need something that I can dive into after a day at the bank. These types of books fit the bill."

I smiled at the memory and then realized my aunt sat glaring at me. "What?"

"I said, the city uses the Rotary Bank just like we do, but their records department is in Omaha. I guess the overhead is cheaper there than locally." She waved a hand, changing the subject. "That doesn't matter. What does is the check is missing and there are only a few people who had access to the office."

"So you checked the account online?" My head was buzzing. This couldn't be happening.

"You think I'm an idiot? Of course I checked our account." She blew out a hard breath. "No, we have to face the facts that someone else deposited the check into their account."

Her implication stunned me. "You think Toby or Sasha took the check? What, like we wouldn't miss $3000? That's crazy. I trust them. Heck, they've been making bank deposits forever. If money was to go missing, it would be easier to skim off the cash."

"Who's to say it hasn't already happened? Maybe they got desperate. You did say Sasha was having daycare issues, right?" Aunt Jackie leaned forward. "And Toby's next to homeless."

"He's not homeless. He's living in the shed until the sub-lease on his apartment is up." My mind started to whirl—wasn't that supposed to have happened already? Why *was* Toby still living in the shed? I turned and looked at the door separating the shop from the office.

"See, now you're putting the pieces together." My aunt threw the pen she'd been tapping across the desk. "I hate even thinking this, but we have to keep the best interests of the business in the forefront of our minds."

"Look, let's hold off convicting either one of them on circumstantial evidence until we find out about the check. I'm sure Amy will get a copy and we'll find the money." I nodded to the computer. "Go ahead and transfer the money out of our savings to cover the event site. We'll put it back when the money shows up."

"I don't have three thousand in the savings. We almost emptied it when we bought the food truck. I told you that."

Now my headache was screaming at me. "I thought we were getting a loan for the truck?" I did need to be more involved in the financial end. Thank goodness I'd planned on taking classes this fall. "Just in case?"

"When I talked to Claire, she advised against it. She said our interest rate on a vehicle that old would be high and if we could swing the purchase in cash, that would be a better business decision. I thought I told you that." She clicked on some keys. "I have a couple thousand in the account, but I've ordered almost that in books for the event." We'd ordered a wide variety so people could donate real books rather than only writing a check during the event.

That had been my brainchild. We'd done a successful book donation for the Bakerstown Child Care center last Christmas and I'd seen how happy people had been to share their favorite book from raising their own children. I dug in my tote for my checkbook. "How much do I need to give you to hold the business over?"

As I wrote out the check, I blessed Miss Emily for the unexpected inheritance she'd left me. Right now, the money was keeping my business afloat. I ripped the check from the holder and handed it to my aunt. "Don't deposit this until tomorrow. I need to transfer money into that account."

She reached for the check but I held it firmly as she met my gaze. "And don't lose it." Aunt Jackie's face flushed as I released the check. Immediately, I felt bad. "Just kidding."

We made plans to sit down on Sunday morning to go over the event details and by the time Toby stuck his head into the office, her color was better.

"Do you need me to stick around late tonight?" He looked back and forth from Aunt Jackie to me, a frown growing on his face. "Something wrong?"

My aunt took a breath and shook her head. "Nothing. Let me get this computer shut down and I'll be out to relieve you. I don't want you going to patrol on an empty stomach."

Toby shrugged. "I've already got my order called into Lille's for dinner. I was going to pick it up on the way home." He looked at me. "You want a ride back?"

I glanced at my watch. Greg would be at the house in an hour. I could walk the distance home in ten minutes and it would take Toby at least that long to stop to get his food. "I'll walk."

Toby closed the door, but not until he divided one more look between the two of us.

I watched my aunt close the laptop. "Let's just keep this between us. Well, us and Amy."

She nodded. "Believe me, I don't want to admit to anyone that I'd left money lying around, waiting to be stolen."

"The money's not stolen." I left the shop hoping that my words were true.

By the time Greg arrived, I'd worked myself into a tizzy. I couldn't believe that either Sasha or Toby would have taken money from the store. Or, for that matter, from me. I'd offered Sasha money more than once to help ease a financial problem she'd been having, but she'd always waved it off, explaining she needed to solve the problem herself. I'd been proud of her determination, I couldn't believe now that it was all a sham.

Greg knocked on the screen but when he saw me sitting on the couch, he let himself in. "You should keep the screen locked at least. What if I'd been some drifter off the highway?"

"Then you would have killed me and put me out of my misery." I saw the surprise flare in his eyes from my answer, so I stood and folded myself into his arms. "Sorry, I'm just worried about something."

"Tell me, maybe I can help." Greg stroked my hair as he held me close.

Sure, he could help. He could start an investigation on the missing money and then arrest the guilty party, which appeared to be one of our friends. Sighing, I sank deeper into the hug. "Just hold me for a minute. Then we can head down to the restaurant. I'm starving and I'm sure I'll feel better with some food in me."

"Whatever you need." He tipped my head up and kissed me, long and slow. I let the warmth of his kiss seep through my body and wash away all the stress I'd felt since I'd talked to Jackie. Afterward, he gazed into my eyes. "Are you sure you're hungry?"

I breathed a quiet laugh. "I'm starving. Do you mind?"

He kissed the tip of my nose. "I'm a patient man. Besides, I've seen you hungry. It's not a pretty sight."

I let Emma in and closed up the house. Toby would be leaving soon for his evening shift, so I didn't want to leave her outside after dark without anyone around. In reviewing the town's security feeds, Greg had seen packs of wild dogs roaming the streets at night. My luck, they'd wander our way and Emma would think they wanted to play.

As we turned off onto the highway, I could see the lights the city had strung all around the beach area. Even though the area was empty, the lights illuminated it like some abandoned carnival show.

I hoped the festival would bring in the customers Mary had promised the group. The Business-to-Business group could get a little grumpy when they'd spent money on an activity that didn't bring in people. Or as Josh had said, the wrong type of people.

"Have you had any complaints about speeding motorcyclists?" I turned away from the beach and watched Greg drive.

He turned down the music. "How did you know?" He shook his head. "Never mind, sometimes, it's like you're in my head. Or do you have a bug placed in my office?"

I smiled. "Maybe I'm just psychic, like Esmeralda?"

"I didn't think you believed in her gift?" He slowed for a set of tight turns in the road. "Don't answer that, I'm not sure I want to know. Anyway, yes, I had three different reports of some guy racing through Main Street at three different times of day. But never when Tim was anywhere close to be able to find him. Esmeralda was ready to shoot the guy herself."

"I saw him during the meeting and then again after lunch. The guy was huge! He about ran over an old lady with a walker. And she was a tourist."

"The reports we got were for a skinny kid. Most of the callers thought he was in high school." He took my hand in the dark. "Heaven forbid, we wouldn't want a tourist to be hurt on our streets. You're beginning to sound like Marvin. It's kind of creepy."

"I didn't mean it that way." Okay, maybe I had, but the woman had been using a walker, for gosh sakes. Didn't the rider have a grandma somewhere? "But I saw the guy, he was football defensive lineman big. I don't know how he didn't blow out a tire."

"Eyewitnesses are typically a little off, but this is kind of crazy." Greg pulled the truck into the parking lot tucked between the highway and the mountain. He turned off the engine and turned to look at me. "You ready to forget what's been worrying you and have a relaxing dinner with the handsomest man on the South Cove police force?"

"I didn't know Toby was meeting us here." I rubbed my finger over the stubble on Greg's face. When he had meetings at night, he typically shaved twice a day. I kind of liked the rough look being unshaven gave him.

"Funny girl." He slid out of the truck and shut the door, walking around to my side to let me out. He caught me halfway down and let my body slide down skimming his own. The guy knew all the right moves. He led me toward the front door. "Let's get some food now, I'm starving."

Chapter 4

On the first day of the Summer Beach Blast Party, I'd arrived at the shop early, but I wasn't the first one there. Kathi Corbin sat at one of our outside tables, looking at her phone. Her blond hair shimmered in the morning sunlight and I wondered if she had been born with that color or had she gotten it under the hand of an excellent hairdresser. She glanced up as I approached and slipped her phone into her Coach bag. If the purse was a knock-off, it was a great imitation.

"Good morning, darling," she crooned in her Texas twang.

"Officially, we don't open for another ten minutes, but come on in." I unlocked the door and held it open for her. "I have a feeling today's going to be crazy, I might as well get a jump on it."

"Your group is so creative with all the little festivals to bring in customers. Back home, we only had the fall homecoming party and the spring shindig. By the time we got done planning for those, we were D-O-N-E, done."

"Did you manage a business before?" I turned on lights and the coffee machines as I walked by the different areas. "I thought Tea Hee was your first venture into the land of retail?"

"Oh no, I worked at my uncle's general store for a few years and then summers during college. I learned a lot about people working the counter there." She stared up at the menu, then looked around. Satisfied they were alone, she reached into her purse and brought out a pair of glasses. She pointed them at me. "You are sworn to secrecy. If you say anything, I'll call you a jealous bitch."

I held my hands up in surrender. "I won't tell anyone, but seriously, why not wear contacts?"

"I've tried them. They make my eyes water. My last eye doctor suggested I use less mascara. And that's not going to happen." She put on the glasses and scanned the menu. She pointed to an item and put her glasses away. "I'll have a skinny mocha double shot."

"Add a piece of cheesecake with that?" I started making her coffee.

Kathi took a deep breath like she could actually smell the items in the sealed dessert case. "I haven't had sugar in years. I can't even think about eating a cookie without gaining a pound or two on my thighs. You have no idea how hard it is to keep a body in this kind of shape."

"The women on the *Titanic* regretted skipping dessert." I handed her the coffee. "Four-fifty, unless I can make you break your no sugar vow."

"You're evil, has anyone ever told you that?" Kathi looked around the shop. "This place is really nice. How long have you owned the shop?"

"Going on six years now. It was a coffee only place until I bought the store. I thought South Cove needed a bookstore. And luckily, so did South Cove." I poured myself a hazelnut-flavored coffee that had just finished brewing. "I think you'll love running a business here."

"I hope so. I've sunk all my savings into the shop. If it doesn't work out, I'll be going on *Cage Match with Miss America* next, just to put food on my table." Kathi handed me cash for her drink and waved away her change. "See you tomorrow."

"Oh, hey, I forgot. Your sister came into the shop yesterday. I didn't realize she moved here with you." I dropped the change into the tip jar and shut the cash register.

Kathi turned back to me and the ashen look on her face didn't match the news I'd just delivered. "My sister?" She shook her head. "You must be mistaken. I only have one sister and she is in Texas caring for Daddy."

"I didn't meet her, Aunt Jackie did. But she said her name was Ivy Corbin. That's your sister, right?" Kathi's face twisted as she processed the news. Apparently, the two women weren't close, which supported Aunt Jackie's argument that there must be bad blood between them.

Instead of responding, Kathi decided to ignore my question. "Look, I've got to get back to the contractors. If you don't keep an eye on them, they tend to disappear for hours. I'm on a deadline here."

And then she walked out of the store, leaving me to question everything I knew about South Cove's newest resident.

Toby held the door open as Kathi walked out. I saw his nod and friendly grin, but the greeting that most women found irresistible, Kathi didn't even seem to notice. He walked up to the coffee bar and filled his travel mug. "She's in a hurry this morning. What did you do?"

"Why do you think I did something?" I swatted him with a bar towel.

He looked around the empty shop. "No one else is here. It had to be you. So spill, what did you girls talk about? Did you tell her the mayor has the hots for her? That would send anyone screaming into the night."

"No, I didn't tell her that." A giggle burst out of me. "Now, I kind of wish I had though."

"See, true evil." He reached around me for the staff schedule and looked at it. "You have me working late Saturday. I can't work the truck that long, I'm on patrol for a double shift."

"I didn't put you late on Saturday." I grabbed the chart and studied the schedule. Well, it looked like I had. Crap. "I'll fix it. I'll work the truck with Nick and Aunt Jackie and Sasha can handle the shop." I corrected the page and handed it back to him. "Any other changes you need?"

"Sarcasm doesn't work on you." Toby scanned the revised schedule. "Nope, everything else is great. Although Sasha's going to be tired of seeing me this week, so it's just as well we cancelled our Monday night date. She claimed she had laundry to do—or maybe she had to wash her hair."

"You guys are seeing a lot of each other. Do I need to write up some workplace policies? What happens if you break up? Will I lose one of you?" I tried to keep the conversation light, but in truth, I was concerned about half our staff dating. Of course, with four, now five people including me, the percentages were a little skewed.

"You know both of us. We're taking it slow and seeing if there's anything there. Besides, she'll probably get fed up with my work schedule and dump me sooner than later. I'm never home." He grinned. "Of course, you know that since I live in your shed."

"Speaking of that, I thought you were getting back into your apartment?" I rubbed a spot of water off the counter, not looking at him. Maybe this was the avenue I could use to ask him about the check.

"You ready to kick me out and build that home gym? That's harsh." He sipped his coffee.

Backtracking now, I leaned under the counter and brought out more cups to stock the front counter. "No, I like having you nearby and I like the extra money. I just thought you'd said your sub-leaser would be out by now."

"He was supposed to be, but he came up with a sob story and I extended his lease. And he upped the rent so I'm getting a bit of money from him each month, which goes into my savings." He looked at the dessert case. "Grab me one of those Apple Caramel cheesecake things. I didn't get time for breakfast before I left home."

I dished up a piece and slid it over to him. He pointed to the paper stuck between the cash register and the coffee machine. "Don't forget to write it down. Jackie doesn't like us eating for free."

I shook my head. "My treat today." I dished a second slice for me and walked around to sit next to Toby at the counter. "So why are you working so many hours? When did you become all about the money?"

"I'm trying to save up to buy a house. You can't imagine how expensive everything is around here. All I want is a little three-bedroom house, but the down payment is holding me back." He wolfed down several bites of cheesecake.

Looking at the almost empty plate, I grinned. Toby could eat an entire pizza by himself. I guess all the hours working kept him active enough to burn off the calories.

"This is one of Sadie's best creations, next to the Triple Chocolate layer one she baked last month. All the girls loved it." Toby held a bite on his fork and waved it at me.

"Don't change the subject. You're buying a house?"

He paused in between bites. "I *want* to buy a house. Right now, Claire says I could swing the mortgage, if I could come up with the down. So that's what I've been working on. Of course, with low interest rates for the mortgage, that also means low interest rates on my savings account." He finished the last bite of cheesecake and took the plates to the sink to rinse. "I guess I need a rich uncle to leave me an unexpected inheritance."

I considered the idea. "Do you have a rich uncle?"

"Not that I know of. Uncle Walter died last year and according to Mom, he was her only brother. I guess I'm just going to have to work for what I want." He picked up the keys to the food truck. "Which means, I need to go get the annex set up. People should be showing up around ten."

"I'll check in on you after I leave here. Nick's starting at noon, which should give you all the help you need until the beach activities close up at eight." I glanced at the now adjusted schedule. "I hope we have enough staffing to get through this week."

"If we have that many visitors, I'll be shocked. Besides, I'm looking for more hours, remember?" He glanced at the office door. "Do you need me to make the deposit as I leave?"

The bank envelope from yesterday sat in my desk drawer. I'd told Aunt Jackie that either she or I would be the only ones making the deposits until we figured out the mystery of the missing money. I hated suspecting Toby and Sasha, but that much missing money was a big deal. When did my life turn into a Nancy Drew book? "I'll take it once Jackie takes over here. I need to talk to Claire about something anyway."

I needed to transfer money so the check I'd wrote Aunt Jackie for the event site wouldn't bounce and cause all kinds of issues. I'd planned on doing the exchange last night, but once we'd finished with dinner, I'd forgotten. Well, I'd forgotten with a little help from Greg. The memory made me smile.

"What?" Toby paused at the office door.

"Go open CBM annex." I waved him on.

He leaned against the doorway, juggling the keys from hand to hand. "Fine, keep your secrets. I'll find out sooner or later anyway. You know guys talk."

"Just go." Now my face heated and I glanced in the mirror that lined the back of the coffee bar. Yep. Red as a Maine lobster.

* * * *

Atomic Power was living up to its name. We'd been able to hear the band for the last block as we walked toward the winery. The good news is the band played a mix of covers from several decades, appealing to the wide generational span that frequented the South Cove Winery. Greg held the door open and we wandered into the almost packed tasting room.

The first day of the festival had been busy. Several business owners nodded as we passed by their tables. I slipped into the first unoccupied table and tilted my head toward Greg. "Looks like I wasn't the only one who needed a drink after today's events."

He kissed the top of my head. "Beer or wine?"

"Get me that new blueberry draft Darla's been talking about." I put my feet up on his chair. "I'll hold down the fort. But don't be too long, I'm too weak to fight for the table."

"I don't know, with the muscles you're building in the training class you should be able to fight off a horde of frat boys with no problem." His lips curled into that lopsided grin that tended to melt my resolve.

"Keep saying stuff like that, buddy. You might just win boyfriend of the year." Leaning back into the chair, I surveyed the room. Although I knew a few of the people, most of the crowd must be tourists staying at the local bed and breakfasts for the festival. A blond-haired woman sat by herself in the corner of the room, watching Blake, the lead singer.

"Who are you giving the evil eye now?" Greg handed me a large beer glass. I took a sip. Surprisingly, it tasted amazing. Not deep and rich like the dark ales I typically enjoyed, but a refreshing change.

I pointed over to the table where the woman sat. "I think that's our new shop owner, Kathi Corbin. She's opening Tea Hee across the street."

"Competition?" Greg took a pull off his beer.

"What?" Turning to look at him, I shook my head. "No. She's not opening a tea shop, it's a tea store. She wants Coffee, Books, and More to serve Tea Hee's special tea blend."

"And you're thinking about it?" Greg leaned back into his chair, watching the band, but listening to me.

"I am. I think a joint promotion is a smart idea. Working together is why I supply coffee beans to Diamond Lille's. Just one more place potential customers get to learn about our business." I nodded to the table. "Kathi looks like she's really into Blake. Tell me he's not married."

Greg turned his head toward me. "And I would know that how?"

"Boys talk. Toby told me that today." My face heated a bit at the memory of what I hadn't told my barista.

He shrugged. "Fine, I do know he's single. Do you want to introduce them?"

I sipped my beer. "Maybe after the set."

We relaxed for a while, just listening to the music. Finally, Blake went up to the microphone and announced, "We're taking a short break. Be right back."

Matt met Blake at the edge of the stage and slapped him on the back. Greg waved the two over to our table and the men went through the greeting ritual. "Hey Jill." Matt smiled at me. "Busy day for you too?"

"Crazy busy." I'd stayed at the shop up until Greg stopped by to get me. We'd eaten dinner at Lille's, then decided to take the walk up to the winery, as this was his last night off until after the festival. The walk-in traffic had died down and they'd closed the beach off at six, so the only one working at the shop was Aunt Jackie. Harrold had brought her a dinner basket from Lille's and as soon as she closed, they'd go up to her apartment to eat. I looked from Matt to Blake, as they were both watching me.

"What?" I looked at Greg.

He laughed and pulled me into a hug. "I told you she didn't hear you."

"I asked what you did." Blake blushed. "No big deal, I was just wondering what shop you ran. I'm still trying to get to know people around here. Playing here's a sweet gig. I'd love to come back. You should see some of the dives where we've been booked."

I caught Kathi's eye and waved her over. "You should meet our newest shop owner."

Kathi's pace was so slow, I wondered if she'd hurt herself working with the contractors at her shop that day. Finally she arrived to the table and I heard her sharp intake of breath. Then as if I'd imagined the weirdness, she put on an award-winning smile and gave me air kisses. "Jill, I didn't see you. When did you get here?"

"Just a few minutes ago." I introduced Kathi to the men sitting around the table..

Kathi just stared at Blake. He grinned and nodded to the beer in her hand. "You ready for another one? I've got to get something before our break ends."

"Sure." She looked down at the bottle like it had magically appeared in her hand.

Matt looked over at Greg and me. "Looks like you two are good. I'll be right back with Blake."

Kathi sank into a chair at the table. She took a long drink of beer. The bottle was almost full. "I can't believe that guy. He looks just like this kid from my high school. I'll admit, I had a huge crush on Aaron, but then he died in a motorcycle accident senior year." She smiled at me. "I don't think he ever even knew my name."

"That doesn't seem possible." Greg held a chair out for me and we sat with Kathi. "You don't seem like the kind of girl guys don't notice."

Kathi pushed a strand of hair back behind her ears. "Oh, you're wrong there. You're looking at the original Ugly Duckling. I was so gangly in school, no one even wanted to be friends with me. I only started doing pageants in college to help pay for tuition. By then, I'd kind of grown into my body and my looks."

"And then you turned your back on your family." An unfamiliar voice spoke from behind me.

I turned and saw the woman who must be Ivy Corbin. She didn't have Kathi's beauty, but you could tell they were related. Same hair, same eye color, same body type. But what worked in harmony for Kathi seemed to fight against each other in Ivy. Her eyes were too close together, her nose a little crooked, and her teeth seemed more canine than human.

"You aren't supposed to be here. Who's watching Dad?" Kathi didn't look at her sister as she talked, keeping her gaze instead on the bar and Blake.

"Like you care? Seriously, I've come to try to talk some sense into you. You have to come back before it's too late." Ivy's voice was suddenly several decibels louder and people at the tables around us started watching the show.

Kathi sighed and polished off her beer. She grabbed Ivy by the front of her shirt and pulled her close. Although she whispered her next words to her sister, I was close enough to hear. "Go wait outside. I'll deal with you there."

Ivy nodded, glancing at Greg, who'd stood when Kathi had grabbed her sister and was monitoring the exchange. Now that she'd gotten her sister's attention, Ivy scurried out the front door without looking back.

Kathi took one last look at Blake still at the bar and then sighed. "Tell him something came up but it was very nice to meet him."

"So that *was* your sister who came into the shop?" I asked the *duh* question and to Kathi's credit, she didn't hand me a sign.

"Family, what are you going to do?" She paused before following Ivy. "You can't control them and you can't kill them."

I sank back into my chair as I watched Kathi leave the winery. Greg was still standing. I put my hand on his arm. "You staying?"

"Just wondering if I should go out there and make sure there's no cat fight." The door to the tasting room was open and I could see Ivy and Kathi walking toward the road.

"Looks like they're taking it somewhere private. Watching those two makes me glad I'm an only child." I patted Greg's chair. "Sit down and relax a bit. Remember, this is your night off."

He sat, but kept his gaze on the doorway until the sisters disappeared down the hill. When they did, he focused back on me. "You should know better than that by now. The head detective never really gets a day off as long as we stay in town."

Matt and Blake returned and I relayed Kathi's message. Blake took a quick peek at the door then shrugged. "I guess I have two beers then."

The rest of the evening sped by and we were just about to leave when Greg's phone buzzed. He looked at the display and mouthed the word "sorry" to me as he walked away from the table.

Darla had joined us and raised an eyebrow. The woman was the local reporter for the *Examiner* along with owning and running the winery. She was always on the lookout for a good story. "Something going on?"

I feigned indifference. "Not that I know."

"Not that you'll tell me." Darla laughed and leaned into Matt. "We've got to go make the last call announcement so people will start paying up and getting out of here. Jill, I'll see you later?"

Matt followed Darla back to the bar. Alone at the table, I took a sip of my beer. I'd been nursing the second one for over an hour and the liquid had grown warm. Pushing the glass away, I watched Greg just outside the door where he could hear whoever had called. From his stance, I knew it wasn't good news.

Leaving the tasting room, I paused outside in the patio area and watched as he finished the conversation. He walked over to me and put his arm around my shoulder. "Date night is over?"

He kissed the top of my head and angled me toward the parking lot. "Yep. Tim's coming over to give you a ride home."

"And you?" Sometimes he'd tell me what was going on if it wasn't too bad. This time, I had a feeling it was bad.

"He's taking me out to the Coastal Inn out on Highway One." Greg watched the road for Tim's lights. The Coastal Inn was a dive motel just inside South Cove city limits. The sign advertised rooms for rent by the hour, day, and week. And clean towels. Yep, it was classy.

"What's happened?" I could barely see his face in the dark parking lot. We stood on the edge of the road, outside the glow of the overhead lamps.

Greg turned toward me and sighed. "They found a body."

Chapter 5

Thursday morning started off busy, mostly with commuter traffic, all wanting to talk about the upcoming weekend and the festival. No one had heard about the dead guy Greg had mentioned last night.

"I wish you'd bring the coffee truck into town and park it in front of my office," a woman said as she handed Jill her credit card. "I bet we could keep you busy all morning. The office gives us coffee, but it's crap. You would think they'd give us good coffee just for the added productivity of the caffeine buzz."

"Robbie, that's a great idea. Of course, we'd have to hire a full-time driver and staff for the truck. Right now, just keeping it open for the weekend has proved a challenge." I handed her back the credit card and her receipt with a smile. "I'm missing my reading time."

"Jill, you should be happy the shop's busy, you're a successful business owner. Enjoy the sales." She sipped her coffee and smiled. "Now I can face my day. I might have to drive back at lunch for a refill."

"Well, the truck's open at the beach so that would save you a little travel time." I waved as she left the shop. Sasha came in right after Robbie left.

She dropped her purse off in the back area. When she returned, washing her hands in the front sink and then putting on her apron, she still hadn't said a word.

"Not awake yet?"

She poured a paper cup full of coffee and drank greedily. "Sorry, I haven't been sleeping well." Her eyes looked swollen like she'd been crying, not from lack of sleep.

"Olivia okay?" Sasha's daughter had started waking up in the middle of the night, wanting to play. The kid could get five hours of sleep and be wide-awake.

Sasha yawned. "Oh, yeah, she's fine. I have her on a better schedule and she's almost sleeping eight hours. I've just had a lot on my mind lately."

"Something you want to talk about?" Toby's comment about Sasha cancelling Monday's date echoed as she pulled a chocolate chip muffin out of the case. As she went to grab the employee purchase list, I took it out of her hand.

"Today's breakfast is on me. Besides, you guys are going to be working crazy hours this week with the festival, I think you deserve a treat." I put the page away. "So how's the library event planning going? Everything going to be ready next week?"

She leaned on the counter and nodded. Swallowing the bite she'd just taken, she sipped on her coffee before answering. "Cat Latimer is confirmed for the event. She just launched the second book in her teenage witch series. The kids loved book number one, so I'm sure we'll have a good turnout. Jackie wanted to go with someone more established, but I like the idea of spotlighting a new author. Of course, if ticket sales tank, it's all on me."

"I've sold quite a few just during my shift. I think we'll be fine." My aunt had mentioned that she wasn't happy with Sasha's insistence on the author to invite, but the girl had stood her ground. I supported Sasha's choice, mostly because she'd been spot on with her decisions about the teen group in the first place. Since she'd started the afterschool book clubs, our young adult sales had tripled.

Sasha nodded. "Probably why I'm not sleeping. I just want the event to be successful. The library deserves a boost."

"We'll be fine. Between the sponsorship from the city, Darla throwing in the drinks, and Sadie and us taking care of the food costs, every dollar from the ticket sales will be a direct donation. Think of how many books the library can buy next quarter for the kids." The thought of the lost check nagged at me. I knew Sasha wanted the event to be successful. Why would she spoil it?

"I don't know how you do it." Sasha finished her muffin and threw away the wrapper. "I get so stressed trying to make ends meet and you have your home and the shop to worry about. And now we're doing this project. Don't you ever worry about money?"

"It's not something I stress about now." Of course, I had the Miss Emily Fund to fall back on if I really needed something. Sasha lived paycheck to paycheck while she was finishing school. I predicted once she finished, she'd get a much better job and we'd be looking for someone new to hire, but I refused to think about that day until it happened.

"I wish I could do that. The financial aid office is running late and if the money doesn't come in before the second week of school, I'll have to push back classes until next semester." She refilled her coffee cup.

"Won't they give you a grace period if it's their fault it's late?" I was starting classes this fall and though I wasn't getting financial aid, I'd been surprised at all the deadline warnings the school sent out, even though I'd already paid for my classes.

"I don't know. I've talked to the office and they keep telling me not to worry." She grinned. "Which makes me worry all the more. Enough about me, where do you want me to start today?"

"Hold on a minute, I need to ask you a question."

Sasha paused, a clean bar towel in her hand. "Do I need to work more hours? I know I said I'd work full time in the summer, but it's been hard keeping Olivia in daycare so long, especially since I had to register last week."

"It's not about the hours," I jumped in. She was going to hate me either way, so I might as well rip off the band-aid. "Did you happen to find the check for the city sponsorship and deposit it?"

"Where would I find a check?" Sasha shook her head. "The only time I do bank drops is when Jackie sends me at the end of my shift. And I don't think that's happened in over a month."

When I didn't respond, she sank into a chair.

"Seriously, you think I might have messed up a deposit." She looked into my face and awareness crossed her face. "No, that's not it. You think I took the money."

"No." I sat in front of her and looked directly into her face. "I don't think you took the money. Unfortunately it seems to have disappeared and as a business owner, I have to ask the questions. I'm sure this is just a bank mix up."

Sasha bit her bottom lip. "I knew this was too good to be true."

"What are you talking about?" Now I was scared. "Did you see the check?"

She shook her head quickly. "I don't know what you're talking about." She stood as a group of women entered the shop, chatting as they came in. "I'll handle this, unless there's something else you need to ask me?"

"No, that's all." I heard the challenge in her voice, but I had known going in that there was no way to get through this conversation without offending her.

I glanced at the clock. I still had to stop by the bank and Amy had set up a practice session at the gym for us on her lunch hour. It wasn't a regular class, but the instructor would be there to help us work through the routine he'd given us the first day. My whole body still ached from Tuesday's workout. Maybe I could call in sick. I sighed. Amy would just come and get me.

"We'll talk more later. I've got to make a bank deposit then go torture myself at the gym." I walked around the counter and slipped off my apron into the dirty clothes hamper. Sasha didn't respond or look at me.

Arriving at the bank, Claire waved me over to her office as soon as I walked in the door. She closed the door behind us and gave me a quick hug before returning to her desk. "I know you're probably here to see if we've heard anything about the check. Let me scan my email. I've been dealing with teller issues all morning. Seriously, don't they teach math in high school anymore?"

"Someone's till not adding up?" I sat in one of the chair and took the bank deposit envelope out of my tote.

"The girl can't count. Her till's fine, but she was all in a tizzy last night when she closed up and she couldn't get it to balance. The computer does all the hard work, why she's having problems is beyond me." Claire typed on her keyboard, then looked over at me. "Preaching to the choir here, I bet. Or are all your employees college graduates?"

"That or attending." I grinned as I leaned forward. "But I'm going to have to hire replacements as soon as they get a good job or decide to leave for bigger pastures. You're working with people who want a career. I'm just providing second incomes for most of my guys."

My thoughts went back to the less-than-successful conversation with Sasha that morning. If the one with Toby went as well, I might be hiring new staff sooner rather than later, as I didn't seem to be winning any friends.

"I'll give you one piece of advice then. Never hire someone who's related to your district manager." The computer dinged and she turned back to her screen. After scanning a few seconds, she clicked open an email. "Here we go."

I waited in silence as she read the email. When she turned back toward me she shook her head. "Sorry, false alarm. They're implementing a new scanning system in the records department and they're having some problems. They hope to have an answer Friday. They tried to trace it through your account, but came up blank, so they're working backwards from the check clearing the city's account, and that's where the scanning problem occurred."

"I really just came in to make a deposit. I appreciate you keeping me in the loop." I stood and she followed me out to the lobby area. She took the envelope and walked it over to an older teller.

"Margie will help you with this." She paused before leaving. "I didn't realize you were doing deposits again. I thought you had delegated the task?"

Dodging the question, I went with a mostly true answer. "I'm heading over to the rec center to work out so I thought I'd handle it. Besides, the shop's busy with the festival going on." Claire wasn't really listening to my answer; she was staring at the young girl helping out a drive-through customer.

"Not like that, Allie. Your check is upside down." She sighed and gave me a quick smile. "Sorry, I've got to go help."

As Margie rang up my deposit, counting out the cash and running the checks through the scanner, I watched as Claire walked the other teller through the deposit process. I could tell this wasn't the first time she'd been corrected when the girl rolled her eyes when Claire's back was turned. I blessed the two, now three, employees I had. At least they wanted the job. This girl seemed like she was more interested in the polish on her nails than learning the right way to process a deposit.

As I waited, I tried to convince myself to relax. This missing money thing was only a blip. Claire would find it and we'd be fine again. Except something in Sasha's pained expression when I'd confronted her made me wince.

Margie handed me a slip and then I remembered the funds transfer. I explained what I needed and in just a few seconds, I had a second slip in my hand. I loved the ease of making banking transactions lately. Besides, I never remembered account numbers to fill out those blank generic deposit slips.

Walking out of the bank, my cell buzzed. Glancing at the caller ID, my heart sank. Not Greg, Mary.

"Hey, what's going on?" I paused in front of the bank. If I needed to go to Mary's South Cove Bed and Breakfast, I'd be turning west. If not, I'd be going east. The sunshine warmed my face as I stood on the empty sidewalk in front of the bank.

"Ashley's in labor. Of course, it could just be a false alarm, but I'm not waiting. I'm taking off this afternoon for Boise. Did you want to go over the preliminary report for the council with me before I leave?" Mary didn't wait for an answer. "I've already sent the PowerPoint to your email and you know what's scheduled. Of course, we won't have solid sales numbers until the next meeting, but they always want to know what their council funding is buying. You can just deflect those questions until the next meeting. Bill should be there to help you out if they get crotchety."

"Congrats. Do they know if it's a boy or a girl?" I'd have to put together a welcome basket of books for the new arrival. And get Ashley's address from Bill.

"They wanted to be surprised. Ashley is convinced it's a boy though. I don't think she even picked out a girl's name. I hope she's right. A girl just won't sound right being called William Anaston the third." Mary paused and laughed at something in the background. "Of course, Bill's pointing out the baby can't really be the third since he won't have the Sullivan surname."

I started walking toward the bed and breakfast. Amy couldn't even gripe about me missing class for this. But then Mary started talking again.

"So I guess if you're fine, I'll just leave now so I can be there first thing in the morning. I should fly, but with rates as high as they are, it would cost a fortune. Lord knows if I'd even get out of here today. No, driving's better. And I should be there for the birth."

I heard Bill talking in the background.

"Yes, I know," Mary yelled back. "He said I won't be there unless I leave, so good luck with the council and let your aunt know I'll call her from the road later this afternoon."

The phone clicked off and I found myself standing in front of the bed and breakfast watching Mary drag her suitcase on to the porch. She started when she saw me.

"Well, look at you. I guess I didn't need to call after all." She looked at her watch.

I kissed her on the cheek and watched as Bill grabbed the suitcase from her. "Don't worry about me, I was on my way to work out when you called."

"Did you have any questions? I guess I went through that pretty fast." She paused as I opened the car door for her.

"Nope. Safe travels." I watched as she climbed into the front seat of their SUV and Bill came around from the back and gave her a kiss.

"Tell Ashley I'll get up there in a week or so. We'll tag-team grandparent this baby." He caressed her cheek. "I wish I could come with you."

Watching them, I realized how hard managing a place like this must be. The Sullivans did take time for themselves, but it took closing down for a week for them to really get a vacation. I was lucky. I could leave the shop in my aunt's care and take off. One more reason I was glad I hadn't opened a bed and breakfast. Well, that and I really didn't like talking to people first thing in the morning.

Bill and I stood together as Mary drove off, waving until she disappeared out of view on Main Street. He turned to me. "You want some coffee?"

"I'm late to meet Amy, so I'll take a rain check." I paused. "You going to be okay, Grampa?"

Bill shuddered. "Man, don't call me that. I can't believe little Ashley's old enough to be married, let alone having kids already."

I watched as a figure came up the sidewalk toward us. Kathi Corbin was doing the walk of shame. Her clothes, the same ones from last night, were rumpled and dusty. And her hair looked like she hadn't even brushed it that morning. She held up a hand. "No talking, no comments, nothing until I get a shower."

I shrugged. "All I was going to say was good morning."

"Is it?" She turned and looked at Bill. "Please tell me you still have coffee available in the dining room."

"Of course."

Bill and I watched as Kathi climbed up the stairs and went into the house, letting the screen door slam behind her. "Late night, I guess," he said.

"Definitely." I said my goodbyes and headed to the gym. Had Kathi hooked up with Blake after leaving the winery? They really hadn't talked much but maybe she'd come back after Greg and I had left. I glanced at my phone again. No text or missed call from him. The case must have turned out to be more than just a dead body. A chill ran down my back. Like a murder.

Amy frowned at me as I walked into the gym ten minutes late. She pointed to the locker room. "Go get changed. We've already started."

We consisted of Amy, Blake, Matt, and the instructor. None of the class members from the police force were there, making me even more curious. I hurried and changed into my clothes and re-entered the gym.

"You're just in time for laps." The instructor grinned as I approached the group. "Today is cardio workout and we're going to test your endurance."

Great. I fell in step with Amy, whose blond hair was in a ponytail that bounced as she jogged.

"Where were you?" she asked. "I called the shop but Sasha said you'd left over fifteen minutes ago. I was worried."

"Bank." I struggled to keep up with Amy's pace. Even though I ran most days with Emma, that was at my own slower pace. I really needed to work out harder. "Then seeing Mary off. Ashley's in labor."

Amy's shriek made me miss a step and I almost fell.

"Seriously? Mary must be so excited." Amy sped up even faster. "This is terrific. I bet that baby's going to be so spoiled."

We continued to talk about the baby and Bill and Mary until the instructor glared at us.

"Ladies, this isn't a church social. Focus on the run. My grandmother can run a faster lap than you're doing."

As we got out of earshot, I muttered, "I don't like that guy."

Amy's laugh echoed in the gym, which garnered us a full-fledged glare from the teacher. After that, we just ran.

Limping home, I saw Greg's truck parked at City Hall. I went in through the side door that took me to the police station. Amy kept going, heading home to shower before returning to her job as City Hall receptionist.

Greg stood by Esmeralda's desk and raised his eyebrows when he saw me. "Rough workout? I'm glad I was too busy to go today."

"Oh, you'll get yours. Don't think demon trainer didn't notice you were gone." I leaned on the counter in front of Esmeralda's desk. The woman kept her desk immaculate. One pen, one message pad, one small calendar, and a stapler. That was it. I knew she kept a book tucked in the desk drawer. She loved reading historical romance, which always made me smile when she came in to buy her weekly supply. "Hey, Esmeralda. You look busy."

"Don't be snide. Just because I keep a clean house doesn't mean I'm not earning my wage." Esmeralda cocked her head and looked at me. "You've lost something."

A chill ran through me. The woman was our local fortuneteller and my closest neighbor, but even she couldn't have known about the missing money. I tried to change the subject. "My mind. How I let Amy talk me into this class, I'll never know."

Esmeralda shrugged. "If that's the way you want to play it. Just know it's safe, you just have to look more carefully."

The phone rang and as she answered the call, Greg took my arm and led me into his office. He closed the door and sat with me on the couch. "Do I want to know what that was about?"

"She's your employee, how would I know?" I felt bad not telling Greg, but I didn't want this to become a big thing until I was sure the money was actually gone. Besides, according to the woman plugged into the vast unknown, I'd find it eventually. For some reason, even though I didn't believe Esmeralda had the gift, her comment made me feel better about the entire situation.

"Okay. So why are you here?" He pushed a curl back out of my face. "Too far to walk home after the workout?"

"You're just mean, you know that right?" I sank into the couch. It did feel amazing just to veg for a second or two. Okay, so Greg could have been right about my real motives for the impromptu visit. "Actually, I wanted to know about your call-out last night. I'm assuming this was a murder and not an old guy dying in his sleep."

"And you deduced that from?" He watched me closely.

Shrugging, I sank deeper into the cushions. No wonder Greg didn't mind sleeping in his office every so often. The couch was amazing. "No one blabbed, if you're thinking of blaming Toby. You didn't call, and you're still wearing last night's clothes."

He chuckled. "You're right. I guess I'm more transparent than I thought."

My eyes flew open. "Is Toby going to be able to work? This isn't going to affect him running the food truck today?"

Greg held up a hand. "Relax, Toby's on his normal schedule. We don't know much about the murder, except the guy checked in a few days ago under a false name. Of course, the motel doesn't ask for any verification or even a credit card. Cash only out there."

"So he's not a local." For some reason, this made me feel better. Sure, it was sad someone had died, but people died all the time. I just didn't want it to be one of my friends.

"Not that I can tell. But I think it's the biker who's been racing up and down Main Street. He fits the description." Greg shrugged and grinned. "And, there's a bike parked outside his room. Yep, I'm a trained investigator, I notice these things."

"Big guy?" I thought about how the elderly woman had almost been smashed by the rider just a few days ago.

"Nope, you were wrong. He's tall, maybe six feet, but if he weighs more than a hundred fifty soaking wet I'll buy you dinner." Greg groaned as he stood and walked across the room to his desk. He pulled me to standing. "I hate it when you do that."

"Do what?" Now that I was upright, my stomach growled, reminding me I hadn't eaten all day. I dug into my tote and pulled out a protein bar.

"Trick me into telling you more than I should." He pointed to the door. "Out of here. I've got work to do."

I took a bite of my protein bar as I walked out. Pausing at the door, I turned back to look at him. He was already typing into some document. "I take it I won't see you for dinner?"

"Not tonight. But I'll be over on Sunday at the latest." He paused. "Are you working the festival that day?"

"Just the morning shift. We're closing the main store and only running the food truck that day." I adjusted the strap on my tote, feeling the weight on my screaming shoulder blade. "Oh, and Ashley's having her baby."

Greg turned to look at me, confusion filling his face.

Before he could ask, I responded. "Mary and Bill's daughter?"

He nodded. "Sorry, my mind is on other things."

I walked out of the office and wondered how bad the murder had been. Just because it was a stranger that lay in the morgue, didn't mean someone from South Cove hadn't been involved or known the guy.

Or why else would he have been here?

Chapter 6

My hair still wet from the shower, I grabbed a bag of grapes and cuddled up on the couch with another YA novel. This one was set in summer and from the few chapters I'd read, the author was amazing at setting the scene. Sasha had insisted I read the book after she'd finished, her exuberance for the story shining through.

Unlike this morning. I paused with the book in my lap and wondered if money worries was really what had my YA specialist in the doldrums. The girl was always on the go. Between school, work, and Olivia, I didn't think she had a spare moment to herself. I made a mental note to suggest a girls' spa night out for Sasha and Aunt Jackie once this summer festival was over. We all would need a break then.

An hour later, with my stomach growling, I sat the book down and went into the kitchen. I chopped veggies for a salad and put a chicken breast on to grill. Sitting down fifteen minutes later to eat, I heard the knock on the door.

I filled my mouth with a large bite of the salad, chewing my way through the living room. Peeking through the side window, I hurried and swallowed. Swinging the door open, Darla pushed a potted plant into my hands and moved me backward into the living room, not waiting for an invitation.

"Hey Darla, what are you doing here?" I knew what she wanted, but it's always fun to play the game. Especially when they bring you presents. I sat the plant on the table near the door. The fern was in a Mexican-inspired clay pot that would look amazing on the front porch. And maybe if I kept it outside, it wouldn't die on me. Greg had started calling me the foliage serial killer, since most of the plants he'd bought for me had wound up in the bottom of my trash bin.

Darla had sat on the couch, Emma in front of her with her head on the visitor's knee. "Oh, I thought we could chat a bit. I'm doing a story on the Summer Festival and I wanted your take on how it was going so far."

I crossed the room and sat on a chair across from her. "Good, but I don't have any solid numbers for you. Mary said it would take a few weeks for those and, as you probably know, she's gone to Idaho to help Ashley with the new baby."

"But you have the food truck down at the beach. This is your first time doing an annex, so to speak. How's that going?" Darla sat straight, her pen at the ready.

Crap, I hadn't even checked in with the truck this morning. They could be out of everything and just close up shop while Toby or Nick ran to the store for supplies. My gaze darted to the kitchen where my lunch sat. New plan, get rid of Darla, grab a slice of bread, swipe it with a tablespoon of peanut butter, and walk down to the beach. I'd eat the salad once I made sure the food truck was okay. "Honestly, I was just going down to check on the guys. I didn't hear how it went last night. They probably reported to Aunt Jackie."

"Oh." Darla put her notebook into her purse and with her head tilted away from me, she asked the real question she'd come to ask. "So what happened out at the Coastal Inn? According to the manager, your boy still has room 110 yellow-taped off as a crime scene. Tilly's a little upset since she thinks she's losing her walk-up business. People don't like to rent where there might be cops hanging around."

"Sounds like you know more than me." I moved the book to the center of the coffee table and lined it up with the long edge.

"Liar. You know something, I can tell by the way you're avoiding the question." Darla leaned forward. "Do you know who it was? Tilly was a little vague on the guy's name."

"When I check into a hotel, I have to show my driver's license and a credit card. I take it Tilly didn't get this from the dead guy?"

Darla laughed so loud Emma jumped from the spot where she'd been begging for attention from the new visitor. "Tilly doesn't even look at the guest sign-in register anymore. How many Mr. and Mrs. Smiths can there be in the world?"

"But this guy wasn't an hourly customer. He'd been at the Inn all week. Didn't she get any information about him?"

Darla smiled and I realized I'd leaked some information. But the good news was, it hadn't come from Greg. I'd seen the guy racing up and down Main Street. Or at least I thought it was the same guy.

"I guess her recordkeeping skills aren't completely up to par." Darla pulled out her notebook and scribbled something. "I take it you found out this from Greg?"

"No." I paused, then, knowing I had to say something, I gave her the least amount I could. "I saw him drive past the shop on Tuesday, the day of the meeting. Didn't you see him?"

She thought a moment, sticking the cap end of the pen into her mouth. "I remember Josh mentioning something about unreliable types but I thought we were talking about the festival."

"We were, but the sound of the motorcycle was what got Josh all hot and bothered." Well, besides the fact that Aunt Jackie was sitting with Harrold and Austin had stolen his spot next to Kathi. I wondered if his interest in the new shop owner was real or if he was trying to make my aunt jealous. Darla's next comment brought me back to the conversation.

"That's kind of a brief glimpse, how do you know it was the same guy?"

I ran my hand through my now dry hair. "I don't," I admitted. "Except I saw him again later that afternoon when he almost ran over a woman in front of Diamond Lille's. He had on the same cut, one with a big pig on the back. I remembered seeing the pig when the motorcycle passed."

"A pig? The local gang has a coyote or a wolf; I can never get that straight. Who would have a pig?" Darla wrote the word pig and underlined it.

"No clue. But I've got to get down to the beach and check on the truck. Do you want to walk down with me?" I didn't really want the company, but maybe Darla would let something slip and I could figure out who had been killed at the no-tell motel without asking my boyfriend.

Darla stood and shook her head. "I've got to open the winery in a few minutes. Are you and Greg coming by tonight?" she asked, her tone hopeful.

"I probably won't see him until after the festival is over. I'm working Sunday morning at the food truck, but I'll probably go back later for the fireworks." I wondered how many customers we'd have that late in the evening, but Aunt Jackie had reminded me that we could sell apple cider and hot chocolate as well as coffee. Still, I thought we'd sell more if we figured out an ice cream menu. Maybe coffee ices? This weekend's sales records would help make my case. Ice cream and a small display of books.

I was talking to an empty room. Darla had already left the house so I walked to the door and waved when she looked up at the house from her subcompact. She looked so uncomfortable, crammed into the small front seat. The vehicle had South Cove Winery painted on the side with a "follow me" sticker on the back along with a wine glass. She seemed to love it. I personally liked driving something a little bigger.

I shut the front door and locked it. Emma looked up expectantly and I debated taking her with me. Since I wouldn't be actually working the truck, I decided she could come along and after clicking the leash, we headed to the beach.

To my surprise, the coffee shack had a long line. Looking at the women standing there, I realized why the line was so long. Toby's girls had followed him from the coffee shop to the beach food truck. I bet Sasha was bored out of her mind at the main shop. I knocked on the side door and a frazzled Nick stuck his head out. "What?"

His eyes flew open even wider and he put his hands up. "Gosh, I'm sorry, I didn't mean to be rude. We're just slammed."

"How long has it been this way?" I nodded to the line.

Nick looked at his watch. "Since just after noon? We were busy in the morning, but nothing like this."

"How's your supplies? Do you need anything?"

I saw Toby pull the boy back into the trailer. "You go make coffee. I'll chat up the boss."

"You like having a minion." I grinned. Emma barked a short hello. She liked Toby, especially after he moved into the shed a few months ago. I had a feeling they played a lot of catch when I wasn't home. Toby didn't seem to sleep much, if at all.

"I love having a minion. And Sadie raised him right. He's polite, charming to the ladies, and a hard worker. He could probably take my job in a few years." He turned his head back into the truck when he heard a large bang.

"Sorry," Nick yelled. "I'm okay."

Toby smiled at me. "I need to get back. The kid is all thumbs. Did you need something?"

"Just wondering if you needed supplies or if I needed to make a bank run?" With this crowd, my idea of having a low-selling weekend was going out the window. So much for ice cream.

"Nah, I stopped at the shop on the way here for cups and stuff. We may need to restock tonight before we close up, but I dropped the money bag off with your aunt from last night's take and she had a new one for me this AM." He cocked his head. "I guess she didn't tell you?"

I needed to be more active in this area. Especially after Aunt Jackie lost the city's check.

Another crash sounded in the truck. "Sorry," Nick yelled again. "It's fine." Although this time, he didn't sound as confident. Toby and I looked at each other.

"You better go." I shortened Emma's leash, as she was leaning too hard into the truck, where a piece of cheesecake now sat on the floor just out of reach. "Call me if you need anything."

I circled back around to the front of the truck. A twenty-something woman with purple stripes in her blond hair grinned. "That man could call me if he didn't need anything."

I smiled and headed back across the parking lot to get away from Toby's girls. Sometimes they could get a little intense.

"Hey, Gardner. Come over here, I've got a bone to pick with you." Lille stood at the edge of the parking lot watching the food truck.

I knew she hadn't been happy when Austin had sold the truck to us when his wife passed, but that had been months ago. I wondered what I'd done now. I stopped a few feet away to give Emma a chance to greet the restaurant owner. "Hey Lille, what's going on?"

"Who said you could steal my best worker?" She pointed at Nick now handing a coffee cup to the woman who'd spoken to me about Toby. I watched as the woman reached up and ruffled his hair and then tucked a bill into the tip jar.

"I didn't know you offered him a job this summer. I talked to Sadie and she said he was free to work." I felt a little confused. I hadn't even been sure that Lille knew Nick had been her dishwasher before he'd gone to school. Tiny, the cook, typically hired all the back of the house staff.

"Whatever, just don't screw with him. The kid needs money for college." And with that, Lille climbed on her Harley, strapped a helmet on, and roared out of the parking lot.

I looked down at Emma. "Totally weird, don't you think?"

She woofed. Which either meant, "You got that right," or more likely, "Why aren't we running?"

I turned back and watched Nick and Toby for a minute longer. The two were laughing about something a customer had said. Nick's face looked beet red. I needed to talk to Sadie and ask her about Lille's behavior.

The answer could be Lille is Lille. But there felt like there was something more in the way she watched the boy. Protective, mother bear even. If I didn't know Nick was Sadie's son, I would have thought Lille was his mom.

Looking both ways, we crossed Highway One and headed back to the house and my salad.

I could see the house when Ivy crossed over the street and waved me down. "Hey, you're the woman that owns the coffee shop, right?"

I put a smile on and turned, ignoring my growling stomach. "That's me." I held out my hand. "I'm Jill. You're Ivy, Kathi's sister."

She shook my hand vigorously. "That's me. Sorry about the outburst last night. Sometimes we Corbins don't realize other people are around when we get into family stuff."

"No worries." I looked at my hand that she was still shaking.

She dropped it like she'd been burned. "Sorry. I'm a total klutz in the social department. I never was comfortable talking to people." Ivy blushed red. "Look at me talking your head off. All I wanted to say was how much I love your little shop. I've always wanted my own store and that would be exactly what I would open if I had the money."

"Are you going to work with your sister?" I looked down at Emma who was smiling at Ivy, asking for some attention. The dog liked her and that made me relax a bit with the woman.

Ivy leaned down and gave Emma a hug, patting her as she rose to her feet. "Pretty dog." She looked toward the beach. "I better get going. I'm looking forward to seeing the Pacific. I've never been this close before."

And then she ran down the road toward the beach and the ocean. I was unlocking the front door and letting Emma inside when I realized Ivy hadn't answered my question.

After eating, I settled back on the couch. With Greg busy with the investigation and the rest of town celebrating the Summer Festival, I was on my own for the evening. I could go down to the beach, but I'd probably wind up working the food truck and sending Nick and Toby home. They wanted the hours, so instead I curled up and started reading.

My phone buzzed just as I finished my book, putting it on the table with a satisfied sigh. Sasha had been right, again. The girl could pick a book as well as I could remember a regular's drink order. I glanced at the display.

"Hey you. How's the shop going?"

Aunt Jackie huffed into the phone. Sometimes she reminded me of the tigers I loved to visit at the local zoo. "What, you expect it to fall apart because you're not here?"

I closed my eyes. Great, she was in one of her moods. In the past, they occurred mostly when she was dating Josh and he'd done something stupid. "You called me, what's up?"

"I just wanted to remind you to do the bank deposit tomorrow. I didn't see a deposit slip in the office drawer so I'm assuming you have the envelope with you?" I heard the door chime and my aunt call out, "Have a good evening."

"I'll have you know, I made the deposit. Check online if you don't believe me." I turned on the television, hit mute, and thumbed through the guide wondering why I had over three hundred channels with nothing to watch.

"The system is down. Why didn't you leave the deposit slip in the desk?" Her voice cracked.

"Hold on, are you all right? You're not crying, are you?" I turned the television off and sat down the remote.

"I'm fine. I just wish you would follow procedures so I don't have to make these kinds of calls." And then she hung up on me.

"Apparently, I broke a new rule regarding bank deposits today." I looked at Emma. "Your Aunt Jackie is going off her rocker. Maybe we need to send her off on a vacation."

Emma lifted her head and looked at the door. Realizing no one was there, she lay back down and fell asleep.

I chalked my aunt's edginess up to losing the check earlier this week, but before I went to bed, I did a Google search on dementia, just to see if she had any symptoms.

When I decided her actions didn't fit the symptoms, I deleted the history. No need for her to find that on my web history by accident.

She'd kill me for sure.

Chapter 7

Walking through town first thing in the morning was the best part of my day. The street sweepers had already removed the dirt and trash from the day before. The city greenhouse guys were walking through town, watering the flowers. Besides them and the birds chirping in the trees, the town was an empty slate. Anything could happen today. Anyone could walk into town. I'd had my share of celebrity sightings. But mostly, I liked the days when normal people came in and surprised me with their unique lives.

I saw Greg sitting at the iron table in front of my shop as I crossed the street. I planted a quick kiss on him as I pulled out my store keys. "What's the occasion?"

He pulled me down on his lap and kissed me more thoroughly this time. When he was finished, he ran his thumb across my lips. "Can't a guy miss his girl?"

Smiling, I leaned my head into his chest. "I missed you last night too." I'd gotten used to spending our evenings together so when he was on a case or out of town, I felt his absence. I rested there for a second, listening to his heartbeat. "Darla came by yesterday to pump me for information about the dead guy at the motel."

"Information you?" He chuckled. "I have to give her credit, even with a full house at the winery this week, she's keeping on the story like white on rice."

"She said that the guy had been staying at the hotel for a while. Do you have an identity yet?" I didn't want to raise my head but I knew I'd start having customers arrive soon and the commuters would want their coffee.

"I have to say I've been proud of you staying out of the investigation." He nuzzled the top of my head with his lips. "Darryl Corbin."

This time my head did raise and I stared into his face. "You're kidding. Any relation to Kathi and Ivy?"

"That's the interesting part. Apparently he's from the same small little town outside San Antonio where Kathi and Ivy lived. I'm assuming some kind of relationship. I'm actually waiting for our new shop owner to arrive across the street so I can ask her a few informal questions." He nodded to the building still only partially renovated for Tea Hee.

"So this *wasn't* just an 'I miss Jill' trip." I stood and unlocked the door. "I'm disappointed, mister."

He came up behind me and nuzzled my neck as I put my keys back in the tote bag. Chills ran down my body and a smile curved my lips. I met his gaze in the reflection of the window. Heat seared through me as I saw the desire in his eyes.

"Wrong place, wrong time." I pulled open the door and flipped on the lights. Crossing over to the coffee bar, I turned on the machines and after throwing my tote into the back, washed my hands. "You want something?"

"Yes."

I shook my head and laughed. "Let me rephrase that. Do you want some coffee?"

We locked gazes for a second, then he laughed as well and sat on a stool at the bar. "Please."

I started the two main coffeepots and then a smaller one for my few decaf drinkers. I pulled out a slice of Sadie's Apple Caramel cheesecake and sat it and a fork in front of him. "Here."

He took a bite, then groaned. "Just when I think her creations can't get any better, she outdoes herself. Seriously, if we weren't dating, I'd marry Sadie just for her food alone. I can't believe she's still single."

Of course, we both knew that Sadie had been dating recently but when Austin broke it off to return to his wife, my friend's heart had been broken. She'd forgiven him, but she wasn't ready to jump into the dating pool again. "I think she and Pastor Bill have been spending a lot of time together lately."

Greg nodded. "I could see that. Bill's a good guy. He was on my basketball team last year at the gym. Pretty good defender with a nice three-point shot."

"You judge a guy based on his sports ability?" The coffee had finished brewing so I poured us each a large cup using the wide-mouth porcelain cups we'd brought in last month. Drinking out of them made me want to slip down onto the couch and read while I enjoyed my coffee. I hoped my customers would succumb to the same inclination. But right now, I just wanted some time with my guy.

"Not just that, but if a guy is a good team member, you can trust him on and off the court." He shrugged. "It's just been my experience. Take it for what it's worth."

I thought about the guys Greg played sports with. I'd assumed he pulled the same set of players for his team each time because they were friends, but maybe there was more to it. I'd always been a sit-and-chat kind of friend. Well, except for with Amy. Now we were taking an exercise class together, which gave me something to complain about during our talks. Of course, Amy liked to discuss the actual class.

I wanted to ask him more questions, but then he turned around and stood. "Got to go. Your new neighbor just arrived." He kissed me and headed out the door. I hadn't realized he'd been watching the street using the large mirror over the coffee bar while we talked.

"See you later," I called as he strolled to the doorway.

Greg paused and smiled at me. "I'll stop by the food truck about noon on Sunday and we'll go get lunch at that new Cajun place in Bakerstown. Will you be off by then?"

"I'm working the morning shift, then coming back to close up either Sunday night or Monday morning. You can drive the food truck back to its normal parking spot behind the shop if we do it Sunday." I put on my hopeful face.

Greg laughed. "If that's how you want to spend No-Guilt-Sunday, I'll do it. But I'd rather sit on the deck and drink a few beers with you."

I shrugged. "Then I'll close up the food truck on Monday morning. Emma is missing her guy."

"Sounds like a plan." He put up a hand waving goodbye and walked out of the shop. I saw him jog across the road and as he left, Ivy Corbin entered the shop door.

She smiled at me as she walked over to the counter. "You do grow men fine out here."

"I think so." I took Greg's cup and empty plate off the counter and sat them in the sink. "What can I get you?"

"Large coffee. I'm heading down the street to talk to every business owner in town. Who knew finding a job would be this difficult? I put in an application at the winery and the diner, but so far, nothing." She pulled out her wallet and handed me a credit card. "And a girl's gotta eat."

I poured the coffee and sealed a lid on top. Handing her the cup, I picked up the credit card to run the charge. "So where are you staying?" I knew Kathi was still at Bill and Mary's bed and breakfast, but she had money.

"I'm at a place down the road, but I need to find someplace cheaper before I run out of credit cards." She signed for the coffee and stuck it back in her purse. "Do you know anything about the Coastal Inn? It looks cheap."

"It is inexpensive, but there's a family-owned motel just a few miles down the road. It's not as fancy as the bed and breakfast, but it's clean." I wanted to add "safer" to the descriptor, but felt like maybe that was implied. Even without the crime scene tape, the Coastal Inn gave off an air of danger and malevolence every time I drove by the place. I handed her a South Cove map and circled the Ocean Motor Court. "It's just past the Inn on Highway One."

The maps had been Mary's brainchild and I loved them. As part of their chamber of commerce dues, each business got a spot on the map and several, like mine, had paid for advertising slots on the back. I used them to direct tourists to other businesses, and I'd seen many people using them to plan their walking tour of the town.

A rumble came from the outside, and we both turned toward the noise. As the sound grew, the large motorcycle I'd been seeing around town sped past, the guy still wearing the pig on his back. My eyes widened and my arm went up in a fist pump. This guy was huge—and alive. Which was more than I could say for Darryl Corbin. When he'd passed by, I shook my head.

"Seriously, they need to catch that guy. He's been a menace to anyone walking across the street for a week. I'll be glad when his vacation ends and he goes back to wherever he's from." I paused, then looked at Ivy. The girl had paled under her sun-kissed cheeks. "Hey, are you all right? You look like you've seen a ghost."

Ivy turned back toward me, her eyes wide. "Maybe I have." She held up the map. "Thanks for this."

I watched her as she disappeared out the front. I glanced at the clock. The shop hadn't been open for a full hour yet. Ivy was from the same town as the dead guy. Maybe she knew him. Kathi had been busy running through the pageant circuit, but according to her sister, Ivy had been taking care of her father. Greg was interviewing the wrong sister.

I thought about Ivy's reaction to the biker. She'd been jumpy, but had there been something more?

I decided she was one person I needed to get to know better. If I'd been Greg, I would have asked her to sub in on my sports team. I needed to find a way to get her off her game and talking.

It was time to invite Ivy to lunch—except I didn't have a phone number to reach her. Nor did I know exactly where she was staying, except it was down the road.

I got busy with my morning commuters and forgot about Ivy. Everyone who stopped by the shop wanted to talk about the crime scene tape they'd seen on their way in. Did I know about the murder? Who on earth could or would do such a thing? Did I think that the murder would hurt the Summer Festival attendance?

The last question concerned me, and I didn't have a good answer. Now, more than any day, I wished I had Mary to ask. She knew all about ways to minimize conflict or bad publicity. But she was busy being a new grandmother. I powered through the questions and tried to put a positive spin on the investigation.

Or at least as positive as a murder could get.

The bell rang over the door and Josh Thomas lumbered in wearing his typical black suit with a white dress shirt and black tie. When he and Jackie had been dating, she got him to purchase new shirts so at least the one he wore wasn't threadbare. When he first opened his shop in South Cove, I thought he took his antique persona too literally. His clothes mirrored his love of the old and still useful.

"Hey Josh, what can I get for you?" I put on my sales smile, even though I knew he was probably here with his weekly list for the monthly Business-to-Business meeting. Somehow, he thought if he promoted his ideas on a regular basis, I wouldn't file his lists in the round filing cabinet.

He was wrong.

He glanced around the room and the empty shop seemed to encourage and deflate him at the same time. He stood at the counter and looked up at my menu like he'd never seen it before. "I guess I'll have a large coffee, no cream or sugar."

Surprised, I almost asked if the coffeemaker in the shop was broken. But a sale was a sale. "Sure, can I get you something to eat with that?" I went to pour his coffee knowing he'd turn down any treat. The only time he ate cheesecake was when we gave it away during the monthly meetings. The guy could squeeze a dime pretty tightly.

"I'll have one of those apple things we had a few days ago." He cleared his throat, then added, "It was really good. Sadie's a great baker."

I about dropped the filled paper cup. Grabbing a sleeve for the to-go cup, I sat it on the counter. "Sure. You want that to go, right?"

He took out his wallet and pulled out a twenty. "No, I'll eat here."

I glanced around the empty shop as I ducked to grab the cheesecake. This wasn't good. Josh hadn't been around the store lately, not since Aunt Jackie and Harrold had started dating. Maybe he was finally breaking out of his shell, or more likely, he had council business to discuss with me.

I put the filled plate on the counter and rang up his order. "Seven dollars even." I nodded to the twenty. "You want me to take it out of that?"

"Please." Now he just seemed amused at my unease.

I counted back his change and he took his time returning the bills to his wallet, making sure they were all facing the same way before closing the black leather.

He looked around the room again. "Why don't you pour yourself a coffee and come join me. I've got something I'd like to ask you."

Great, here it comes. The thought almost spilled out of my mouth, but I clenched my teeth together. "Sure." I grabbed my still-full coffee cup and followed him to a table. The wheeze in his breathing sounded more pronounced since I'd last seen him.

He settled into a chair and took a sip of his coffee. "This is really good. Did you know I bought some of your beans before, when…" He paused and I knew he was thinking about the past. He used a hand to brush the thought away. "Never mind, that business isn't what I came to talk to you about."

"Council business? All you really need to do is send me an email the week before the meeting and I'll add it to our list. I can't always guarantee that the agenda item will be added." Then I threw Bill Sullivan under the bus. "You probably know that Bill has veto rights on the topics discussed. It's part of the agreement with the city."

He nodded, looking thoughtful. "That's understandable."

I was floored. Who was this guy and what had the alien pod monster done with Josh? I just stared at him, not knowing what to say.

"Sorry, I'm getting off track. What I wanted to ask you is if you could see your way to watch my shop for a few weeks. Kyle will work the business, but he's still young and needs to have someone to check in with him. I'd also like you to make any bank deposits while I'm gone." He pushed a piece of paper toward me.

I studied the list, stunned at the request. I didn't think Josh liked me enough to even say hello as we passed on the street. Now he wanted me to help run his business? I pushed the paper aside. "What's going on?"

"I told you, I need you to help me out for a week or two. I'll try to be available by phone the second week, but I can't promise anything the first week." He took his own copy of the list out of his pocket and smoothed the creases. "Now is there anything on this that you'd like me to go over?

The bank manager has already been alerted to your limited access to the accounts. If you need additional funds made available because Kyle finds a piece to purchase, you have the authority."

"I don't understand."

Josh cleared his throat. "Fine, we'll go over the list. Number one, please check that Kyle is opening promptly at ten. We don't get a lot of customers that early, but I have a few regulars who enjoy shopping before the weather turns hot."

I put my hand on the paper, causing him to look up at me. "No, I mean, why am I helping? Where are you going? On vacation?"

He shook his head. "I wouldn't ask you to do me such a big favor for a romp in some tropical island. I just need you to help. You've been very successful with your own shop and I'd appreciate it if you could see your way to doing me this favor."

I stared at him. "Aunt Jackie might be a better choice. She's more familiar with your shop."

He held up a hand. "You can't tell your aunt about this. I'm sure she's too busy with her work and," he swallowed hard, "other things to be bothered with this."

"But," I started but before I could press him, he stood.

"So if you have more questions, please let me know. I'll be leaving on Friday and back no later than a week from Tuesday. Although I'm sure it can't take that long"

I watched him walk out of the shop, his shoulders drooping, and wondered what was going on with the man. I'd corner Kyle later when Josh wasn't hovering and find out. The kid adored his boss, but if something was going on, he'd know.

And if he didn't, I'd make Josh tell me his plans before he left tomorrow.

Chapter 8

When Sasha arrived, she looked better than she had yesterday. Her eyes were clear and I didn't get the impression she'd been crying. Maybe whatever was bothering her had been dealt with or she'd gotten good news about next semester's financial aid. If she'd still appeared worried, I was going to tell her I'd front her the money for tuition until she got her aid. I didn't want her to have to push off school any longer than necessary. Having Olivia had already put her behind in her schooling. The girl worked hard, she deserved a break now and then.

"Hey boss, has the place been dead without all the chicks from the school coming in?" She shook her head. "I drove by the beach parking lot and it's filled with cars. I didn't even have to stop to know they were following Barista Babe."

Sasha had started calling Toby that a few months ago. I thought it was funny, but it made him uncomfortable. He knew he drew women into the shop, he just didn't like the idea it was because he was cover-model handsome. The boy did have some substance under all that good-lookingness.

"I've had a steady stream of customers since we opened. Not swamped, but enough to keep me busy. Your shift may be a little slower if all the traffic stops at the beach, but there's enough places with sales happening, we shouldn't be dead." I thought of Josh and his strange request. He liked Sasha. Maybe he'd let something slip to her when he'd come in for his afternoon coffee. "Do you know what's going on with Josh?"

Sasha tied her apron behind her back and then poured out the coffee to make a fresh pot. "He seems better. Breaking up with your aunt did a number on his head, you know that right?"

"I mean, do you know if he's doing something next week? Maybe a vacation?" I still hoped that something positive was behind the strange request. However, I didn't hold out much hope. The man had looked scared. That was never a good thing.

Sasha set up the first coffeepot to brew and dumped out the second pot. She shrugged, not looking at me. "Not that he told me about. What did you hear?"

The man hadn't really sworn me to secrecy, or if he had, I thought I was still being vague enough that it didn't break his confidence by asking. "Nothing."

Sasha raised her eyebrows, clearly not believing my response. A door chime sounded saving me from having to respond.

"I'm running to make a deposit, then out to the truck. Anything I need to take?" I scooted behind her to get my tote out of the office along with the deposit bag Aunt Jackie had locked in the desk.

"Nope." Sasha stepped behind the cash register and greeted the customers. The couple must have been visiting for the festival since I didn't know them. I half-listened to their order, then left through the front door. I turned left toward the bank and ran right into Esmeralda.

"Whoa, sorry." I held up my hands, not quite sure we wouldn't wind up on the cobblestone sidewalk.

When she regained her balance, Esmeralda ran a hand down her skirt to smooth the crinkles. "You're off balance."

"Typically happens when I almost knock someone over." I wasn't in a mood for her cryptic answers.

"I didn't mean physically." She grabbed my arm, swaying in the morning sunlight. "You've lost something."

"Yeah, you said that before." I tried to step around South Cove's resident fortuneteller and my neighbor. The woman liked to play with my head. She'd even admitted she was good at reading people. My worry about the missing money must be showing on my face.

The fingers of her hand tightened around my arm, keeping me grounded to that spot. "You need to keep her safe. The dark is near but it's not aimed specifically at her. If she's kept safe, the evil can't find her."

Cold chills ran the length of my body. Esmeralda sometimes seemed to know too much. Things that she couldn't know, even with mad body language skills. Aunt Jackie wouldn't have told anyone about the missing money. Well, she might have told Mary, but her best friend was out of town.

I whispered my question, hoping to reach whatever power was talking through Esmeralda. "Who do I need to keep safe?"

As I spoke the words, the spell broke and the fog cleared from her eyes. The vision was gone and my neighbor was back. Esmeralda smiled. "I'll do my best to keep Maggie inside for the festival. I know you worry about her."

Maggie was a jet black kitten that had adopted both me and Emma. She tended to cross the road to visit when she thought Esmeralda had a message for me from the great beyond. I believed the cat liked sleeping in the afternoon sun on my front porch. Either way, I worried about her getting hit by a car as she crossed back and forth. "That would be good, especially this weekend. Mary says our traffic should double."

"It's sweet for you to worry about my Maggie." She released my arm, staring at her hand like it had acted on its own. "Did something happen?"

Now I did walk around her. No use bringing up the vision. Esmeralda would want to read my palm or do my tarot cards or something to make sure there weren't additional vague premonitions to give me and I didn't have time for that. Once my errands were done for the day, I was curling up on the couch and reading.

I didn't get even close to the couch for over two hours. The lines at the bank were long. People were grumping at the new teller for mistakes. Then when I got to the food truck, they were almost out of coffee cups, so I had to run back to the house to get my Jeep. Then to the store and back to the truck. I'd just pulled out a bottle of water and the book I'd been dying to start when my cell rang.

"Yes?" I tried to keep the annoyance out of my tone. I probably failed.

"Where are you?" Aunt Jackie's voice was low like she was in public and didn't want to disturb the people around her. The noises in the background sounded familiar, but I couldn't place them.

I opened the book and read the first line. "At home. I'm a little busy right now, can I call you back?"

"Unless you're finishing getting ready for the planning meeting, I think you need to talk to me."

"Wait, what planning meeting?"

A long, drawn-out sigh echoed into the phone. "The library event? Sasha asked you to step in for her so she could keep the shop open today. We always meet for lunch on Thursdays."

I slapped my palm against my hand. I'd forgotten all about the meeting. "Lille's, right?" I glanced at the clock. One-thirty. I would only be a few minutes late if I hurried.

"See you soon." My aunt clicked off and I grabbed my purse and my keys. Hopefully Lille's parking lot wouldn't be packed. I would just walk, but the tone of my aunt's voice had informed me I was already in trouble for not being on time.

I let Emma outside and ran to my car. I got the last slot in the parking lot and ran into the restaurant. I spied my aunt and two women sitting by the window. Nodding to Lille who stood at the hostess stand glaring at me, I weaved my way through the tables, filled with mostly tourists.

My aunt took in my rumpled clothes and sniffed as if I'd shown up in pajamas.

I slipped into a chair and smiled at the women. "Good afternoon. Sorry I'm late, I'm Jill Gardner."

The woman closest to me held out a hand. "Monica Chatman. I'm the head librarian for the school district and this is Kori, she's an assistant."

I shook both women's hands, but I got the feeling that Kori didn't much like the title Monica had bestowed on her.

"Actually, I'm the marketing director for the library," Kori explained as she shook my hand.

It was Monica's turn to sniff.

"Anyway, so glad to finally meet you. Sasha raves about you." Kori ignored the pointed barb, not even breaking stride talking to me. "She's been so helpful, as I'm trying to set up a teen-based marketing program."

"We adore Sasha." I took out my notebook and a pen. Opening to a clean page, I looked around the table. "So what are we meeting about?"

"Dear, we don't just jump into business. We usually have something to eat first. I'm sure you're hungry after your busy day."

My aunt's comment made it seem like she knew what a mess my day had been. Who was her source? Hoping she was just making conversation, I nodded and put the notebook to the side. "Sorry, I don't mean to be rude."

"No problem. I was the same way when I first started working for the library back home. Now Texas is a place that likes their social routines. We'd have a meeting to decide on the agenda for the meeting we were having the next day." Kori sipped her tea. "You all move a lot faster than my former co-workers ever did."

"I didn't realize you were from Texas." My aunt looked at me, the question forming on her face before she asked. "What part?"

"Just a little town near San Antonio. I doubt if you've heard of it."

"I can't remember exactly where, but our new tea shop owner is from the San Antonio area."

Kori put her hand on the table. "You're kidding me."

I held a hand up in a mock pledge. "I swear to God."

No thunder crashed into me as I stood there, so apparently my vow hadn't offended the big guy. "I think she said she was from Melaire. Have you heard of it?"

A big grin filled Kori's face. "That's where I worked right out of college. I ran the children's division for the local library. It was such a small town, I'm sure I've either met her or some member of her family. What's her name?"

"Kathi Corbin. Her sister Ivy's currently in town too. Although, I'm not sure that she moved here." I looked at Aunt Jackie. "Did you get the feeling she just needed a temporary job when she talked to you about the shop?"

My aunt gently shrugged. "I didn't let the conversation get that far since we aren't currently looking for additional help. It didn't feel right to let her keep hoping."

"I know both women. Kathi's quite the celebrity since she was a runner up in the Miss Texas beauty contest. She talked to my teen group one Saturday about career choices for women, but all the girls wanted to hear were her pageant stories." Kori pushed her long bangs out of her eyes. "I guess it's the age group."

I didn't know since I had only been in one beauty pageant in my life when I was just starting high school. Back when I thought I could do anything. I had a ton of confidence, but the girl who won had been groomed in contest lore since she was five. She had the walk, the smile, and even the best answers. And she had a stage mother who didn't mind stepping on other contestants' evening gown hems.

"So is their mother still alive? Kathi said that Ivy was the caretaker for their dad." I watched Carrie bring refills for everyone's iced tea and then tap a pen on her pad.

"You guys wanting food?" Carrie glanced at Lille who still glared at the table.

I picked up my menu. "Of course. Bring me the Cajun Grilled Chicken salad, with the vinaigrette on the side."

As the others ordered, I sipped my tea. I didn't know why I was so intrigued by the Corbin family, but there was definitely something Kathi wasn't telling us about her impromptu move across the country to start a new life. After Kori ordered, I reminded her of my question.

"Oh, the mother? I don't know. I got the feeling she'd been gone a while. Kathi's dad never left the house, or at least, I never saw him out in town."

I formatted another question but my aunt kicked me under the table. I leaned down and rubbed my calf.

"We'll get started now. I'm excited to bring you all up to date about the author and the plans for the presentation and signing." Aunt Jackie took the reins for the next hour as I sat and took notes. I'd really let myself get behind in the planning process and most of the information was a surprise to me as well as the librarians.

As we said our goodbyes to Kori and Monica, I pointed to my Jeep in the parking lot. "Can I give you a ride back?"

"I think I'll walk." My aunt surveyed the sky for any rain clouds. "I need to stretch my legs for a bit before I take over for Sasha."

"The bank was crazy busy when I made the deposit today." I hoped my opening would lead her to tell me that she'd found the missing check. And remind her I was doing all the bank trips.

"Claire stopped by the shop just before I left. She's ready to kill that new teller, but what can you do?" My aunt kissed me on the cheek. "I'll talk to you tomorrow."

She paused at the sidewalk edge and looked both ways. A blue sedan stopped to let her cross the street. Just as she was halfway across, a black motorcycle sped around the car and past Aunt Jackie, knocking her back onto the pavement. I ran to her side. The woman from the car beat me to her and on the other side, a truck stopped, blocking traffic.

Aunt Jackie struggled to stand, but as soon as she was up, she doubled over in pain and leaned against the car.

I looked her over. "Are you all right?"

He face was ashen as she shook her head. "Something's wrong with my ankle."

I dialed 9-1-1 and when Esmeralda answered, I quickly explained what had happened. Before I got off the phone, Greg had pulled up in his truck.

"Is it just your ankle? You aren't hurt anywhere else, are you?" He kneeled and touched the skin where even I could see the angry red marks.

"I'm perfectly fine, except for my right foot. I can't seem to put any weight on it." My aunt pressed her lips together and I could see the pain in her eyes.

"The ambulance will take thirty minutes to get here. I can meet them on the highway if she's okay to be moved. Did you see what happened?" He took me to the side. Harrold had left his shop and joined the group clustered around the blue sedan.

"That motorcycle guy with the pig on his back sped around the car waiting for Jackie to cross. I think he must have frightened her because she stepped back, then she was down." I put my hand over my heart, trying to slow my breathing. "It happened so fast."

Greg gave me a quick squeeze. "I'm taking her to meet the ambulance. Follow me in your Jeep." And then he walked back over to the group, picked Aunt Jackie up in his arms, and carried her to the truck.

I put my hand on Harrold's arm. "Do you want to ride to the hospital with me?"

He turned and looked at me like he'd never seen me before. Then he nodded. "Let me lock up the shop and I'll be ready."

I didn't have to wait very long for him to climb into the Jeep. I'd moved the car to wait in front of his shop after the traffic had cleared and Greg and Aunt Jackie were long gone. I didn't know if we'd see the ambulance, but I knew Greg would follow and stay with her until I got there.

The ride to Bakerstown was quiet. Harrold and I were both lost in thought. I parked the Jeep in the emergency room lot and we hurried into the hospital. "Jackie Ekroth? She was just brought in by ambulance?"

The lady at the desk nodded, then typed some keys. "We show she's been admitted, are you family?"

"I'm her niece." I looked at Harrold who shrugged.

"You go ahead. I'll wait out here." He walked over to the coffeepot and poured himself a small Styrofoam cup. Coffee spilt over his hand as he raised the cup shakily to his mouth.

I followed him and patted his arm. "I'll come let you know what's going on as soon as they tell me."

Then I followed the greeter who stood waiting to take me back into the treatment rooms. The swinging doors led us to a hallway so white it made me nauseous. The hall was wide enough for two or three stretchers to race toward the next door. The woman turned in front of me and motioned toward a door. "She's in there."

I walked in and the sight of Aunt Jackie lying on a hospital bed made my head spin. Greg stood at the foot of the bed. They stopped talking when they saw me.

"What are you doing here? You should be relieving Sasha at the shop in a few minutes. She has to pay extra if she's late picking up Olivia, you know." My aunt waved me out of the room with her hand. "Go on. I'm just fine. Greg said he'll drive me back when they finish with my wrap."

"You thought I wouldn't come? The bone's not broken?" I aimed the question to Greg, not trusting that Aunt Jackie would tell me the truth.

"Just a sprain. And a few scrapes. She's very lucky." A nurse squeezed in next to me and went to the top of the bed. "And we need to do a tetanus shot since she hasn't had one for at least several years. Older patients don't bounce well."

I could hear my aunt's sniff at the reference to her age. "I wouldn't have even fallen except for that horrible motorcycle gang member." She turned toward Greg. "Who's on your list of possible suspects?"

Greg patted her hand. "Can't say I have a list. I wasn't there to see the guy, remember? I'll have to check the security cameras to see if we got a good shot." He paused and looked at me and I saw the 'this time' that he didn't say. Now he believed my description of the larger motorcycle guy. And since the other one was dead, I guess he was thinking about more than Aunt Jackie's accident.

"So you're letting her out today?" I watched the nurse take Aunt Jackie's blood pressure.

She marked something in her chart before answering me. "In about thirty minutes she'll be on her way home." The woman frowned at my aunt. "To rest. You need to stay off that foot as much as possible."

"I'll bring her home with me." There was a pull-out couch in the office and even though it wasn't as nice as my guest room, at least she wouldn't have to go up and down the stairs. "I'll drop her off, then go back to her apartment and gather some clothes, then I'll go back and take over for Sasha. Nick can drop off something from Lille's when he takes his lunch break."

I had convinced myself that this might just work, especially if I could keep Emma outside so she wouldn't knock Aunt Jackie over and break some other part.

Aunt Jackie snapped her fingers to get my attention. "Jill, listen to me. I'll stay with Harrold."

I stopped my mental planning and focused on my aunt. "What?"

"I said, I'll stay with Harrold. I've been staying there most nights already." She leaned her head back on the pillow. "If I ever get out of here, that is."

"That's my cue to see if the ortho guy is ready to do your wrap." The nurse left the room.

I stared at my aunt, unable to formulate words. Not only had she turned down my offer of help as her only relative, she'd just admitted she'd been living with Harrold. Or all but living there.

"Close your mouth dear, it's not attractive." Her eyes were still closed but her lips curved into a grin. "We've been meaning to tell you, but I guess this is as good of time as any."

"Tell me what?" This had been a crappy day and I was one announcement away from stopping at the Bakerstown Dairy King for a banana split.

A shoe scraped the floor behind me and Harrold walked in, the greeter holding back the curtain. "Look who I found."

Aunt Jackie opened her eyes and smiled as Harrold walked around to the side of the bed and kissed her gently on the lips. He took her hand and squeezed. "Are you all right?"

"A little banged up, but nothing serious." Aunt Jackie nodded at me. "I believe it's time to make the announcement."

"Go ahead." Harrold dug into his shirt pocket. "I've got the hardware right here."

I watched as he slipped a large diamond ring on my aunt's left hand. She kissed him then turned to me.

"Harrold and I are getting married."

Chapter 9

"They hardly know each other," I ranted as Greg drove me back to South Cove. We'd left my Jeep with Harrold to drive Aunt Jackie back home. "I can't believe she's even thinking about marriage again. She dated Uncle Ted for four years before they even got pinned."

Greg rolled down his window and rested his arm on the open windowsill, not saying anything.

"Are you going to just sit there, or argue with me?" I ran my fingers through my hair three times before I took my hands and put them under my thighs, hoping to keep them from randomly pulling every hair out of my head. "Let's stop for a milkshake."

"We already drove past the last drive-in about ten miles ago. We'd have to turn around and I don't think you want Sasha to be even later in picking up Olivia." He turned the volume on the stereo down. "Your aunt is a grown woman. She can make her own decisions."

I sank into the truck's seat defeated. I knew this might happen someday, but now? My emotions were all jumbled. "She looked so happy. The two of them were just beaming at each other like teenagers who decided to go to the prom. Don't you think it's too soon?"

Greg didn't answer for a few minutes then as he drove past the turn off for The Castle, he shrugged. "You're not going to like what I'm about to say."

"Go ahead, I don't think today can get worse." I studied the coastline, knowing that I needed to get Emma out there to run. That would help burn off these feelings. Running cleared my mind. The problems didn't go away, but they seemed more solvable after the activity.

"They don't have a lot of time to waste." Greg was right and his words hit me hard. I didn't like thinking about my aunt's age or the number of years we had left.

The truck slowed as we turned a corner and saw The Coastal Inn parking lot filled with news vans. Greg turned on his blinker and maneuvered the truck into the crowded lot. "Sorry, honey. I've got to see what's happening. Hopefully it's just a slow news day."

I dialed the shop as I watched him make his way through the people and into the office.

"Coffee, Books, and More. How can I help you?" Sasha answered after the second ring.

"Hey, it's Jill. I'm almost in town, but Greg had to stop and check out something. I promise I'll be there soon." I watched as several of the local stations tried to get Greg to answer a question as he walked through.

"You must be at the Inn. I've been watching the newscasts. Someone has a hostage in one of the rooms."

I sat up straighter. "You're kidding, right?"

"I swear. The maid went by a room and saw a woman holding a gun on a man. Now, no one will answer the door in the room." Sasha murmured something that I couldn't make out. "Crazy, right?"

I considered my options. If this was true, Greg would be here for hours, dealing with the issues. "I'll walk into town from here. Just give me a few minutes."

"No hurry, when I heard about Jackie, I had my mom pick up Olivia and bring her down. I'm good to work until closing. As long as you don't mind a little girl curled up on your couch reading." Sasha paused. "Is Jackie all right?"

I thought about the question. My aunt could have been seriously hurt, but I was grousing about her love life? I tried to shake the vision of her in that hospital bed out of my head. And then, the look on Harrold's face when they had arrived at the hospital and only family had been let in to see her. I was acting like a completely spoiled brat. "She's fine. Luckily nothing's broken. She does have a bad sprain and will have to be off her feet for a week or so."

"That's going to drive her crazy." Sasha giggled and a grin curled my own lips. Being slowed down was going to make my normally super active aunt just a little nuts. And Harrold got to deal with all of that. I was beginning to feel sorry for the guy just a bit.

I thought about my perfectly timed schedule for the week. "So if you're okay closing, I'll check on the truck before I go home and then tomorrow, I'll work a longer shift and you can come in and close. What time would be good?"

We made plans for Friday and Saturday to cover the store, but I knew I needed help with the food truck for those days since Toby's time was now going to be limited and I couldn't leave Nick there alone. This was one of those times we needed a sixth employee. My aunt's shifts were just one task of the many she handled. I'd worry about the others if and when she told me I needed to step in. First, we needed to get through the weekend.

Greg knocked on my window and I rolled the glass down. "Hey, I'm going to be stuck here for a while."

"I heard. Who's been taken hostage?"

Greg ran his hand through his hair, clearly frustrated at the question. "And how did you hear this?"

"Don't worry, I didn't go traipsing around your crime scene. Sasha saw it on the news." I peered at him. "Don't you trust me at all?"

"It's not that I don't trust..." He turned as a reporter shoved a microphone in his face. "Look, I said no comment. If you want an official statement, come by City Hall in an hour and we'll give a full update."

The reporter sulked away and Greg turned back to me. "The news got it wrong. There was no hostage situation. Just a family dispute. Nothing serious. No guns, no bloody parts, just a fight."

I reaffirmed my commitment not to watch the local news programs. If anything big was happening, it would show up on my Facebook feed.

"Of course not, that's not sexy or even interesting," Greg continued. "Like I said, slow news day. Once they hear my official statement, I bet they won't even do a retraction after blowing the situation up to this frenzy pitch." He held out his keys. "I know you have to get back to the shop. Do you want to drive back to your house? I'll have one of the guys drop me by to pick up the truck."

I pushed his hand away. "I'll walk back to town. I can stop and check on Toby and Nick, then just head home. Sasha's got the shop covered. I need to make some calls and find a warm body for the truck tomorrow. There's no way I can leave Nick there alone."

Greg opened my door and swept me into his arms for a quick kiss. "You're the most understanding girlfriend in the world. You know that, right?"

"Glad you noticed." I squeezed his arms. "Call me tonight. I don't think I'll be able to do much on Sunday."

"There goes Greg's No-Guilt Sunday," he complained, but a smile on his lips was echoed by a twinkle in his eyes. "I'm sure you can make it up to me in some small way."

I slapped his arm. "Go work. I've got problems to solve."

Greg looked over at the police line where the news vans were still parked, and a row of reporters watched us. "Me too."

As I walked away, I heard the litany of questions barrage Greg as he walked back toward the motel office. Darla said she'd interviewed the office manager. Maybe I should stop by the Inn with a basket of cookies tomorrow and see what she told our local reporter. Yeah, right after I worked a double shift and found someone to work the food truck. No, this was one murder investigation that Greg was going to have to handle all on his own.

I had too many other problems to deal with, including dealing with my aunt's big news of the day. What was Josh going to say? And for that matter, where was he going that I needed to make bank deposits for him?

Lost in thought, I power-walked the bike path that ran between the motel and the beach. *One good thing*, I thought, *I should get my steps in today*. The sun was low in the sky, but I could hear the crowd at the beach still going strong. We'd close the truck about six, which would give Toby time to run by his place and get a quick shower before clocking in for his evening shift.

The guy had more energy than I did. And I wasn't going to complain about it today.

"I'm surprised to see you out here."

I jumped, grabbing my tote, and turned toward the beach side where Ivy Corbin was climbing up the stair access to the road. I relaxed my shoulders, but kept my hand on my tote. This woman was starting to ring my warning bells for some reason. Not that I knew or trusted Kathi, but her sister was just enough off-center she made my skin crawl. I looked up and down the road.

"Did you walk all this way?"

"I like the fresh air. I used to walk from the farm all the way into town twice a week when I lived at home. I learned to shop light at the store, and if I was going to the library, paperbacks were my friends." She fell in step with me. "Are you heading back to town or the party down at the beach?"

"The beach to check on the food truck and then home. I'm about partied out." I hid a yawn behind the back of my hand. "It's been a long day."

Ivy considered me, then glanced over her shoulder. "Did you hear what was happening at that hotel down the road? I swear I've never seen so many news trucks."

"False alarm apparently. That's where I started walking. My boyfriend is the police detective here in South Cove, so he had to stop to handle the issue." I could smell the food cooking now. Diamond Lille's had opened a booth where they were serving gourmet burgers for the festival goers.

"So did you hear what was happening?" Ivy asked the question a second time and I glanced over at her. "Why were the news crews even there? Was there another dead body?"

I shook my head. "I don't know the details, but I heard it was a family dispute. Probably a husband and wife got into it and the maid overreacted. But who knows."

"Did you hear about the murder there a few days ago?" Ivy's voice held an undercurrent of excitement. Was she one of those drama vampires? People who liked it when bad things happened to others? My internal alarm bell was clanging like a fire alarm had gone off. I paused and looked at her, but Ivy was staring back in the direction of the Inn, like she expected someone to come after her.

"Just that some guy died. Nothing exciting." We were steps away from the parking lot. For a second, I'd considered asking Ivy if she could work while Aunt Jackie was out, but there was something holding me back. For a visitor, the woman was excessively interested in the bad things that were going on in South Cove. Maybe I could talk to Kathi about her. I really needed to hire someone soon. Like, for tomorrow's shift.

When I reached the food truck, my cell rang. "Sorry, I've got to take this."

Ivy just waved and headed down to the beach, directly to Lille's burger booth. Maybe she'd already found a job? I sat on a bench on the edge of the parking lot and answered my cell. "Hello?"

"Your aunt wants to talk to you." Harrold's voice sounded amused.

"Is she okay?" I kicked myself for leaving the hospital so soon. I should walk back up to the Inn and get Greg's truck. If he was still there. I glanced at my watch.

Harrold's voice brought me back to the conversation. "She's fine, she just wants to make plans for tomorrow."

"Wait, what?" I realized I was speaking to dead air. Harrold had already passed the phone to my aunt.

"Jill, you'll need to deal with my shift tonight." My aunt's voice sounded normal, no pain or tiredness coming through the phone.

"It's already handled. You need to rest. I can figure out staffing without your assistance from the hospital bed." I'd expected to hear from her about staffing, but not until tomorrow at the earliest. Typical Aunt Jackie, wanting to keep her finger in everything.

"I know you're probably stressing about the festival staffing. We've talked and Harrold and I will deal with my shift tomorrow at the shop. I won't be able to help out on Sunday in the truck, but we were closing the shop anyway, so you should be fine."

I rolled my eyes, even though she couldn't see my reaction to her martyr offer. "I can deal with the shop on my own, you don't have to come in."

"Now that's just a lie and you know it. Harrold and I can staff the shop. His son has already agreed to manage The Train Station on Saturday. I'll stay off my feet and on the couch while Harrold does all the heavy work." I heard him chuckle in the background.

"I'm being called into servitude," Harrold called out from Jackie's bedside.

A grin landed on my lips. "Welcome to my world," I shouted back, knowing he probably couldn't hear my response.

"Now, don't be cute." My aunt brought me back to reality. "If the festival wasn't going on, I would stay out of the shop and on the couch reading or watching old movies. I just can't leave you in a lurch, not now."

"I could hire someone temporarily." I still worried about Aunt Jackie pushing herself too hard.

"No need. The doctor said I should be dancing by next weekend. I'll have Sunday through Tuesday off. Just plan for me to be gone on Wednesday too just in case and deal with tonight's shift. Other than that, I'll be there." My aunt's words had a finality to them that told me it wouldn't do any good to argue.

"If you're sure." I had to admit, it made my life easier. I watched Ivy chatting up Lille at her booth. If I called around, I might be able to find someone who wanted a few hours, but the summer hiring had already drained the pool of available help in the area. Hiring Ivy was off the table. There was just something that bothered me about Kathi's sister.

As I said my goodbyes, I realized I hadn't asked her about Josh's strange request. He'd asked me to keep it from Jackie, but I wondered if she knew what the antiques dealer was planning. Probably a shopping trip for some estate sale. The guy kept his dealer life under wraps, hoping that no one would get the good stuff before he could manage to buy it all cheap.

I tucked my phone into my tote and headed back to the food truck to check on supplies. When things were back to normal, I was going to have a long talk with my aunt about hiring another part-time employee. At least during the summer when we were doing the food truck, we needed more manpower we could trust.

Toby greeted me as I walked into the truck. "Hey boss, how's Jackie?"

"Word spread quickly." I explained her injuries and that she and Harrold were still at the hospital, but heading home soon. As I talked, I checked the supplies. It looked like they'd barely been touched. "Slow day?"

Nick sighed. "No, heavy day. I just restocked everything a few minutes ago. We wanted to be ready for tomorrow's opening. And Toby let me drive his truck." The kid's grin lit up his face. "It's rad."

Toby handed me the deposit bag. "I've already set up the drawer for tomorrow. But here's today's deposit." He held on as I reached for it, watching my face. "Unless you want me to make the deposit on my way to the station?"

I pulled it out of his hand. "I'm heading that way anyway. I'll do it." The bank had already closed for the day but they had a drop box for business deposits. I'd walk into town, check on Sasha, let her know the change in plans, and then drop the deposit for both the truck and the shop. If Lille's wasn't too packed, I'd stop there to grab food before I went home.

"Okay, then. You realize you could tell me if something's going on, right?" Toby's question made me nervous. The guy could read me like a book and he knew something was up besides Jackie's injury. I just hoped Claire would figure out where the money went. If we didn't get an answer tomorrow, it would be Monday before we'd hear anything else. When I didn't respond, he looked beyond me toward the ocean. "I'm on beach patrol tomorrow afternoon and Saturday through the fireworks but I'll stop by to see if you need anything."

"Sasha will be relieving you at ten, and then she and Nick will work the late shift. I'd love it if you'd check in with her. I'll be at the shop until Aunt Jackie and Harrold come in to replace me."

"Jackie's feeling that good?" Toby asked.

I shook my head. "No, she's feeling *that* stubborn."

* * * *

By the time I got home that night, the sun had already begun to set into the ocean. A faint breeze carried a mix of summer florals with the always present salty sea smell that made me feel at home. There was a packet leaning against my front door. In dark block letters, someone had written on the front–For Jill Gardner's eyes only.

There was only one person who would leave that type of message for me. I took the envelope into the house and laid it on the table as I let Emma out and poured myself a glass of iced tea.

I pulled out a formal power of attorney, several deposit slips, and a ten-page document explaining how to make a bank deposit. Josh had left his instructions.

Chapter 10

Antiques by Thomas was closed when I walked by the next morning on my way to open the shop. That in itself wasn't unusual. Coffee, Books, and More opened four hours earlier than Josh's place. I glanced up at the apartments above the store. Lights shone in the one on the left where Kyle, Josh's assistant, lived. The second apartment, the one where Josh lived, was dark. He'd left South Cove.

A part of me worried that this was about Aunt Jackie and Harrold. Josh had been devoted to my aunt so when she'd started dating Harrold, Josh had been crushed. I knew when he found out they were taking their relationship even further, it would hurt him even more deeply.

I glanced over at Tea Hee. The outside of the building looked almost ready to open. The construction crew had built a fake porch on the building, complete with picket fence railings. They had painted the entire thing white to make the shop look like your grandmother's house. If your grandmother lived in a little southern town, that is. Several wooden rockers sat on the porch, just waiting for someone to take a load off. I wondered if Kathi was still on board with us serving her signature tea at the shop. I made a mental note to make sure I talked to her about the joint venture. And maybe we could talk about her sister and what was going on with the family.

As I unlocked the shop's front door, Greg's truck pulled up across the street and I paused in the doorway. This was two days in a row he'd met me at the shop when I'd opened. I could get used to starting my day with the guy. I waved as he got out of his truck and he paused, looking back at Tea Hee. He crossed the street and met me at the door.

"Hey, you." He pulled me into a hug. "How did your evening go? I saw Harrold dropped off your Jeep last night."

"Yep. I have to admit, he was really sweet and concerned about her." I leaned against the doorway. "I guess I could do worse than Harrold for a new uncle."

"You're still freaked out, aren't you?" Greg ran his hand over my hair and pulled me into a hug. "It's going to be okay, one way or the other. You know that, right?"

I relaxed into his hug. "I'm being a spoiled brat about this, aren't I?"

"A little, but I think you're more concerned about making sure Jackie's okay. And there's nothing wrong with that." He kissed me on the head. "I've got to go to work."

I looked up at him. "I thought you'd come to see me and have coffee?"

He shook his head. "Sorry honey, I'm on the clock. I need to talk to your new neighbor."

"Why?" I held up a hand. "Forget I asked. I already know what you're going to say. You can't tell me what's happening in the investigation."

He tapped me on the nose. "You're learning. Maybe I'll see you tomorrow out at the beach. I just hope tonight's not too crazy. I don't think Toby's been sleeping much."

"Are you telling me that I'm going to have to cut his hours?"

Greg shrugged. "I know he's trying to buy a house. He can't keep burning the candle at both ends. Let's just keep an eye on it. I'd hate to force him to make a choice."

We said our goodbyes and I went into the shop to make coffee. I glanced at the work schedule for the next week. With the festival going and Jackie limited in what she could do, I needed Toby. Besides, I worried about how much traffic our Barista Babe brought into the shop. If Greg told him he had to quit the second job, I'd be hurting in more ways than one.

Life was ganging up on me this week.

Instead of brooding, I got busy. I did all the morning and evening chores, hoping that Harrold and Aunt Jackie could handle the walk-in traffic.

It was noon when Kathi Corbin appeared in the shop. She collapsed into a stool at the counter.

I handed her a glass of water. "What can I get for you?"

"Double shot espresso." Her hands shook as she lifted her water glass.

I started the coffee, but kept my eyes on her. "Are you all right? You look frazzled."

Kathi drank down the entire glass of water. Then she sighed. "I'm sure you know that Greg came to see me this morning."

"I saw him, but he didn't tell me what he was doing." I kept my eyes down as I finished her coffee.

"Well, he wanted me to come with him to the county morgue. The body that they found out at that motel on the highway was someone I knew."

I stopped pouring the coffee. "Who?"

"The motorcycle guy that died a few days ago?" Kathi started to explain.

I finished pouring her espresso and handed it over. "I don't mean what body. How did you know him?"

"Oh." She took the coffee from me. "Darryl was my cousin. I told you I used to work for his dad at the general store. Uncle Pride died a few years ago and Darryl thought he needed to take on the role of family patriarch, even though he doesn't have an idea of how to run his own life, let alone a family."

"I'm sorry for your loss. Did you know he was in town?" First Ivy, then her cousin. There was one thing both of those people had in common: Kathi. If I was investigating this murder, I'd be looking at the former beauty queen's motives hard. But I was sitting this one out, even though my fingers were itching to find out more.

She sipped her coffee. "No. Ivy told me that Darryl wasn't happy and had sent her here to bring me home, but I never expected him to come in person. I mean, it's not such a big deal, right?"

"What's not a big deal?" I was confused and didn't know what she was talking about.

She put the cup down and put on the fake smile I'd seen at the meeting while she was entertaining the crowd.

"Family stuff." Her face brightened. "On a brighter note, guess who has a date this afternoon?"

I pursed my lips and pretended to think. "Let's see, you?"

She nodded, her blond hair bouncing with the action. "Blake stopped over at the shop this morning and we got to talking. Of course, he's busy with the band every night until Monday, but we thought we'd go wander around the festival for a couple hours Saturday. Just like two tourists, getting to know South Cove."

"It's a great time to check out the other shops on the street." I wished I had time to do my liaison thing with a few of the businesses this week. It would be great PR not only for the Business-to-Business meeting, but also for Coffee, Books, and More. "I'm stuck working most of the weekend since my aunt was hurt yesterday. I'm glad it was minor, but I know how you're feeling about your cousin. It's hard to put that kind of stuff on the back burner when it's family."

"Oh, no. Well, tell her to get better soon. Summer is a bad time to be laid up, you miss out on so many fun activities." Kathi pointed to the display case. "Why don't you get me up a couple of those cheesecake slices? Maybe if I feed my construction guys they'll work faster."

I knew when I was being sidelined, but I didn't take it personally. I just changed my tactic. As I boxed up the treats, I posed a new question, trying to keep her talking about her family. "So how long is Ivy staying? I heard she was looking for work. Is that just until you open and then she'll be working with you?"

The color drained from Kathi's face, even with the perfectly applied makeup. "She won't be staying long. In fact, she'll probably return to Texas with Darryl's body. Someone has to deal with all the arrangements, and Daddy isn't up to that kind of stress."

"Is your dad ill?" I thought about Kori's statement that she'd never met the guy.

Kathi took a twenty out of her purse and laid it on the counter, making a big deal of looking at the clock. "I had no idea it was that late. I really need to go." She grabbed the bag and quick stepped to the door, faster than anyone should be able to walk in that high of heel.

"You forgot your change," I called after her but she didn't even turn around.

She raised her hand in a farewell gesture and called back, "Keep it."

I rang up the purchase and put the tip into the jar. Toby and Sasha split the tip fund at the end of the week. And now, I guess Nick would be cut in on the windfall as well. I knew Toby probably brought in more of the cash during his shifts, but he was the one who insisted on the equal shares. Apparently for him, it went to the house fund. For Sasha, I expected it made sure Olivia had food and paid for daycare. And now with Nick splitting it even more, I hoped it wouldn't cut into her budget too deep. Of course, summer was our busy season, so maybe she wouldn't even see a decrease. The missing check entered my mind again.

My thoughts hovered around Sasha and her financial situation for the next hour or so. I knew it wasn't my business, but I also knew the girl was fretting about something. Something she wasn't talking about.

Harrold wheeled Aunt Jackie into the store precisely at three PM. He grinned as he pushed her toward the couch. "Your relief shift has arrived."

"Such as it is," Aunt Jackie muttered.

I walked over to the chair, catching his eye and raising my eyebrows in a question. Harrold just grinned. "Don't mind her. She's been grumpy all day."

"You've been treating me like an old lady all day, no wonder I've been out of sorts." She tilted her head, presenting her cheek for a kiss. "How's the traffic been today?"

I bent over and gave her a quick kiss on the offered cheek. I sent my thanks upward for the wave of gratitude I felt that she hadn't been more seriously hurt. "Busy. I've talked to the guys over at the truck and they've been swamped. They've had a line since they opened. Sasha's replacing Toby and then she and Nick will man the truck until close."

"Purchasing the truck was a smart business decision." My aunt's statement wasn't one of pride, but more just the facts.

"We're going to have to hire more staff if we use it often." I thought about the long weekend ahead and knew I didn't want to spend all my time working in the small truck kitchen. Even without really cooking anything, that metal box would be steaming hot by the middle of the day.

My aunt waved away the idea. "We'll be fine for a while. Besides, this is our maiden run. And we have Nick until school starts. With what that college of his costs, I'm sure he'll welcome the hours."

Harrold had gone to the counter, washed his hands, and donned an apron. "So who wants to show me how to make coffee?"

Welcoming a distraction, I trained him in how to run the cash register, make the menu coffee drinks, and where we kept the extra cheesecakes just in case he sold out. It was almost four by the time Aunt Jackie told me to leave.

Glancing at my watch, I shrugged. "I have to make Josh's bank deposit anyway." I froze, hoping Aunt Jackie hadn't heard, but I felt her gaze bore into me.

"Why?" Her tone was cold and hard.

I grabbed our own banking pouch and tucked it into my tote. "I told him I would." When I got to the door, I added, "He's out of town for a while." Then I powered through the door before she could ask a follow-up question. I figured my cell would ring in about two point five seconds, but that I could ignore. At least I knew one thing. Josh's disappearance was a surprise to my aunt as well.

The bell rang as I pushed open the door to Antiques by Thomas. Kyle stood at the counter, working on a laptop. His smile deepened as I walked toward him. "Hey, neighbor."

"Hey, yourself. How has business been today?" I had a funny feeling my aunt wouldn't be the only one to call tonight and I wanted to be able to give Josh an update when he checked in about the store.

"So so. I had a guy come in and ask about selling some pieces, but since I didn't know what Mr. Thomas would offer, I had to just take his name and number. Mr. Thomas said I might be estimating purchases later this year, but for now, I'm in sales only."

"I'm sure it's a science." I didn't know much about the antique business except I was sure Josh's business plan consisted of four words. Buy low, sell high.

Kyle pulled out a matching bank deposit bag to our own and handed it to me. "I think it's more of a feel thing. Thanks for doing this. I know it made Mr. Thomas feel better about being able to leave me alone in the shop."

"No worries, I have to do my own deposits anyway." I took the pouch and considered how much they looked alike. Was this the cause of the missing money? It could have been an honest mistake by someone at the bank. I slipped the deposit bag into my purse. Distracted by the idea, I asked about Kyle's boss. "So do you know where Josh went this weekend?"

Kyle frowned, his hand tapping on the counter as he considered my question. "He didn't tell you either?"

I glanced at my watch. I still wasn't good at sneaking information out of people. "Oops, if I'm going to make it to the bank, I better get running. Let me know if you need anything while Josh is away."

I dashed out the door and heard Kyle call out a goodbye, but I'm sure he knew I was avoiding the question. So Josh hadn't told the one guy who worked with him where he was going either. This was getting curiouser and curiouser. He could be trying to buy an estate before anyone got wind of the sale, but I didn't think so. This felt more personal.

I mulled over possible answers to the Josh mystery as I walked to the bank. When I got there, the line was almost out the door. Margie's line was ten people deep, but the new teller, Allie, was filing her nails.

I headed to the new teller's window. The bank was closing in a few minutes and I didn't want to be carrying around both our shop deposit and Josh's all the way home. She didn't look up when I put the moneybags on the counter, keeping her eyes on one of her glittery nails, which I swore had real gold mixed in the polish color.

When she didn't speak, I did. "Your window is open, right?"

She looked up at me and rolled her eyes. "Duh. I guess people just like Margie more than me. I haven't had a transaction all day."

I wanted to tell her that maybe she needed to learn some social skills, but I didn't need an argument. Let Claire teach her employee customer service skills or figure out a way to fire the boss's relative. Instead, I pushed the bank bags closer since she hadn't attempted to pick one up. "These are both commercial deposits so there's a mixture of cash, coins, and checks."

The girl opened one and sighed. "This is going to take forever." She glanced at the clock. "I'll need Claire or Margie to walk me through this kind of deposit." She zipped up the bag and put it and the other one under her counter. "You can pick up your deposit slips tomorrow."

"Usually Margie does it while I wait." I wasn't sure how to press the point, but didn't want to take a chance of more money going missing.

Allie pointed to the line. "Well, she's got a ton of people and Claire just stepped out for a district meeting with my dad. So there's no one to help me with this. You're just going to have to wait. You do want the deposit done correctly, right?" She opened each of the bags, took the deposit slip out, and made a copy on the printer behind her. She shoved the paper toward me and then picked up the nail file again. When she saw I hadn't moved to take the copy, she cocked her head. "Can I help you with something else?"

Like she helped me at all? I shook my head. I'd wanted to talk to Claire about the missing deposit, as she said she should have a report from Nebraska today, but since she was out of the branch, asking Allie would be a waste of time. I took the pages and folded them into my purse. "Nope, I'm good. Have a nice day."

She didn't respond. I glanced at Margie, who met my gaze and shrugged in a non-verbal 'what can you do' message. But at least she saw me come in, so if the bank bags disappeared, I had at least one witness and I had the photocopy. Poor Claire, this girl was going to ruin her branch's reputation.

I shouldn't be thinking bad things about someone I didn't know, but Allie had instilled absolutely zero confidence that the deposit would be done tonight. More likely, she'd hand it over to Margie in the morning and have Margie "show" her how to process a commercial deposit for both mine and Josh's deposits.

Tomorrow, I'd come in earlier, or just wait until Monday when I had all day. I hated leaving money in the store, but we had an old safe built into the floor, so nothing should happen.

I started walking toward the beach, wanting to check in with Sasha on how the traffic had been with CBM Annex, or as most people called it, the food truck. I wasn't convinced yet that the truck was worth the extra staffing, nor was I convinced we actually had enough staffing to do it right. Thank God Nick had decided he'd done enough dishwashing for Lille's for a lifetime. As soon as Sadie had mentioned he was looking for a summer job, I'd hired him on the spot. Or at least his mom had called and let me hire him over the phone. The kid was a hard worker.

As I walked by Diamond Lille's, a Harley pulled out of the lot and I saw Lille wave to the rider. Before she could disappear into the restaurant, I called out to her. Even across the parking lot I saw her roll her eyes. I didn't really want to deal with Lille with an attitude, but I took a deep breath and hurried over to meet her.

She took a pack of cigarettes out of her purse, lit one, and walked over to meet me in the middle of the parking lot where she'd set a bench and, more importantly, an ashtray. She blew out a puff of smoke as I walked up. "What do you want?"

"Good evening to you too." Holding my hand up, I tried to stop the next words out of Lille's mouth. "Sorry, bad habit. I've been dealing with people all day. Anyway, I needed to ask a favor from you."

Now she raised her eyebrows in the universal 'are you freaking kidding me' motion. Instead of speaking, she took another puff off her cigarette. Then as she exhaled, she asked, again, in a softer tone, "Seriously, what do you want?"

"Did you hear that my aunt was almost run down by a motorcycle? Luckily she didn't break anything, just a bad sprain to her ankle and her pride, but it could have been worse." I paused, wondering how to say what I wanted to ask without sounding like a royal jerk. "Another elderly woman was almost hit earlier this week, right there." I pointed to the road in front of Diamond Lille's.

"I heard about both incidents." Lille put out her cigarette even though it was only halfway smoked. "But I still don't know what you want from me."

Pulling up my big girl panties, I pressed on. "I wondered if you could talk to the local motorcycle, uhm, club you know people from and see if this rider is from there. All I know is he is a huge guy and wears a cut with a pig on the back."

A smile curved on Lille's lips. "You're saying he's a porker?"

"I don't know what the name of the, uhm, club is. I thought maybe someone from the local group could help us identify the guy and then Greg could go tell him to slow it down while he's in town." I exhaled, not realizing how fast I'd been talking.

"You can call them gangs, I know that's what you're thinking." Lille tucked her half-smoked cigarette back into her pack and stood from the bench. "I don't know if I can help, but I'm tired of these guys coming in and making problems for the local group. They're a bunch of sweethearts."

Sweethearts that ran the local drug trade, I thought but was able to keep the words from flying out of my mouth and getting me on some sort of gang hit list—or kicked out of Diamond Lille's. "I appreciate it."

Lille walked back to the restaurant's side door. She paused, then turned back. "How's Nick doing?"

"He's a hard worker, you must be sad you lost him." Now those were words I hadn't planned on saying. Lille's face turned a brighter shade of red, but then she actually smiled.

"You're right, I am sad. I got used to the little twerp being around." And with that, she left me standing in the parking lot.

Chapter 11

By the time I arrived at the food truck, Toby had already left to get ready for his police shift and the crowd around the truck had dissipated. I opened the side door and climbed in. Nick was on his phone and turned beet red when he saw me.

"Sorry, Miss Gardner. I was just answering a text from a guy at school. We're debate partners." He turned off the phone and shoved it in his pocket. He scanned the truck for something to do.

Sasha put her hand on the kid's shoulder. "Why don't you go take a break? We haven't had a customer in a few minutes and I need to talk to Jill."

"You sure? I could restock the cups. They look a little low." He stepped toward the storage closet.

Sasha stepped in front of Nick. "Go take a break. Come back in fifteen and then you can restock everything. I don't want to be worried about breaking any child labor laws because we didn't let you go to the bathroom. Just don't sneak a cigarette. Your mom would kill me."

"I don't smoke." Nick climbed out of the truck and I saw him check his watch. The kid would be back before fifteen minutes had passed. I would bet my house on it.

Sasha waited until he was out of sight before turning to me. "Look, I want you to know that I wouldn't steal from you or Jackie or the shop."

"I know that." I pressed my lips together. Actually, I *had* thought there was a chance, but from the way she reacted when I asked her, I knew she couldn't have taken the money.

"Now, see, I don't think you do. I mean you seriously asked me if I'd just happened to deposit a check for Coffee, Books, and More into my account—a check that supports the literary event I'm working my butt off to make successful." Sasha put her hands on her hips. "I'm building a life here for me and Olivia, but if you don't trust me, maybe I should be looking elsewhere."

"I don't want you to leave." I sank back against the counter. "Frankly, I don't know what happened to the missing money. All I know is the bank says the check has been cashed."

"There's no way I could have switched up deposit slips without someone noticing. Have you thought about that?" Sasha rubbed an imaginary spot on the stainless steel counter, not looking at me. "I want you to trust me."

"Sasha, if you're telling me you didn't take the money, I believe you. It's not that I think you or Toby *would* steal, I just can't imagine what happened to that check. Nothing more will be said of the issue." My lips curved into a small smile. "We need you here. Who else would run the teen clubs with such style?"

Her lips twitched. "You'd probably have to shut them down. Can you see Toby talking to a group of teenagers? He'd do the 'don't drink and drive' lecture every month and tell them about his most recent busts instead of talking about a book."

Looking to change the subject, I refocused the discussion back to Nick. "How's Nick doing?" I looked around the neat as a pin truck interior. "Looks like you have him cleaning every minute you're not busy. I don't think it was this clean when we bought the truck off Austin."

"Probably wasn't." Sasha shrugged. "I can't help it. It's like my own little store so I want to keep it shiny. Silly, right?"

"Who am I to judge? Especially when it makes the store look amazing." I leaned on one of the counters. "Seriously, how are you doing? Is there enough traffic to keep this place open out here?"

"Maybe not yesterday. I think after Toby got hit with his cosmetology students, the place kind of died off. Today, it's been slow and steady since I've been here. I doubt we'll get many more customers tonight though. I thought if we were really slow, I'd close up about seven."

I looked at my watch. It was six now and since I'd arrived, there'd been no customers. "Let's make it six-thirty. Then Nick can help you clean up and you both can get out of here at a reasonable time."

"Sounds good to me. Just before you got here that Ivy chick showed up and wanted to talk. Ballsy, that one." Sasha wiped off the counter as they spoke.

"Why do you say that?"

"She asked if she could come in the trailer and sit and chat." Sasha shook her head. "It's like she was raised in a barn. She thinks all she has to do is ask and someone will do something for her. You should have heard her go off about Kathi and how her sister had all the business owners blackball hiring Ivy."

"It hasn't been that way at all. I can't get Kathi to say anything about her sister being here except how Ivy would be going back to Texas sooner than later." I grabbed a bottle of water out of the small fridge under the front counter. "Believe me, I've tried to get the gossip. The only thing I learned was the girls' cousin was the motorcyclist that was murdered at the Inn a few days ago."

"Wow, did Greg tell you that? I thought you didn't talk about cases?" Now I had Sasha's full attention, the wet rag stilled on the counter.

"Not Greg, Kathi. She said Greg took her down to the morgue to identify the body this morning." I thought about our conversation that morning. "I have to say, she wasn't too broken up about him being dead. I don't understand their family dynamics at all."

"Well from what Ivy told me, Kathi was the favorite child. Her dad and the rest of the family treated her with kid gloves from the day she was born." Sasha dropped her voice. "Apparently there was a little love triangle issue and that's why Kathi left home for here."

"I can't see anyone not choosing Kathi unless the other woman was Miss Universe or something. Face it, the girl is gorgeous, and men, sometimes, are stupid."

"Sometimes?" Sasha started to giggle and I joined in.

The door slammed and we turned to see Nick standing there staring at us like we were deranged. "Sometimes, what?"

I cleaned out the till, leaving them enough to get them through the last few open minutes. I'd refill the cash register to start the day with tomorrow, as I was working the food truck first shift, then going to relieve Aunt Jackie and Harrold at the shop for a few hours. If this weekend didn't kill one of us, we'd be lucky. Too few people and too many hours and slots to fill. I made a mental note about talking to Aunt Jackie again about at least hiring more part-time staff to help out when we had events. And since I was starting up school in a few months, I didn't want to be missing classes just because we didn't have anyone to keep the store open.

I said goodbye to Sasha and Nick and trudged home, holding my tote a little closer. I would stick the moneybag into my office safe as soon as I got to the house. I had just crossed the highway when I heard my name being called from behind me.

"Now what," I muttered. I realized in my busyness, I hadn't eaten all day. As soon as I got home, I was opening a can of soup and making a sandwich.

Ivy Corbin was behind me. She crossed the highway, dodging traffic as she ran. When she reached me, she put her hand on her heart. "I really have to start working out more."

"Did you want to talk to me?" Even I heard the grump in my voice. Ivy blinked at me. "Sorry, I'm starving and I get a little snarky."

Ivy pointed toward town. "I'm walking into town. I thought we could go together. I'd hate for you to have to walk alone."

"I'm only going as far as my house, but you're welcome to tag along until then." I started walking again and for a few minutes we were both silent. I was beginning to wonder if Ivy had talked herself dry with Sasha when she finally spoke.

"Do you like my sister?"

The question surprised me. Echoes of teenage angst oozed out of Ivy as we walked. I considered my answer carefully. "She seems nice. I haven't really talked to her that much, so I can't tell exactly what kind of person she is, but yeah, I could see liking her."

Ivy seemed to consider what I'd said.

When we reached my driveway, I paused. "This is my stop. Thanks for walking with me."

"Great house. Looks like someone's done a lot of repairs." She craned her head around the garage. "And another shed back there? You have a great setup here."

"Thanks." I jingled my keys in my hand. All I wanted was my soup and to crawl into a hot bath and forget about today. "So I'll see you later?"

"Don't trust her." Ivy stared at me with wide eyes.

The statement came out of the blue, then I realized she was talking about her sister. "Kathi? I'm not supposed to trust Kathi?"

Ivy nodded.

"Tall order on no evidence." I shrugged. "I guess I'll just have to take your words under advisement."

As I walked away, I heard her call out. "If you want to keep your boyfriend and your nice little life, don't trust her. She eats people like you for lunch."

* * * *

Emma greeted me at the door, whining to be let out. I should have stopped on my way down to the beach, but I hadn't thought about it. The good news is she hadn't had an accident. The bad news was she really, really had to make water, as my grandmother used to say.

I flipped through my mail, separating out the majority of the envelopes promising lower interest rates, pre-approved loans, and flyers for the local mall stores. If I got real mail, it was typically a bill. Today didn't disappoint. My water and credit card bills had arrived on the same day. I put them both on the desk and after turning on the shredder, all the financial junk mail turned into confetti. Or, what I loved to use to start a fire in my backyard fire pit. Greg marveled at my skill in fire building. I just knew how to increase my chances of being successful.

With that thought in mind, and a pot of condensed soup on the stove heating up, I pulled out my journal and started writing. By the time I'd finished, I had written down everything that had been bothering me, even if they didn't have anything to do with the murder.

I drew a line down the middle of a page. On the left, I wrote down random thoughts about the missing money. I wished Claire had been at the bank today, I had wanted to find out what she'd learned. The event was coming up soon and I didn't want this hanging over my head for weeks afterward. I paused and put "call Claire" on my Monday to-do list. Then I made a list about Kathi's cousin's death. Darryl Corbin. Son of the family patriarch, Uncle Pride. I guessed that role had passed to Darryl when the uncle had died. With Darryl gone, did that role fall to one of the female survivors? Pushing aside my curiosity about family traditions, I asked the bigger question that was bugging me—what was he doing in South Cove?

I opened my laptop and started a search on Darryl Corbin in Melaire, Texas. I got a few hits. Darryl had been the quarterback at the local high school during his tenure there. According to the local sports reporter, the team had hit a rough patch under his leadership, losing more games than they won. Another link led me to the uncle's obituary. At the bottom, the paper had listed out his surviving relatives: unmarried Darryl, two nieces, and a brother, which must be Kathi's daddy. With him ill, he didn't seem likely to take on the role, especially since Darryl had taken over after his father's death. On the other hand, now the family didn't need much of a patriarch since it was down to just three people on Kathi's side of the family.

No smoking guns there. When I returned to the search field, I changed the name to Kathi and got a ton more hits. Mostly about the pageants she'd entered over the years. Most of them she'd won, but when she got into the bigger venues, like Miss San Antonio, she'd stalled her win/loss record. And after her run for Miss Texas, there was nothing. No appearances, no talks, and no sign of the hometown beauty queen, at least on the internet. I checked the date on the Miss San Antonio mention. Four years ago. What had Kathi been doing in those four years? Was that when she worked for the uncle's store?

I changed my search again and looked up businesses in Melaire. The city council webpage was woefully out of date, which reminded me to check out South Cove's page. I switched over to the site and scrolled through some pages, making notes about changes and updates needed. Then I forwarded the notes in an email to Amy for her to address on Monday. And if she had questions, we had the workout class together on Tuesday. One more thing off my long list of to-dos.

Going back to the Texas site, it bothered me that I didn't see a general store listed either on the council's page or as I searched the web. Maybe they didn't have a web presence, but you would have thought Google would at least have an address, phone number, and picture of the front of the building. But there was nothing I could match up to what I knew about the place.

I closed down my laptop and finished eating my soup, staring at the list of questions I'd written about Kathi and her family. I had focused on the wrong angle. That was the problem.

I turned the page and started writing questions just about the murder and why Darryl was even here. I wondered if Darla had gotten anything new from her interview with the motel clerk.

I picked up the phone and after dialing, reached her. "South Cove Winery, can I help you?"

"Hey Darla, it's Jill. You busy?" It was a dumb question; I could hear the music and the crowd milling around the tasting room.

"Swamped with customers. It's great. What can I do for you? Are you and Greg coming down?"

"Actually, I wanted to know who you talked to at The Coastal Inn. I've been thinking about the murder and wondered what she knew about Darryl."

There was a pause on the phone. "Sorry, I didn't catch most of that, but why do you care about the murdered guy? Are you investigating on your own again? You know that drives Greg crazy."

"Are you going to tell me who you talked to?" I kept the question short, knowing full well she could hear me.

"Only if you share what you know. I'll come by the truck tomorrow morning and we can talk." With that, Darla hung up the phone.

I glanced at the clock. Almost nine and I felt like I'd been awake for days. I took my bowl to the sink, let Emma outside one more time, and walked around the house, locking doors and turning off lights. I grabbed a book I'd been reading and a bottle of water and let Emma inside.

Glancing out the window, I could see the little light shining over the door. The rest of the shed was dark. Toby would be out on patrol until five, when he'd come home for a power nap, then return to his patrol duties promptly at noon. Greg would be handling the morning shift at the beach festival. Then Toby, and finally Tim, unless things got out of hand. In that case, all three of them would be called in to handle whatever issue arose.

I guess Greg might have the same staff issues I did. I'd have to make sure he came by for some coffee.

* * * *

As I got ready to work the coffee truck the next morning, I texted Greg an invitation to stop by when he had time. I knew he was probably busy with the festival and the murder investigation, but I hoped he could spare a few minutes for me. I kind of missed the guy. Besides, I wanted to ask if he'd found out anything about Kathi's uncle while he was investigating. Something about the family felt off, but maybe it was just a difference in culture I was sensing.

I gave Emma a new bone and locked my sofa pillows in the office. The girl had a bad habit of eating them and I didn't want to tempt her any more than necessary. She stood by the back door, waiting for me to click her leash on her collar.

I bent and gave her a hug. "Sorry girl, no runs today or tomorrow. We should have our beach back by Monday though."

I heard her chuff and knew she wasn't happy with the answer. Emma loved to run more than I did. Okay, she loved to run, and I did it so I could eat more cheesecake. Never mind the reasons, it all worked out in the end. Today she'd have to settle with hanging out at the house alone.

I locked the doors and headed down to the beach to start my shift. I hadn't worked the food truck since our first trial run. Although I didn't love working in the little shop as much as Sasha did, it was fun to change up the atmosphere and hopefully gain more customers. I hadn't figured out a way to combine the book experience with the mini coffee shop, yet.

I was considering the pros and cons of adding an outdoor rack when I arrived at the truck. A few of my commuter regulars were there, waiting for me to open, including Claire LaRue, the bank manager.

I unlocked the door and opened up the windows. "What do you guys want so I can get it started?"

I listened to the called out responses and started up the hazelnut blend, as well as our signature dark roast. Most of the six relaxing and soaking up the morning sun drank their coffee pure. Black with no cream or sugar. I noticed Claire hadn't joined in the order call out so after I served up the regulars, I leaned over the counter where she stood waiting.

"What's up?" It's never good when your banker tracks you down to talk.

"Don't look at me like I'm an IRS auditor." She leaned on the truck. "I realized last night after I got home that I'd told you I'd call and I didn't. So I'm coming over to tell you I still don't know what happened to the deposit."

"Isn't that kind of weird? I mean, don't you guys have some sort of system?"

Claire shrugged. "We do, unless something happened when we were uploading the deposit. The clearing center in Nebraska has verified the check cleared, but can't track the account down due to server issues. Between you and me, the new system isn't working at top speed yet. The IT guys have all descended on the center and they swear the system will be fixed in hours, not days. But as I think about your deposit, all I can come up with is someone made a mistake."

"So you don't think the check was deliberately deposited by someone else into their account?" I glanced around the parking lot, but we were alone.

"You think someone stole it and put it into their account?" Claire tapped her fingers on the counter. "I don't see how that could happen. I mean, Margie knows all the businesses in town. If someone tried to change an actual check, she would have alerted me immediately."

I blew out a breath. I'd hoped the deposit would show up, and not in Toby's or Sasha's account. Claire's explanation on why this wouldn't occur made me even more confident. I nodded to the coffee bar behind me. "What are you drinking today?"

"Large skinny mocha with whipped cream." Claire shrugged. "I'm feeling like I need a pick me up. I'm heading into the bank to try to train Allie one more time. If she can't learn the job this week, I give up. Let her dad hire her in his office."

I made the drink and slipped a sleeve on the cup. "Four-fifty. Unless I can talk you into a slice of cheesecake?"

"You noticed I said skinny mocha right?" She handed me a five-dollar bill and waved off her change.

I dumped the coins into the tip jar and grinned. "With whipped cream. You know that has calories, right?"

"A girl's got to splurge sometimes. I'll give you a call Monday morning as soon as I talk to the Nebraska branch manager. We will find out what happened." Claire walked back to her car and slipped behind the wheel of the upscale sedan.

I poured myself a coffee and watched the sun come up over the mountain. The only thing bad about working the truck was it didn't have a back window so I could see the ocean. I would have to be satisfied with my mountain view.

Traffic kept me busy until about ten. Greg walked up right as I'd served the last customer in line.

"Hey beautiful. Get me a large, black please." He leaned against the truck and ran his hand through his hair.

"Uh oh. Has it been that bad already?" I poured the coffee, put on a lid and a sleeve, and handed the cup to him. "Be careful, it's hot. I just made a fresh batch."

He closed his eyes and inhaled deeply over the cup. "I swear, just the smell of this is giving me a boost. You're the best girlfriend ever. Have I told you that before?"

"Once or twice." I brushed the too-long hair out of his eyes. "So what's going on?"

Greg sipped his coffee and then shrugged. "Long nights trying to figure out this whole Darryl mess. I suppose you've heard the gossip around town."

"No gossip, but Darla should be here any minute. You want me to ask her something specific?" No way could he say I didn't warn him that I was talking to Darla. And I'd kind of said I was investigating, in a roundabout way. He hated when I stuck my nose in what he considered his business, but to be frank, I kind of liked figuring out what happened. It was like watching all those crime shows, but in real life.

"Just tell me you're not trying to solve the murder." He looked into my eyes and then held up a hand. "Wait, don't say a word. I don't want to know. If I don't ask, you don't have to tell me and I won't have to lock you up in one of my cells for safekeeping."

"As long as I have access to my books, I might enjoy the break from real life." I sipped my coffee imagining a day or two with nothing to do but read. "Hey, do you know anything about Kathi's uncle? I guess he ran the general store, but once he died, everything online just disappeared."

"I've been looking into her family tree a bit. Actually, I've had Esmeralda call and talk to a few residents in their hometown, but so far, nothing strange has come up." He stared at me for a long minute. "You think the murder is about family?"

"Who else knows all your deep dark secrets?" Leaning against my forearms, I stretched out of the truck to try to see around the truck to the beach. No luck. I sighed and fell backwards into the truck. "Anyway, all kidding aside, Kathi came by and told me she'd identified the body as her cousin."

Greg's brow furrowed. "That's funny, since she barely looked at the body and I had to threaten her with obstruction before she'd tell me. So why would she start blabbing her relationship with the deceased to everyone?"

"I know you're not doubting me, right?" I pointed at his coffee. "We break up, there's no more free java for you."

He reached up and pulled my head down into a quick kiss. "I don't date you for your coffee." His blue eyes twinkled. "Besides, Toby would still feed my addictions."

"You're a brat." I nodded to the woman standing behind Greg. "How can I help you?"

She looked at Greg and almost dropped her purse. She waved him up to the window. "You go ahead."

Greg held his cup in a mock salute. "I'm already taken care of. Thanks for the offer, though." He grinned at me. "I might stop by tonight with dinner if you're going to be home."

I held my hands outstretched. "Just give me a call and I'll let you know what's going on."

"It will be late," Greg warned as he walked away. He tipped his hat to the woman still in line. "You have a nice day, ma'am."

I swore the woman almost swooned. When she came up to the front of the van, she was still half-twisted around, watching Greg walk out of sight. I guess the man had a certain air about him.

"What can I get you?" I asked, grabbing a cup to start her order.

She pointed to Greg. "I'll take one of those and a large decaf."

Pouring the coffee, I smiled. "I can provide the decaf, but finding a guy like Greg is a lot harder than it looks. Which is why I'm not giving him up, to anyone."

"You'd be a fool to let him slip through your fingers." The woman put a ten on the counter.

I handed her the coffee cup and smiled. "I guess mama didn't raise no fools here."

The woman laughed and waved away her change. "Keep it.'

As she walked away, Nick Michaels came up to the trailer on his bicycle. He padlocked it to the trailer and hurried into the service area.

"Did I miss the rush? I knew I should have come in early, but I couldn't get a hold of anyone."

"You're right on time. If I worked you too long your mom would have a word or two with me." I dumped the almost empty pot of dark coffee.

He stood at the sink and washed his hands. Sadie had raised a great kid. "She knows I want to make as much money this summer as I can. There's a cool Semester in Paris program I want to get into for junior year. But I have to have the deposit in October. So I'll take as many hours as you can give me."

"Well, if we keep doing these festivals, I'm sure you'll get more than enough hours this summer." I counted out the money and set up the cash register for his shift. "Are you sure you'll be okay for a couple hours? Sasha will be here at two."

"I'll be fine." He crossed his arms and looked at me. "What, don't you trust me?"

Trust is earned, not given, I thought. But I nodded. "Of course I do. I just don't want you getting overwhelmed all by yourself."

He puffed up his chest. "Just call me Super Barista. I can make two mochas and plate up a serving of cheesecake with one hand tied behind my back." He shadowboxed across the trailer.

"Call me if you need help. I'll have Jackie come down to watch the shop and I can be here in less than five minutes." Laughing, I tucked the bank bag into my tote. "Do you need anything before I leave?"

He shook his head. "I'm good." He looked around at the already prepped trailer and pulled a book out of the backpack he'd wore on his bike ride. "I even have something to read while I wait. Of course, this exact book is stocked in the store, so I'm trying some subliminal messaging. Buy your coffee and your next escape at Coffee, Books, and More."

"Smart idea," I said, and truly meant it. When I first opened, my marketing strategies had been more hit and miss. Mostly I bought books each week and watched what sold. Now that Coffee, Books, and More had three book clubs along with a staff-suggested book of the month club, I was selling a lot more books to tourist and town folk alike. I thought about Nick's idea; we did a lot of hand selling in the store. Maybe it was time to set up a Staff Recommends shelf. I'd bring the idea up at the next staff meeting to get a list from everyone.

"I took a marketing class last semester. It was great. If I wasn't going pre-law, I'd major in marketing. It's so much fun. You design a plan, implement it, then start over when it works or doesn't. You never really fail, you just find ways that don't work." He grinned. "No pressure there."

Chapter 12

As I walked home, I remembered I also needed to stop by Antiques by Thomas. I hoped no one would realize how much cash I was walking the streets of South Cove with, but honestly, I didn't want to get the Jeep out. The road was already crowded with cars and finding close parking would be a nightmare.

Nope. I'd just pretend like I was on my way to work, just like a normal day and forget about what was stuffed in my tote. I paused for a bit at home to let Emma run outside as I grabbed the other deposit bag out of the safe. Then, I headed back into town. My cell rang as I was passing Diamond Lille's.

I answered with what I hoped was a cheery hello. I was already five minutes late, and in Aunt Jackie time, that was over an hour. She believed in being thirty minutes early.

"Where are you?"

My aunt wasn't much for small talk. "Just now in South Cove. I've got to make a quick stop and I'll be there to pick up the deposit."

"Fine." And the line went dead.

I was in real trouble when my aunt used the 'f' word. *Fine* meant everything but fine. I crossed the street and entered the antiques store. The smell of the past filled my senses. I always felt like I'd stepped back in time when I walked into the store. This time, Kyle wasn't at the counter. I rang the little bell and waited. The chime echoed through the shop.

I stood by the counter for a few seconds, and glancing at my watch, I knew I needed to get moving. The bank would close at noon and I still had to stop next door for my own deposit. "Kyle? It's Jill Gardner. Do you have a deposit ready for me?"

Something banged in one of the far rooms. I'd been shopping at Josh's store before. The place was crowded with boxes, furniture, and odds and ends. I didn't know how he sold anything. Most days the place looked more like a storage shed for hoarders than a shop for collectors. I called out again. "Kyle?"

"I'll be right there." His voice seemed to be coming from the far back room. I turned toward that direction, wondering if I needed to go find him. Maybe he had been trapped in the maze all morning.

I turned and started toward the sound of his voice, but then he popped out of the room on the left, all covered with dust and dirt. When I first met Kyle, he could have been a poster child for a street kid. He had so many piercings, I was sure he couldn't walk through the metal detectors at the airport. And he had not one, but both arms covered in full sleeve tattoos. Now he had removed the metal from his face and wore button-down dress shirts covering his ink. "You okay?"

He nodded, then took a cobweb out of his hair and brushed it off onto his jeans. "It's bad back there. I'm working on clearing out some boxes."

I watched as he circled around the counter and then handed me the deposit bag. Again, it looked just like mine. I tucked it in the tote. "I forgot to get the bags from the bank from yesterday's deposit. Are you open tomorrow?"

"Nope. Closed on Sunday and Monday. Then I've got three days before the boss comes back." He looked nervously toward the back room. "I hope I'm done by then."

"Done with what?"

The door chimed and a well-dressed couple entered. The woman glanced at her husband after taking in the front display area. "I love places like this. You can find anything."

Kyle smiled at me. "I'll see you on Tuesday evening." He came around the counter and turned his entire focus on the couple. "Welcome to Antiques by Thomas. What are you dreaming of finding? I might be able to help."

The woman tittered and started to explain the piece she was looking for. I circled around the trio and headed back out to the street. A few steps from the shop, I heard a noise and I found myself pushed back against the building. The ocean of people on the sidewalk parted and a motorcycle screamed through them on the sidewalk. Apparently the line of cars looking for parking spots had slowed the guy's progress so he'd decided that people moved easier.

This time I stepped forward and tried to get his license plate as he blew past me. Covered with some type of plastic, I could only make out a few letters. "A, X, 1," I muttered as the crowd started walking again. I dove into the shop as soon as I was close to the door and pulled out my cell, dialing 9-1-1.

"South Cove Police, how may I help you?"

"Esmeralda, a biker just flew up Main using the sidewalk as his personal lane." I headed to the back where Aunt Jackie sat, glaring at me with the deposit bag in her hand.

"You need to get to the bank before it closes," she said as she shoved the bag in my free hand.

"Hold on." I turned away from my aunt and focused on the call.

"I know. My board's lighting up now. I just sent Greg a text, but he's down at the beach. I don't think we'll catch him this time either. I've got to go. I've got five calls on hold."

"Wait, I got a partial plate." I read her off the digits and then hung up.

My aunt was staring at me. "What have you gotten yourself into now?"

Frustrated, I tucked the new envelope into my tote. "You didn't see the motorcycle fly through the crowd on the sidewalk? It's a wonder no one was hurt."

"I heard a ruckus out there, but we were busy with customers." She stared at her wrapped foot. "Besides, I can't really run to the window every time I hear something now, can I?"

Harrold walked over and stood near me. "You're coming back to relieve Jackie, right? She needs to take a pill and lie down for a while."

"I think I can make my own decisions on what I need," Aunt Jackie snapped. "If you're so bored, why don't you go run your own shop?"

"Aunt Jackie." I looked at her. "Go upstairs and relax. Harrold will watch the store while I'm gone, then he can come upstairs for you to apologize or he can go home. It's up to you."

The two of them stared at me like I had gone mad. Then Aunt Jackie shrugged. "He doesn't have to wait for an apology. I'm hurting and grumpy."

"You're pushing yourself too fast." Harrold said, then held his hands up in mock surrender when she glared at him again. "Sorry, I can't help myself. I worry about you."

She smiled at him but her face held the pain still. "I'm going upstairs. Come up when you're ready and we can reheat that potato soup I have in the freezer. I have some rolls we can eat with it."

Harrold watched her leave and then nodded to me. "The sooner you go, the sooner you'll get back. I was just putting on a good face for your aunt, but I don't know how to make any of your fancy drinks. I've been pushing the plain coffee all morning."

"Give them free cheesecake and have any customers who order something you don't know how to make wait for me. I'll be back in fifteen minutes tops." I figured it would be longer, but I didn't know if Harrold would let me go if I was totally truthful. I paused at the door. "You're good for her, you know."

He shook his head. "You have that wrong. We're good for each other."

Greg called me before I reached the bank. "You okay?"

"I take it Esmeralda told you I called about the biker on the sidewalk incident." Greg's call made me feel all warm and gooey. He'd send the grumpy me up to bed if I was blowing a gasket, just like Harrold had done to Aunt Jackie. "I'm fine. I got a partial plate."

"She told me that too. The other callers didn't get much more than big guy and black motorcycle, so I'm glad you were there. I worry when you're in the middle of these things. But I'm getting used to it." Greg paused. "I've got to go. Plan on dinner tonight. I feel a need to be close to you."

"Oh, that's sweet. I'm missing you too." I pulled the door to the bank open and walked into the cool air-conditioned lobby.

"Actually, I'm thinking keeping you close might be the only way to keep you safe."

"Not funny. Look, I'm at the bank. Call me when you're on your way and I'll tell you where I am." I looked at the two lines. Allie's was shorter, but I knew that was a bad idea. I'd wait out the line for Margie. Harrold could hold the fort for a little while longer.

A chuckle filled my ears. "I wasn't joking." He hung up on me and I put the cell in my tote and then pulled out the four bank bags.

I heard the groan from the woman behind me as she calculated the time it would take to process my transactions. Then as I watched, she stepped over and got into Allie's line. *You're going to regret that move, lady.*

Margie's line continued to shorten, and the other one didn't move at all. I saw the line jumper compare our lines several times before she tucked the deposit back into her purse and disappeared out the door. If Claire didn't get this girl trained soon, or transferred out to another branch, she'd have customer service complaints to the head office. If she didn't already. Finally, it was my turn at Margie's window. I piled the four bags on the counter. "Sorry about all of this."

Margie shrugged. "No worries, you guys are easy. I like doing your deposits. You should see what some of the other businesses bring in. At least your cash is in some sort of order."

"You may not like one packet. I'm in charge of doing the deposits for Antiques by Thomas for the next week. I'm not even looking into the bags, just bringing them in and taking back the deposit slip." I had a feeling Josh was meticulous in his money handling, but who knew how Kyle completed the task.

"Still not a problem, but you didn't hear that from me."

I watched as she quickly sorted the cash, counting it out for me to view, then scanned all the checks. She had all four deposits done and the bags and slips back to me in less than five minutes. Harrold would be happy to see me walk through the door. "Thanks. Hey, Allie was going to run yesterday's deposit after I left. Can I get the bags and slips from her without going through her line?"

I saw Margie scan the computer screen in front of her. "I don't see a deposit yesterday." My heart dropped. If Allie had lost my deposit, that was one thing, but if she'd lost Josh's, I'd never hear the end of my irresponsibility. I kicked myself for not insisting she just muddle through the deposit. "Hold on, let me ask her."

Margie walked over and I could see Allie shake her head. Then Margie pointed at me and asked her something again. This time the girl seemed to ponder the question and her face brightened. She ducked under the counter and came up with two bank bags. My two bank bags. Margie said something, grabbed the bags out of the other teller's hands, and marched back to her window.

She opened a bag and took out the contents. "Sorry, it appears that she forgot to make your deposit. I'll talk to Claire to make sure you don't lose any interest because of our error."

She hadn't made the deposit? "How is that even possible? I thought you all counted out your tills every night?"

Margie wouldn't meet my eyes. "We do. But if someone hides work, it's hard to track. Look, I'm really sorry and I will talk to Claire. I suppose you could call our hotline and complain if you really want to, but it would only look bad on management, not the specific teller."

"That's okay. No harm, no foul." I folded the four bags she'd already given me and tucked them back into my tote. I tried to lighten the mood with a joke. "Just know I'll be standing in your line from now on, even if you're swamped."

"You and everyone else in town," Margie muttered as she finished processing the deposits.

* * * *

After rescuing Harrold and extracting a promise that he and Jackie would be back down at four, I opened my laptop and scanned my emails for anything to do with next Friday's library event. Aunt Jackie's accident had come at a bad time. Between the festival and my aunt running on four of her normal fifty cylinders, we were up against some deadlines. RSVPs were coming in to the store email and I had to get a final number to the caterer on Monday. We had offered the gig to Sadie and her Pies on the Fly business, but she'd turned us down saying she wanted to attend as a guest, not work the event.

I added names to the spreadsheet that we kept accessible in the cloud or somewhere on line. I didn't really understand the way it worked, but I loved the ease of updating the document. Aunt Jackie, Sasha, me, and even our two librarian sponsors could update the list as we gathered RSVPs. I'd just finished the last of the credit card charges for the event tickets when I noticed Blake and Kathi walk by the front of the shop. She was pointing across the street at her still-in-restoration building and as I watched, they crossed, weaving through traffic. The sight of Blake holding her hand made me smile.

The door chime sounded and Darla strode in. "Sorry about this morning. I got tied up at the winery. Who orders the usual amount of alcohol for a festival weekend? My night manager, that's who. I don't know what the girl was thinking."

"Did you get the problem solved?" I knew from experience that deliveries from Bakerstown were in short supply on weekends—and pricey.

"Yeah, but Jake's going to expect a favor out of this one, I can already tell." She leaned back and stared at the display case. "Slice me up some of NY's finest. I can't help it, I love that stuff."

"Something to drink with that? A latte?" I knew Darla was partial to full-octane mochas.

"Hazelnut coffee. I've been working my butt off all week. I know we do these festivals to bring in business, but this has been crazy." Darla looked around the shop that for the moment was empty except for the two of us. "You're kind of slow, huh?"

"Here, yes. But the truck has been hopping. I think most of the morning foot traffic has moved down to the beach. The first band started at one. They'll be going until ten tonight." I sat the cheesecake and coffee in front of her and she slid onto one of the counter stools. I grabbed a bottle of water for me and went around and sat next to her. "I'm here until four, then Greg and I are doing dinner at the house, then back to the beach to close up the truck. Wash, rinse, repeat tomorrow."

"Oh, the joy of owning your own business. Did you ever think it would be this demanding?" Darla took a bit of the cheesecake and groaned. "Sadie is a magician with her ovens. This is heavenly."

If I was going to ask her about the murder, I had better do it now, before the sugar coma hit. "So did you talk to the manager over at The Coastal Inn? Did she have anything to tell you about the murder?"

Darla's fork paused midway to her mouth. She looked at me, then the cheesecake, then back to me. Finally, she resolved her internal struggle and sat the fork down. "Are we talking on or off the record?"

"I'd rather you not quote me for your article, if that's what you're asking." Not that I had anything to share that Darla probably didn't already know, but it was good to set up the ground rules first.

She took a sip of coffee and pulled a notebook out of her purse. Paging through, she paused and read the notes. She dropped it on the table and considered me. "I'm going to trust you. Besides, knowing you, you probably want to solve the crime more than write something for a competing paper."

I held my hand up in a salute. "I swear I'm not working for any type of journalistic endeavor. Does that cover everything?"

"Just about." A smile creased Darla's face. "So when I went to talk to Tilly, the guy had signed in as Joe Cook. Which apparently wasn't his name. But I bet you already know that."

I nodded. Everyone knew who had been killed by now, and I didn't get the info from Greg, so it wasn't a problem confirming Darla was right. "Darryl Corbin. He is, well, was, Kathi's cousin."

"I think even in death, they stay cousins. He's just the quieter of the two." Darla leaned closer. "Did you know Ivy was seen visiting his room with another guy?"

Wait, could there be a fourth cousin? The obituary for Kathi's uncle had only listed Darryl and the girls along with their dad, so if not a relative, maybe the guy was Ivy's boyfriend? I'd never seen where Ivy was staying, she just appeared in town or out on the beach. Where was she living? Not at The Coastal Inn. Definitely not at Main Street Bed and Breakfast with her sister.

Darla pointed her now empty fork at me. "Where'd you go just now?"

"I didn't move." Confused, I looked down at my body, confirming I hadn't moved even an inch.

"In your head. You were doing some heavy lifting up there. What were you thinking about?" Darla took another bite of her cheesecake. After she swallowed, she continued. "And don't tell me nothing. Your eyes were twitching like you were in REM sleep, only you were wide awake."

I didn't answer her question. Instead, I asked one of my own. "Did Ivy Corbin fill out an employment application with you a few days ago?"

Darla nodded. "She said your aunt sent her up my way. Why?"

Excitement flew through me like a kid the night before the state fair. "Because job applications have the address and phone number for the candidate, right?"

"You want to know where Ivy's been living." Darla pulled out her cell and dialed a number. When someone picked up the other end, she directed them to go into her office and pull the employment folder. "I'll wait."

I looked at her and she shrugged. "The kid's pretty new. He wanted me to call back in a few minutes because he was setting up the band. He'll learn that the boss comes first, always. Or at least, I hope..." She broke off her tirade and listened. "Yep, that's the one. Find an application from Ivy Corbin and give me the home address and phone number."

She flipped her pad to a clean page and wrote down the information. "Thanks," she said then hung up on her employee.

I looked at Darla. "Well?"

"She lists a Texas address as primary, but right under that is a local hotel. One I'd never even considered Ivy staying at. She's got a room at The Castle."

Chapter 13

The Castle was the primo hotel-slash-tourist attraction in the area. When Craig Morgan ran the place, he was friends with the mayor and sucked up all the city's marketing funding. After he died—well, was killed—his ex-wife took over management of the place. We were all much more cooperative now.

Rooms at the art deco museum were pricy. How was Ivy managing with no job and no visible means of support? And why was she looking for part-time work when she could save a bundle by staying somewhere cheaper? The problem nagged at me during the last few hours of my shift. Luckily, I got a rush of customers right after Darla left, which lasted until just a few minutes before Aunt Jackie and Harrold emerged from the apartment.

Aunt Jackie looked rested and her cheeks were actually pink. She'd been so drawn when I sent her upstairs, I had begun to worry that we'd have to close either the annex or the shop without the manpower to keep both open.

"You look better." I kissed her cheek as she hobbled around me, using crutches to stay off her bad ankle.

"Don't start with the *I told you so*. I was perfectly fine before I left, but I'll admit, the nap did feel good." She set up on the couch and waved me over. "Bring that laptop over here and I'll go through the event sign ups."

"Already done, or at least up to two o'clock today. Then I got busy with customers." I still took the laptop over. "You could look over the to-do list I've started and see if there's anything I need to do tomorrow or Monday. I can't believe this thing is happening in less than a week."

"Did you hear from Claire?" My aunt didn't look up from the computer screen as she reviewed my work on the spreadsheet.

"She said she should know more on Monday. I guess they're doing some sort of computer upgrade." I kept my voice low, hoping Harrold hadn't heard our conversation. "It's been a mad house over there too."

I explained about the new teller, including the part where Allie had almost lost our deposit. I had to leave out the part about me doing Josh's deposits since Jackie would ask why and where he was, two questions I didn't know how to answer.

I glanced at the clock, almost four-thirty. "I gotta run. I'm meeting Greg for dinner at the house."

"A thoughtful man would have taken you out so you didn't have to cook." My aunt sniffed.

Sometimes I didn't know if she liked Greg or if she just tolerated him on my behalf. "He's been crazy busy this weekend too. Besides, I can throw something together faster than it would take us to drive someplace to eat."

"I ordered in a pizza from Lille's for later tonight." Harrold flung a white towel over his shoulder. *Barista Babe, Senior Division*, I thought, trying to keep my grin on the inside. "Why don't you two come down and eat with us? Jackie, isn't that a great idea?"

Jackie rolled her eyes at me and then turned on Harrold. "No, I don't think that's a great idea. I'm sure you only ordered one pizza and have you seen the boy eat? I swear, we'd be lucky to get a piece of crust when he was done."

"So not fair." I grabbed my tote bag. "Partially true, but still unfair to talk about someone who's not here to defend themselves."

"Having a healthy appetite is never a bad thing in anyone." Harrold leaned against the couch, holding my aunt's hand. Another sweet moment. The universe seems to be telling me something. Like how my life could be someday.

"Anyway, I'll talk to you tomorrow. You are off the hook for your shift at the food truck. There's not enough room in there for you, your crutches, and your personal slave." I nodded to Harrold.

"Then I'll see you on Wednesday. I have a follow-up appointment on Monday so we'll ask him to release me for a full schedule." My aunt put her reading glasses back on and stared at the computer. I'd been dismissed.

"It will probably be more like a few weeks before you can count on having her full time." Harrold squeezed Aunt Jackie's hand. "Although she is pretty stubborn."

"You've noticed that?" I hurried out the door before I could hear my aunt's response.

I dropped off my extra bank bags to Kyle along with the deposit slips. "Put these in the cash register where they'll be safe." I could have hung on to them, but honestly, I was afraid if I lost them, Josh would blame me.

"Good idea." He put them into the register while I watched. "I'm closing up for the night but I didn't make any more sales after you took the deposit. So I'll just put the cash drawer in the safe for Tuesday."

"Sounds like a plan." I put my hand on the doorknob, but turned back. "Have you heard from Josh?"

"You mean since he left on Friday?" Kyle shook his head. "Man, I'm beginning to worry about the dude—I mean, Mr. Thomas. He never goes a day without checking in on the store, even when he's on big buying trips. Have you heard anything?"

I wanted to ease his fears, but I was climbing on the crazy bus along with Kyle. Josh should have at least checked in. Josh could be hiding something. Something could be wrong. I would mention his disappearance to Greg tonight. Maybe he could look at John Does and hospital admit lists to assure me that Josh really was just on a vacation. One he didn't want us to know about. To Kyle, I said the only thing I could: "I'm sure he's fine."

Kyle nodded and I could see him swallowing hard to keep back the crack in his voice before he answered. "I'm sure you're right."

As I walked home, I couldn't help but wonder which of us had lied more convincingly. I sent a prayer up for protection for the wayward Josh.

I'd had time for a shower and a quick change of clothes before I heard Greg's truck pull into the drive. I was sitting on the back porch in the swing sipping iced tea. I could see him climb out and then reach back in to the cab and pull out a bag. Even from my distance, I could see the logo. Diamond Lille's. It was like Greg had overheard my conversation with Aunt Jackie earlier and brought dinner just to spite her. The man was an angel. No matter how it happened, I was ecstatic about not having to cook. He saw me on the swing and announced. "Dinner is served."

I put the book down that I'd been reading and stood to greet him. I motioned for him to set the bag on our outdoor table. "I'll go get plates and silverware. What do you want to drink?"

"Iced tea will be fine." He sank into a chair and started pulling out containers. Fried chicken, mashed potatoes, gravy, and a side salad. When I was growing up a feast like this only happened on Sundays. I brought out real plates and he dished me up my meal, making sure I got the breast piece rather than a thigh. He handed it to me. "This okay? You've been starving yourself since your aunt was hurt."

I took a bite of the mashed potatoes and felt the tension ease from my shoulders. Food shouldn't ease my concerns this much, but it did. At least for a while. And so, since I had an unhealthy relationship with food, I ran. This meal would mean I needed to run a marathon. And then maybe an extra couple miles.

I didn't care. "It's great. I didn't realize how hungry I was."

We ate in companionable silence for a while. Greg threw Emma a biscuit and she wolfed it down like it was a marshmallow. He shook a finger at her. "If you don't chew your food, you can't enjoy the flavors."

Emma looked up at him like he was the smartest person on earth. Besides, she still wanted another biscuit.

When we'd eaten our fill, I glanced at my watch. "When do you need to go back?"

"I thought I'd walk down with you and leave the truck here. Parking in the lot is a nightmare. When are you going?"

"I'm closing so I need to be there by seven to start the process. Sasha will handle the late walk-ups and I'll get everything ready for opening tomorrow." I leaned back and closed my eyes. "I'll be so glad when the festival is over. Remind me never to support one of Mary's ideas again."

"You will, you know it." He threw Emma another biscuit and she ate it as quickly as the last. "Have you heard anything about the baby? Weight, name, hair color, sex. I hear all those things are important."

"You forgot length." I shook my head. "I need to call Bill and see what's going on. I just haven't had the time."

"You'll see him Monday night."

A distant roar filled my ears. "Monday night?"

"You're giving a report to the council on the festival. I know I saw your name on the agenda." Emma dropped the wet, slobbery ball at his feet and wiggled her butt in anticipation. Greg shook his head at the dog before returning his gaze to me. "Don't tell me you forgot."

"Another reason not to support one of Mary's crazy ideas. Frankly I'm trying to forget, but people keep bringing it up. I hate going to those things, especially when Mayor Baylor is on a roll about something." I looked at Greg who was watching Emma throw the tennis ball in the air for herself and catch it. The dog was talented and knew how to entertain herself. "Maybe you could read my presentation. Say I was sick with something, like a cold or the plague or maybe swine flu. That way they'd be glad I didn't attend."

Greg watched Emma for a bit longer, then turned back to the table. "What, has Amy already turned you down?"

"Flat." Sometimes I hated that my boyfriend understood me. I couldn't pull anything over on him, not lately. "You any further on the murder investigation? Or have you been breaking up fights at the beach all day?"

"About half and half. Of course, part of my day was dealing with the fallout from that idiot driving his motorcycle down the sidewalks of Main Street. Just once, I'd like to have someone close by when he's pulling one of these stunts." Greg pushed his fork through his mashed potatoes absently.

"I asked Lille if the guy was local. She said no one local would wear a pig as part of their colors. Apparently that's low class even for a biker gang." I ate the last bite of chicken and eyed the bag. Was I still hungry or did I just want more because of the perfectly awful day, no, week, I'd been having? I decided that a wing wouldn't hurt and pulled one out of the bag, breaking it apart as I continued. "Who knew even gangs had pecking orders?"

"Oh, I think there's a lot you don't know about gangs or motorcycle clubs." Greg pointed his fork at me. "And I'd rather you didn't go off and try to find out more information. This guy doesn't care who he hurts, from his actions today. I'm just glad the only incident so far has been your aunt's ankle. I really have got to figure out why he's here."

Greg had that faraway look he got when he was thinking about a problem and I wondered if he realized what he'd even said aloud. I finished my chicken and looked at my watch. "Ugh, I've got to get back to the truck. Are you done?"

It was kind of a rhetorical question since Greg belonged to the clean plate club and he'd earned his membership that night. The only thing left on his plate were leg bones from the chicken. He stood and looked into the bag. "Should we put these leftovers in Toby's fridge? I don't think he's had time for a real meal for days now."

I nodded. "The key's on the rack by my kitchen door. Make sure you leave him a note too. I'd hate to see this go bad because he didn't realize it was there."

Greg followed me into the kitchen, wrote up a note, grabbed the tape and the food bag, and then went out to my backyard where his second-in-command lived. I had to say, I kind of liked the company now and then. Toby had coffee and donuts with me on Monday mornings, keeping me entertained with his stories from late night patrols as well as interesting customers that had come into the shop the week before. The one thing we didn't talk about was his dating Sasha. Toby kept that side of his world separate and since the two of them worked for me, I appreciated that. The boy had gotten his heart broken, not too long ago, from a woman that he'd thought had been the one. Now he was protecting it from both Sasha and her daughter. A practice that was probably good for him, but maybe not so great for Sasha.

I cleaned up the dinner dishes, rinsing and putting them into the dishwasher, and put the trash into a can in the laundry room where I could lock Emma out when I wasn't around. The girl did love dumpster diving.

I was ready to go by the time Greg returned. He slapped a bank deposit bag down on the table. "You need to make sure your employees return these to the shop after they make a deposit. Claire's always complaining about having to buy new ones for the local businesses."

I stared at the bag, not wanting to touch it. Toby hadn't done a deposit in over a week. Why would he have a bag in his apartment? I unzipped the bag and there were two deposit slips. The one looked like our normal take for a day. It was the second one that had me shaking inside. It was for three-thousand-dollars and had a different account number than the first one. I sank back into my chair. "Crap."

Greg sat next to me. "Are you okay? You're doing way too much. You need to slow down, or you'll be the one in the hospital."

"I'm fine." I fingered the deposit slips. Monday, I'd take this into the bank and let Claire tell me who owned the account number on the slip. I just prayed it wasn't Toby.

With Emma in the house with a chew bone, I locked up the house and we started walking to the beach. I tried to focus on anything but Toby and the money. "Hey, did you know that Ivy was staying at The Castle?"

He didn't even look at me as he responded. "And?"

"Don't you think it's a little out of her price range? I mean, she was looking for work a few days ago and now we find out she's living in one of the most upscale hotels in the area?" I was thinking aloud, more than asking him a question, but his words surprised me.

"And why are you so concerned about where someone is living? He put his hand on my arm and stopped our progress to get my attention before we continued. "Please tell me you're not trying to investigate this murder."

"Of course not, I just thought it was interesting, that's all." The lie felt heavy in my mouth. Thinking about my conversations with Kathi and Darla, I knew I'd been investigating all along. Especially after I found out the dead guy was Kathi's cousin. Something in all this craziness wasn't adding up right and I wanted to get it solved.

I had actually written up a suspects pool in my notebook. The only thing I hadn't done was label the page "people who could have killed Darryl."

As we continued our path down to the beach, I wondered if I'd ever stop my investigations. I knew it was a bone of contention between Greg and me. Was it my fault that I found things interesting and wanted to learn as much as I could?

The kiss he gave me when he left me at the food truck was brief and I could tell we both felt like there were things unspoken, but we didn't have time for a real fight, and I wasn't sure what I'd say if Greg gave me an ultimatum.

If I didn't stop sleuthing, would we have to break up?

I let the food truck door slam behind me as I entered and Sasha spilled coffee on her hand as she jumped.

"Ouch." She sat the cup down and grabbed a napkin as she looked at me. "Are you okay?"

I shook my head, tears filling my eyes. I so wasn't okay, but I didn't want to talk about it. I didn't even want to think about it. I found a napkin, wiped my eyes, and as Aunt Jackie would say, bucked up. Which basically meant quit being emotional and just do the job at hand. The relationship stuff could wait for another day. "Fine, I'm just tired."

Sasha seemed to consider this as she handed the now-full cup to the waiting customer. "Enjoy the festival," she called out the window, then she turned to me. "Mercury is in retrograde. Which means you shouldn't make any decisions about relationships or business ventures until after the twentieth."

I poured a cup of coffee for myself and leaned against the counter, looking at her. "I didn't know you believed in all this horoscope stuff. Or have you been talking to Esmeralda?"

I would have sworn that Sasha blushed at that question, but with her dark skin tone, I couldn't really tell. I did see her gaze drop and she grabbed a rag, washing up a spill that I couldn't see. "So, yeah, I went and got a reading the other day. She had come into the store and when she touched me, she said that things were happening in my life that we needed to explore."

"I wish I could do that to sell coffee." I sipped the dark brew, letting the warmth ease out the crazy I'd felt just a few minutes ago. Sometimes just saying nothing was the best response to a problem.

"Don't tease. It was really helpful for me to sort out some things that had been bothering me. I wasn't sure what was happening in my world and when she told me that the climate was wrong to make any big decisions, I realized she was right." Sasha squared her shoulders. "And I think the advice can be given to you as well. You looked ready to shoot a bear when you walked in, and I know you and Greg just had dinner together."

"We did. And nothing's wrong." I put my coffee down and grabbed the closing checklist that Aunt Jackie had modified for the truck.

Sasha shrugged. "If you say so. Just remember, no big decisions."

"Until after the twentieth. I get it." I didn't like being snippy, but even if I put on a happy face, Sasha would see through it. That's what happens when you work closely with someone. They know your moods. And this was one time I didn't want to examine my feelings even if it meant keeping my co-worker at arm's length. *Greg and I are fine* became my mantra as I worked through the checklist. And as I finished the close, I'd almost convinced myself of the fact.

Almost.

Chapter 14

Toby came into the truck right at nine. He grabbed a cookie from the display and leaned against the counter, right where I'd been two hours ago with my conversation with Sasha. The truck wasn't that big, so leaning areas were limited.

"What are you doing here?" I had just turned off the last machine and was putting the cash register money into a bag.

"Greg gave me a dinner break and told me about the leftovers in my fridge. Since I'm heading that way, I thought I'd walk you home." He pointed to the coffeepot I'd just turned off. "Did you dump that yet? I could use a refill."

"Go ahead. I was just about to shut it down for the night." I looked around the small kitchen and grabbed my tote. I knew I needed to ask him about the bank bag in the apartment, but maybe this wasn't the right time. Not that I thought Toby would go all serial killer crazy on me, but stranger things have happened. "Dump whatever's left and let's go."

I'd closed up the outside of the truck and was just locking up the windows when he came out, turning out the lights as he left. He held out his hand. "Give me the keys and I'll lock the door."

"I can do it." I moved in between him and the closed door and turned the last lock. The truck had been vandalized once before I'd bought it. One of the things I'd had done as the truck was being repainted from the cheery Good For You Desserts truck that never opened was to get all new locks installed. Now, Aunt Jackie and I had the only keys, besides the one I left in the shop for whoever was opening the truck.

"Fine. Just don't tell my mom. She'd be upset to find out that I didn't act like a gentleman."

We walked toward the house in silence. Finally, Toby looked up at the stars. "Nice night."

"You don't have to make small talk." I looked over at him. "I appreciate you walking me home, but it really was unnecessary."

"Like I said, I was heading this way." He shrugged. "You're in a mood."

"I'm not in a mood," I snapped back. Okay, so maybe I was. Taking a deep breath, "Sorry, I'm beat and grumpy."

"So is my other boss. You two have a fight?" We crossed the highway and now headed up the small hill to my house. The county had put sidewalks all the way from Diamond Lille's to the highway for easier access to the beach for tourists. I also appreciated not having to share the side of the road with traffic.

"No, we didn't have a fight." That much was true. We probably would have one in the future, but as for tonight, there had been no argument. Just the unease that things were a little off between the two of us. "Mercury in retrograde," I murmured.

"Oh, don't you start that too." He groaned as we turned into my driveway and we paused at the gate to the front yard. "Sasha's been out of sorts for a month now, blaming it all on this retrograde stuff. I'll be glad when the darn thing moves."

That made me smile. Before I opened the gate, I turned to look at him. "Greg put some leftover chicken in your fridge tonight. And found one of our deposit bags." I paused, waiting for his reaction.

"Cool. I'm starving and I didn't want to have to go get something." He stepped toward the shed, but noticed I was still standing there with my hand on the gate latch. "So what's the other shoe that's got you all wound up?"

"Why did you have a bank bag on your table?"

Toby grinned. "It's been there for over a week. Every morning I swear I'm going to take it to the shop and it's still sitting there when I get home. Lately, it's been a contest to see when I'd finally remember to bring it back." He groaned. "Jackie's not upset about the deposit slips not being put into the cash register like we're supposed to, is she?"

"You knew about the deposit slip policy?" I swore as soon as this weekend was over, my aunt and I were having a sit-down where we talked about all the rules she'd developed for the shop. I was tired of being out of the loop. I pushed the thought away. I was getting distracted. "No, she's upset because one of the deposits didn't hit the shop's account."

"Wait, you're saying that shop money was stolen?" He put a hand on his cell. "We should call Greg."

"Hold on. I don't have all the facts yet. But it looks like the missing deposit was one of the two in your bank bag." I could see him physically react.

"Good, I would hate to think we had a thief in the area." He looked toward his apartment and I was certain his mind was back on the chicken. I needed to ask the question.

"Toby, did you put a three-thousand-dollar check from the city into your account?"

He had started walking to the shed but my question stopped him cold. "You think I took the money?"

"You didn't answer my question." I wasn't going to apologize. I had a right to know.

He looked at me for a long time. "No, Jill, I didn't put any money that's not my own into my account. I won't steal from you or anyone."

With that he turned away and walked to the apartment, pulling out his key and entering without another word.

And I felt like a heel. I went into the house and locked the front door. I let Emma out for a quick potty break before we trudged upstairs with a book and a bottle of water. I was done for the day. If I kept having conversations about missing money with my staff, pretty soon I'd be back to working all by myself. I could still hear the music playing out on the beach and I wondered when Greg would pull the cop card and have them shut down. I glanced at my clock; it was already ten-thirty and the last band had been scheduled to end by ten. But the music was nice as it floated into my bedroom on the evening breeze and I fell asleep listening to the eighties cover band that somehow knew all my favorite songs.

* * * *

The alarm blared in my ears and I kept trying to turn it off, but then I realized I was still dreaming. This time, I sat up in bed and took the alarm into my hands. I thought about pitching it across the room, but just turned it off, knowing that tomorrow I'd have a day away from the shop.

A day crowded with errands, but at least I didn't have to juggle the truck and the shop today. One last day for the truck, then we'd park it until the next festival. But before we opened for the fourth of July, I'd make sure we had hired another part-timer or two. Aunt Jackie and I were going to have this talk about more staffing or the truck would stay parked. I was beat.

I let Emma out, poured a cup of coffee, and headed back upstairs for a long, hot shower. I didn't have to open the truck until nine, so I had some time to properly caffeinate myself as well as enjoy the Sunday paper. Typically, Greg hung around on Sundays and we read the paper together, but I didn't think I'd see him today, no matter that he'd implemented the No-Guilt-Sunday rule. Keeping our distance for a while was probably the best idea.

By eight forty-five I had the truck open for business. Except there weren't any customers. The partiers from last night were all sleeping in and the festivities for the morning hadn't started up yet. So I took a book out of my tote and grabbed one of the folding lawn chairs we kept in the storage compartment and sat out in the sun.

I supposed I looked like Austin with his beachside bike rental outlet on most summer weekends. We all knew he wasn't truly there for the customers, instead just enjoying the sunny California summer morning. I heard the waves crashing on the beach behind me and smiled as I opened the book and got lost in the story.

I didn't have a single customer until ten, a good hour after our start time, and even then, it was sporadic until noon when people started showing up and ordering iced drinks. I made a note in the notebook I kept in my tote bag to adjust beach sales time, at least on Sundays. That would help with the staffing issues right there. We could open at eleven and not miss too many sales.

Managing the food truck was a different world and I was enjoying learning more about the best practices. It was just killing me trying to keep up with the staffing and extra duties right now. And nothing would really change until fall.

Except in fall I'd be cutting my own hours because I'd be going back to school. Maybe we needed to add more than just a part-time position. I mused over that idea as I served coffee and treats all morning. I was surprised to see Nick arrive and park his bike near the truck. I glanced at the clock as he put a chain around the truck bumper.

"Hey, boss." He turned to wash his hands and put on his apron.

I handed out an iced mocha to the last waiting customer and then turned to face him. "I didn't realize it was that late already."

"You been busy?" He checked the coffee levels and the little signs we had on each, telling the staff when the last batch was brewed.

"Not until eleven. Since then, it's been steady." I took a slice of cheesecake out of the fridge and grabbed a spoon. I was starving.

"You still need me to work, right?" Something in his voice made me look at him.

"Of course, why? Do you need the day off?"

He shook his head. "No, I just don't want you to feel obligated to give me hours 'cause you and my mom are friends."

"Believe me, if I could clone you, you'd get double the shifts this summer. I definitely need you all the hours you can work."

He smiled. "That's what I told mom, but she said I should make sure and not just assume."

Leave it to Sadie to worry about everyone else. "Seriously Nick, if you hadn't joined the staff this summer, I don't know how we could have pulled off this annex thing. And with Aunt Jackie on the injured reserve list, I may need more help."

A voice drew me back to the window. "Hey, you guys open?"

Blake stood under the truck window, a lazy grin on his face.

"Of course." I sat my plate down. "What can I get for you?"

"The largest coffee you have. I didn't get much sleep last night. I went over to Kathi's shop after the gig at the winery and we talked for hours." He pulled a ten out of his wallet and laid it on the counter. "We're playing the two to four shift here on the beach bandstand and then going back to the winery to start our regular gig. I'm loving the hours, but man, I'm beat today."

I hear you, buddy. I rang up the coffee as Nick poured it. "I saw you and Kathi walking through town yesterday. I take it your date went well?"

"Kathi's a winner. She's smart, funny, and of course, beautiful." Blake grinned. "I'm sounding like a high school kid gushing on his first date, huh?"

"I'm glad it's going well." Someone should be happy during this planet thing.

He stuffed his change into his wallet then rubbed his face. "It's way too soon to tell, but it's starting out good. Now if I can just stay awake today through my gigs, I'll be happy." He held up the cup as I handed it to him. "Thanks for the caffeine."

Blake walked away in his tight, worn jeans and an old Lennon tee. Nick stood next to me and we watched Blake leave for the beach grandstand. "I heard his band play over at the winery. They're really good."

"How did you get into the winery?" Maybe there was more to Sadie's fair-haired boy than I knew. "Don't tell me, you have ID that says you're twenty-five?"

He grinned. "You really think a fake ID would work here? All they'd have to do is see me walk in and I'd get booted out and there would be a call down the church phone tree to have the women's group pray for my soul."

"Then how are you hearing Blake's band?" Now I was curious.

"No big deal. Darla lets the kids sit outside at the tables when there's a band. That way, we get to enjoy the music. She's been doing it since last fall."

I was about to ask more about the arrangement when Lille walked up to the truck. "Hey, Ms. Ramsey, how are you?" Nick leaned over the counter to greet his former boss. I didn't know if I'd ever heard Lille's last name before. I guess sometime someone would have had to mention it, but I wasn't sure that was even true.

"Did you come for coffee?" Stupid question, but I didn't understand why the restaurant owner would frequent my shop, unless she wanted a book, which we didn't stock on the food truck annex. Yet.

"Sure. Make me one of those chocolate things. I want it hot, not frozen like some ice cream dessert thing. Stupid way to ruin good coffee." She directed her order to Nick. Then she crooked her finger at me. "Come outside for a second, I need to talk to you."

I met her over near the stairs leading down to the beach. The area was still quiet even though there were people starting to arrive. Lille had lit up a cigarette while she waited.

I stood upwind and asked, "What's going on?"

"Your biker isn't from around here. In fact, the local guys want to talk to him about his antics in the area. Seems his bad acts are causing the cops to crack down on their members. And the club leaders aren't happy with being watched so closely." Lille took a drag from her cigarette. "I was told that they know he's from down south somewhere."

"Mexico?" I frowned, the guy hadn't looked Hispanic. Of course, I hadn't gotten a good look at anything but his back as he sped away.

Lille's jaw dropped a bit and then she rolled her eyes. "Our south. Like the ones who started the Civil War? Georgia, Alabama, Texas. You know, states in the south?"

Now I felt dumb. "Oh."

Lille threw her cigarette on the ground and then put the fire out with her booted foot. She picked up the filter and threw it away in the nearby trashcan. "Anyway, I've got people looking at the clubs down there to see if the mascot on the back matches. It's a long shot. Nothing stops a guy from wearing a cut from a club he's no longer a part of, but at least it might give your boyfriend a clue."

From her tone, I could tell she thought Greg needed a clue in many areas of his life, but I didn't take the bait. I wondered sometimes if Lille just liked egging people on to see what kind of reaction they gave back. "Thanks, I appreciate your help."

The look of surprise on her face told me I'd been right. She shrugged then looked at the food truck. "He's doing all right? You're giving him good hours and paying enough?"

"More than he probably wants right now, but he says he's saving for some overseas program." I paused, wondering if my next question would push our newfound detente. "Why are you so interested in Nick? I can't believe you watch out for all your ex-employees so carefully."

Pain flashed across Lille's face and for a moment, I thought I'd seen the beginning of tears. Then just as quickly as it was there, the normal Lille scowl was back on her face and she glared at me. "You just go on sticking your nose in other people's lives and leave mine alone."

I watched as she stomped back to the truck, paid for her drink, and then disappeared down the stairs to the beach. When I got back to the truck, Nick held out a twenty-dollar bill. "I think Ms. Ramsey got confused when she left the tip. She must have thought it was a one. Should I go find her?"

I was pretty sure that Lille had meant to over-tip so I shook my head. "Put it aside and if she doesn't come back before the end of your shift, put it in the tip jar. I'm sure she's very aware of what she does."

"I don't know. She's careful about money things. When I worked for her she'd come talk to me about where I was going to college and financing stuff. She was as hard on me about grades as Mom." He put the twenty by the side of the till and looked around the truck. "So what do you want me to do now?"

I let him handle the front of the shop while I checked supplies and ran the first cash drawer deposit process. I'd just finished when Ivy came up to the window. She saw me in the back and waved me closer after she'd ordered. "How are you today?"

Sometimes people meld the lines between great customer service and friendship. And most of the time, I didn't mind, but for some reason, Ivy's attention felt fake. If Lille was all dark and broody, Ivy was sweetness and light—but it felt like the dark and broody was hidden behind some mask. "Great. The festival is almost over and I have a day off coming tomorrow."

Ivy nodded with my words, silently commiserating. "My uncle always said a regular routine is best for both customer and proprietor. He never had the shop open on Sundays because he said God gave the world a day of rest and who was he to second-guess the Maker."

The town Ivy and Kathi grew up in must be tiny. "Well, weekends are our bread and butter here in a tourist town, so Monday's our rest day." I handed her the coffee she'd ordered from Nick. "What are you doing today? It's a great day for the festival."

Ivy's eyes darted toward the beach and the activities. "Actually, I'm taking a quick trip back home to check on Daddy."

"Quick? That must be a ten or twelve hour drive? You're flying, right?"

She shook her head, sipping the coffee. "Nope, I'm driving. It's just under twenty-two hours. I should be there early Tuesday."

"Well, I guess I'll see you in a couple weeks when you get back." No way would I drive that long just for a quick trip.

"I should be back Friday. Daddy has a doctor appointment Tuesday afternoon, then I'll start back Wednesday morning." She took another sip of her coffee. "I hope I can keep caffeinated during the trip. Your coffee's the best."

I wasn't sure what to say so I tried to change the subject. "Have a nice trip. Oh, have you talked to Kathi? I hear from Blake that their date went awesome."

Ivy frowned and shook her head. "What date?"

The sisters apparently didn't talk about much. That's another problem in a small town, there aren't many secrets, especially when people see you day in and day out. "Oh, she probably didn't mention it since it was so casual. But from what I can tell, Blake's a great guy. Your sister's lucky."

"She's playing with fire, that's what she's doing."

"It was only a first date. I know I probably shouldn't be gossiping, but he was so happy about meeting her." I wondered if I should have just kept my mouth shut.

Ivy started walking to her car, apparently done with our conversation. She turned back and shook her head. "You don't understand. The guy isn't the problem. My sister is. Kathi's engaged to be married."

Chapter 15

I was surprised when I found Greg on my doorstep with a grocery bag filled with supplies that evening. While he grilled steaks for dinner, I recounted my conversation with Ivy. When I finished, he closed the grill and didn't meet my eyes. "Don't get all bent out of shape, I didn't ask for her to tell me all this."

"I wasn't even thinking about the case." He came and sat by me in the swing, putting his arm around me and scooting me close. "Sorry I was a grump last night."

I leaned my head into his body and drank in the smell of him. "I think we're both a little ragged lately."

"No excuse. I swore I wouldn't let the job get between us ever." He didn't say anything else and I wondered if he was thinking about how his first marriage had dissolved.

I shook the image of him and Sherry together out of my head and returned to the subject of Ivy and her impromptu road trip.

"Don't you think it's weird though? Kathi didn't say anything about being engaged when we were talking about Blake. Maybe Ivy doesn't know the updated info. Couples break up all the time." I cuddled into his side and watched my dog wander the backyard looking for rabbits or maybe a bone she'd buried a few months ago.

"Couples *not* like us, right?" He tickled my side just to see if I was paying attention. I slapped his hand for good measure.

"Why would we break up?" I thought about the look of dread that had come over Ivy's face as she almost sprinted to the car. I'd been expecting her to turn up Main Street toward Tea Hee, but instead, she turned left and north toward a highway that should take her home to Texas. Even though I didn't like the girl much, I worried that she was taking such a long road trip by herself. And then turning around and coming right back. The girl was cray-cray.

"If I broke up with you, I wouldn't know all the gossip or be able to keep you out of trouble when you go sleuthing without my permission. I guess I'm stuck with you forever." He kissed the top of my head. "I suppose I can deal with that."

We sat in silence for a while, the awkwardness gone after our last conversation. Finally, I pulled myself up. "I'll grab the salad and set the table. I can smell that those steaks are almost ready."

He held out his iced tea glass for me to take inside. "Can you get me a refill? I think the steaks should be perfect by the time you're finished in the kitchen." He stood and grabbed one of Emma's tennis balls. He called out to get her attention, then threw the ball out past the shed.

I paused at the doorway, watching him. "How is the investigation going? Are we still on track for the Mexico trip?"

"As long as I get this case closed in the next week or so, sure. Otherwise, I'm probably losing another deposit." He took the wet, slobbery ball from Emma and threw it again, wiping his hand on a towel. "Either we need to stop planning vacations and just take off one day or people need to stop dying."

"Maybe both." I smiled as I went back into the kitchen and got the rest of dinner ready. In a few minutes, Greg pulled open the screen and he came in with the steaks on a plate. Emma followed closely behind, a look of rapture on her face. I'm pretty sure she was trying to use ESP powers to get Greg to drop the plate. Unfortunately for her, dog telepathy didn't work on the guy.

Greg sat the plate on the table and went to the sink with the tongs. He washed his hands, then pulled me into a hug. "So what do you know so far about the murder? I want to keep myself in the gossip loop."

"Why would you think I know anything?"

Greg laughed so hard, we almost didn't hear his phone chirp with the incoming call. He groaned as he pulled the device out of his case, staring at the still-steaming steaks. "Hello?"

The longer Greg went without talking on an incoming call, the more likely it was something bad. This time, when he hung up, I pointed to his plate. "Do you need a to-go box?"

He shook his head. "Nope, I'll walk back to the beach with you when you go shut up the annex."

My blood chilled as I thought of the possible issues that could be behind that statement. Aunt Jackie's accident had taught me one thing.

Stuff happens when you least expect it. "Why? Did something happen to the truck? Or was it Sasha and Nick? Tell me they're all right."

"They're fine." He put his fork down. "I don't want you to jump to conclusions here, so just listen to me, okay?"

I nodded, knowing I was already in the jolly land of conclusions and had filled in the blanks with my own form of crazy town guesses. "Just tell me it's not something with Aunt Jackie. Or Amy. Or Sadie." My heart rate increased with each name.

He put his hand up. "Hold on, I told you I'd tell you the truth. Just stop filling in the blanks without knowing the story."

"Okay." I put my head down, trying to slow my breathing. When I looked back up at him, he held out my tea glass.

"Take a sip." He waited until I had then took the glass from my hand and sat it on the table. "The reason I'm not leaving is there isn't a dead body. I'll have to go over to the hospital later, but right now, the EMTs are out at the beach with Toby. They're handling the situation."

My brain was trying to wrap around the words he was saying, but even with the calmer breathing, I was still freaked out. "So what's the situation?"

He nodded to my plate. "Start eating and I'll tell you." When I stared at him, he waved his fork at me. "I'm serious."

I picked up my fork and knife and started cutting my steak. I took a big bite, then pointed at my mouth. "So what happened?"

Greg paused between bites. "Someone beat up Blake after his set at the beach. He was loading their stuff into his van and he got hit from behind."

"Don't tell me his equipment was stolen too." That would be the end of Atomic Power. The band wasn't making enough to live on, let alone deal with a theft.

Greg buttered a fresh roll, studying it like it held all the answers to the world's problems. "That's just it, nothing was taken. Blake just got the crap beat out of him for no apparent reason."

As we quickly finished our dinner so Greg could return to the beach festival and talk to Toby, I thought about all the bad stuff that had been happening in our little town. All since one specific woman had moved here. Well, I guess I couldn't blame her for the motorcycle guy who had almost hit Aunt Jackie, nor for Josh's strange disappearance. But her cousin dying here in town, that was too coincidental. And what was that stuff about Kathi being engaged? Too many questions were rolling through my mind. Questions I couldn't voice to Greg or he'd tell me flat out to stay out of it. And as long as he didn't tell, I didn't have to listen.

I think we both knew the game I was playing, but Greg gave me some rope so he wouldn't have to say "stay out of it" all the time. Besides, the investigation I was doing was more about Kathi's family than who had killed poor Darryl. *Keep telling yourself that lie and you'll feel a lot better about skirting around the truth.*

We walked down to the beach and when he left me at the food truck, he gave me a quick kiss. I felt his lips traveling upward to my ears and he whispered, "I was hoping to take you on the carnival rides tonight."

My body shivered at the promise of the fun we would have together, pretending we were kids for one night. "Maybe you'll be done before they close the area."

He grinned. "I'm going to try my best. Come find me when you close up the truck."

And with that, he was gone, taking the stairs two at a time and jogging over to where I could see the blinking lights on the edge of the beach. The crowd had thinned and when I entered the food truck, Sasha was the only one there.

"Hey, boss." She looked up from the book she'd been reading as she sat on a stool near the window in case a customer approached. Glancing at the clock, she shrugged. "I didn't expect you for another hour."

"Greg had to come down and deal with something." I wasn't sure why I was couching my words, the information would be on the late news tonight. *South Cove festival costs one man his pride*, I could hear the headlines now. Or, more than his pride. I hoped Blake was just roughed up, not seriously hurt.

Sasha yawned and put a bookmark to mark her place. "I sent Nick home about an hour ago. We were so slow, he cleaned everything twice, just to make sure I wouldn't get hit with a rush and he wouldn't be here to help. He's a good egg."

"Yes, he is." I looked out on the darkening parking lot. "Let's close up. It's Sunday and we both need some time to rest up for next week. Do you have plans tomorrow?"

She held up the book. "Other than finishing this, nothing. Olivia is with her grandmother this week. They're doing vacation bible school and Mom thought it would be easier for her just to stay over."

"A childless week? What will you do with yourself?" I pulled out the cash drawer and started putting away the money into the bank bag, counting as I went.

Sasha pulled down the windows and started cleaning out the coffeepots. She paused and stared at me. "I don't know. It's been so long since I didn't have little-miss-tag-along to take care of, I'm not sure what people who don't have kids do with their free time."

I closed down the truck and sent Sasha home with a few ideas of what she could do this week. When I'd listed off a long bath, she brightened and laughed. "Do you know how long it's been since I could just soak in the tub? I'm pouring a glass of wine, running a hot bath, and staying there until I finish this book or the water turns cold."

I watched her drive away and turned back to the beach. The moon lit up the beach near the water. The rest of the sand was lit by little white lights that Mary had ordered to be hung from booth to booth. And of course the bandstand had stage lights. I glanced over that way to see if the ambulance had left, or if lights still flashed.

No lights, no truck, no Greg. I scanned the beach but didn't see him. He might have gone back to the station to do the paperwork on Blake's incident or he may just be wandering through the crowds. I decided to take one quick stroll through the festival to see if I could find him before heading home. The idea of taking on a few of the rides made my knees a little weak, but I'd love it once the ride was over.

Many of the businesses on Main Street had opened small booths for their wares. The Glass Slipper had a booth and as I walked by, the wind chimes jingled lightly in the breeze, causing the shop's owner, Marie Jones, to look my way. She smiled and gave me a nod of her head. The woman was amazingly strong and recently had been able to deal with the impromptu appearance of an abusive husband that she'd thought she'd left behind long ago.

I didn't stop, knowing that Marie liked it when the shop was quiet. She was a lot like me in that regard, she liked her own space and the hard sell would never be in her tool box. People could like her stuff or not, she didn't really care.

I found Greg over near the dart toss, watching as Nick ran the game. Time after time, Nick broke the balloon, trading his prizes for the next size up, until he finally had a large stuffed dog. He took the dog under his arm and turned around, noticing Greg and I, standing together.

"Now that's something I never expected." He grinned at the two of us, standing together. "Mom said you guys were dating, but I never saw you as a couple. You're both too old to just be dating."

"You're skating on thin ice, kid," Greg warned but in a friendly tone. "I can still run you in for loitering or something."

"But then you'd have to deal with me losing an employee," I joked back. "Mama don't like it when she has to cover everyone's shifts. Besides, I'm sure he meant that *you* were old since he'd never say that about the boss who schedules his work hours."

Nick's face turned so red I could see it in the darkening light. "I didn't mean to say you were old, it's just I don't picture people your age dating. That would be like my mom dating someone." He caught the shock on my face and shook his head. "Man, I need to just shut up, don't I?"

I hadn't been reacting to Nick calling us old, but rather that he didn't know his mom had dated Austin for several months last year. Either Sadie was very good at hiding her other life from her kid, or Nick was just too self-absorbed to notice his mom doing anything outside of the world they'd built together. "Yep, you're getting in pretty deep. I might just let Greg arrest you."

Greg put his arm around me and turned me toward the middle of the carnival. "Come on grandma, I want to take you on Drop of Death before I have to get you back to the old folks' home."

"Ah man, so not funny," Nick called after us. "I said I was sorry, didn't I?"

"You're not going to let him off anytime soon, are you?" I put my arm around Greg as we walked together. "In his eyes, we probably are old. They're the next generation, ready to rule the world."

"Nick's a good kid. He just needs some real life experience." Greg pointed to the first ride, a roller coaster. "I'm not sure we're riding anything. It looks like the place is shutting down."

The man who had been running the ride was now pulling up the safety fences and stacking it on a trailer that had been parked behind the carnival. The man was slender, but his arms muscular and covered with tattoos. For a minute, he reminded me of the motorcycle guy. When had we first seen him, Tuesday? Had the carnival already been here, setting up? I glanced around the midway. Most of the people milling around now were carnies, the festival goers having moved to the stage where the promise of one more fireworks show was just about to start.

"Greg," I began, then stopped. He didn't like me investigating, but wasn't this just a random thought? I took a deep breath and dived in. He'd probably already thought of it, but I was going to say it aloud. "Could the motorcycle guy be part of the carnival crew? This all started on Tuesday. Were they in town then?"

Greg stopped walking and looked down at me. Then he looked around the midway at the people getting ready to pack up and leave. "Hiding in plain sight," he muttered.

I was about to ask him another question when he stepped away from me and took out his cell. He called Toby and Tim and asked them to meet him at the midway. Then he looked at me like he'd almost forgotten I was with him.

"Sorry to do this, but can you make it home all right?"

I kissed him on the cheek. "No problem. Maybe I can find Nick to walk an old lady across the street."

"It was a good idea, Jill. And I need to talk to the managers before everyone takes off for the next festival." He squeezed me. "Sometimes you surprise me."

"I hope that keeps being a good thing." I made my way through the maze toward the parking lot. Now, everyone was at the grandstand and as I began to climb the stairs to the parking lot, I heard the first boom. I turned around and sat on the middle of the stairs to watch the show.

Twenty minutes later, the last finale burst dying down and the music ending, the crowd cheered their support. I finished climbing the stairs and was probably home before most of the festival goers had left the parking lot. Another bonus to living so close to the beach.

Emma was on edge, as she'd heard the firework booms. As I let her out, I followed her out to the porch and sat in my swing thinking about the times I'd seen the guy who had almost hit Aunt Jackie. The timing seemed right, and here I'd been, blaming everything that had gone wrong on Kathi and her extended family. Maybe this too was just a coincidence, especially if Greg did find the beefy rider hiding in the carnie crew.

Emma sat at my feet and whined, sensing my mood. Either that or telling me it was time for us to head upstairs and go to bed. I took it for the latter, and we went inside. I double-checked the locks on the doors before I went, unease still prickling under my skin.

* * * *

Monday mornings my alarm was shut off and I got up when the sun woke me. This Monday, I woke with the night still enfolding the morning, not wanting to give up its hold on the day. My coffeepot hadn't even started brewing when I trudged downstairs to let Emma out. I'd be dead tired tonight after—no make that *during*—the council meeting, but I had too much on my mind to stay in bed any longer.

Checking my cell I saw Greg had left a short text. *One more rabbit hole dug up without a rabbit. Sorry to cut our time short for a false trail.*

A lead I'd sent him on, so I wasn't sure why he was apologizing to me. I should have been the one saying sorry. But maybe that was part of investigating, like inventing, going through all the ways it wouldn't work before finding the one way it had.

I opened my notebook and started making a to-do list for the day. I had to drop off deposits at the bank, talk to Claire about the lost money, finish the last minute arrangements with the caterer for Friday night, write up something for a partial report to the council on the festival, stop by The Castle and The Coastal Inn and—I paused.

What was I doing at the two places where Ivy had been either staying or seen visiting? Just bringing cookies for Business-to-Business marketing? Or was I hoping that I'd learn something new about the murder or the elusive motorcycle guy who'd hurt Aunt Jackie? And, the thought popped into my head, were they really the same thing?

I added talking to Kathi to my list and then glanced in the fridge. I'd also have to make time for a grocery run, as the meal we'd cooked last night had mostly come from the food Greg brought and had cleaned out what little food I'd had in the house.

The coffeepot beeped and I went to fill my cup. Time for some liquid power-up before I started my day of rest with a load of laundry and cleaning the bathrooms. As I sipped the coffee, I added one more thing to the list, after starting laundry and before the bathroom chore. Time to take Emma for a run now that the festival goers had left our beach.

We were on the home stretch of our run when I heard the sound of a Harley revving. I looked up, and stopped in my tracks. There on the edge of the hill where the parking lot sat, a black motorcycle and its oversized rider sat, watching the surf. I felt the guy's eyes pass over me like I was just another piece of trash that had washed up from the tide.

Even from this distance, I could tell it was the same rider.

Chapter 16

I debated going to talk to him or just calling Greg, but before I could do anything, including move from the spot I seemed glued to, the bike engine revved again and the rider turned it toward the highway and disappeared.

Now I did run toward the hill, taking the steps two at a time when I reached the entrance to the parking lot, but by the time I arrived, there was no sign of the guy either in the lot or on the highway that ran between our town and the Pacific Ocean. I walked back to the spot where he'd been parked on the grassy edge.

A piece of silver gum wrapper lay on top of the sea grass. I picked it up using the tips of my fingers to bring it closer to examine it. A strong smell of mint still hung onto the paper and I knew this had come from the rider and not been left from yesterday's activities. I put it into the second poop bag I always kept on hand. I'd needed to add one more stop to my list, dropping this off to the police station and convincing Greg to check it for DNA or prints or something.

My cell rang as I stood there, staring at the spot. I wanted to make sure I wasn't missing something.

"Hey Jill, I know the shop isn't open this morning, but any way you can drop by the bank? I've found your deposit." Claire's voice boomed over the small speaker in the phone. "Where are you? I swear I can hear gulls."

"You can. I'm on the beach, just finishing up my run." I pulled the phone away from my ear and check the time. "I can get there in about twenty minutes, will that work?"

"As long as you're here before eleven. I have a meeting with my district manager in Bakerstown at noon. He's not very happy that I terminated his little girl. I'd like to get your problem off my desk, before someone else starts sitting here."

"That's nice of you, but do you really think he'll can you?" That was so cold, firing someone just because they made a good business decision.

"Let's just say he doesn't have a rational bone in his body. I don't suppose you could bring me a large coffee. It's going to be a heck of a day."

That made me smile; no matter what, people always wanted their shot of joe in the morning. Luckily, I kept a supply of my favorites at the house to brew for my own enjoyment. "No worries, I'll hook you up."

An older couple slowed their pace as they heard my words. When I waved at them, they blanched white and hurried down the stairs. I'd made the wrong impression, again. I put my cell away in my tote and then looked around the area one more time. The food truck gleamed in the morning light. Add one more thing to my already crowded Monday list; I needed to get the truck moved back to its spot behind the shop.

First, Claire. I had a slice of cheesecake in the fridge to give her as well. Finding the money was triple amazing and she deserved a treat for that.

I made it to the bank with two minutes to spare. Claire was working a teller line, but waved at me as I came in. I motioned toward the seating in the lobby. She nodded and I went to sit, taking a book out of my tote and getting in a few pages while I waited.

A chapter later, I heard my name and looked up to find Claire standing over me. "Must be a great book, I've called your name three times and was beginning to worry you were in some type of coma."

"A reading coma. I rather like that." I tucked the book away in my tote and stood to follow her into her office. I handed her the coffee mug and then dug in the tote for the bag with the cheesecake. "Here's a little something extra to make your day better."

She peeked into the bag and smiled. "You may want to take it back once I tell you the news."

"You didn't find the deposit." I sank into one of her guest chairs. Losing three thousand wouldn't kill me, but it was a lot of money, just the same.

She opened the container and dug the plastic fork I'd brought along into the Key Lime Cheesecake. "Oh, gosh, this is heaven."

I waited for the food coma moment to pass, then handed her the receipt we'd found. "You did find the money, right? That appears to be the deposit slip."

Waving her fork at me, she paused and took the deposit slip and looked at it before taking her next bite. "We found the money. It had been deposited into your savings account."

"So why couldn't Aunt Jackie see it online?" Now I was worried. Had my aunt just missed the deposit?

"Not the business account. Your personal account. The second savings account you call the Miss Emily Fund?" Claire took another bite of the treat. "There is no way that should have happened. I don't think we've ever made a deposit into that account since you set it up. This had to be Allie's doing. That girl was a menace."

"I didn't think I even had slips for that account." At least the money was found. We could play the blame game for days, but all that really mattered was the end result.

"I can't explain how she did it. Heck, I'm going to have to go back through weeks of transactions just to make sure that nothing else weird is going on. I'm betting this is just the start. It's a good thing your aunt called me last week." Claire leaned back into her chair and closed her eyes. "I'd hate to think of what could have happened if we'd been audited before I realized what she was doing."

"So back to hiring?" I thought about Ivy and wondered if she would be more of a hindrance than a help. Of course, that wasn't fair to the woman. I barely knew her and didn't know anything about her background. Darla had her job application. I wondered if she'd found anything we hadn't known.

"I have a folder in my desk." She leaned down and pulled out a three-inch thick file. "Most of these can't pass the background check, so that's where I send the applications first. Then out of maybe one hundred apps, I interview probably five people. I'll get these sent over to the investigation company this week and if they find someone that I like during the interview, in a couple months, I'll hire someone and hope they stay for longer than it takes for the folder to fill up again."

"Did Ivy Corbin apply here?" I still wasn't sure what I was looking for, and didn't know if Claire could tell me anything anyway. So I lied. "She left her credit card at the shop and I wondered if you had any phone numbers where I could reach her?"

Claire thumbed through the pages. "I think so, hold on." A smile curled her lips as she pulled a set of papers out of the pile. "Success. It's been a good day. We found your deposit and now I found a needle in a haystack. Now if we're really lucky, we'll be able to read the contact numbers. You won't believe how many people don't even put a phone number on their application. Like, how am I supposed to schedule an interview?"

I leaned toward the desk and did my best to read upside down. I recognized the street address Ivy had listed as The Castle. Someone would have to be a celebrity to afford to live there full time. Or old family money rich and Kathi had mentioned the family wasn't well off. So who was paying the bill?

I had another stop to make on my way to Bakerstown. Hopefully Brenda Morgan, the Castle manager, would be in her office this morning and willing to chat.

"Here we go. I've got a cell and a message number. Do you want both?" Claire had her pen poised over a note pad.

"Sure. Does it say who the message number is? I mean, if it's Kathi, I could just drop the card there, but it didn't seem like they were on the best of terms."

"Robert, no last name. It's the same area code as Ivy's though. Maybe he's in Texas where she's from."

As I left the banker's office, I mused over the name Robert. I hadn't asked what Kathi and Ivy's father's name was, so it could have been him. I doubted it though, if he was as infirm as it seemed, taking messages from a sick bed seemed a little off. At least the message number wasn't Darryl's. I only knew of two people Ivy knew in the area. One was dead, and one wasn't talking to her. Neither one was named Robert.

I wondered if Toby would run the number to get a name without telling Greg I was snooping again. The last time he helped out with one of my investigations, Greg had been in the loop.

I drove the Jeep up the winding hill to The Castle and parked in the lot. I paused at the entry gate and gave my name to the girl selling tickets. She called up to the office and then nodded me through. I smiled as I walked through the gate and made my way to the cabana.

Brenda stood at the open door and flung her arms around me as soon as I walked up. "I'm so glad to see you. I can't believe it's been so long. What have you been doing? What brings you out to my neck of the woods?"

After being released from the bear hug, I felt guilty. I hadn't been a good friend and now I was only here to find out information from her on one of her residents. I slipped into a chair and dropped my tote on the ground. "I'm good. On my way to town to get supplies." I looked around the office. "You've done a lot of redecorating. It's beautiful." When her husband Craig had run The Castle, the office had reminded me of those old gentlemen's lodges where they drank scotch and women weren't allowed, unless they held a serving tray. Now it looked like classic old Hollywood.

"Thanks. I've been digging through the storage bins and you wouldn't believe all the great stuff that's in there, just gathering dust. I wanted it to feel more upbeat and fresh than before." She sat next to me on the sofa. "So tell me why you're really here. I've got a tour starting in twenty minutes."

"Am I that transparent?" Her gaze made me squirm a bit.

She leaned into the couch. "I'm very good at reading people. Living with Craig taught me that skill and it's worked well for me ever since. So don't feel bad, what do you need?"

Hoping I wouldn't sound stupid, or worse, stalkerish, I just dug in. I explained about Kathi moving to South Cove, then her sister showing up, then the cousin being murdered. Even to my ears, there didn't seem to be any connection except they were family. "She's living here. And what I want to know is who's paying the bill. Can you tell me that? Is that breaking confidentiality?"

Brenda didn't answer. Instead, she stood and walked over to her computer, tapping a few keys. "It looks like a Robert Marshall's credit card has been used to pay for the room. She's been here a week and from what I can see, likes her room service. But the room's on hold this week, as she called to change her reservation."

"I knew that. She's gone back home to Texas until Friday." There was that name Robert again, but this time it came with a last name. At least one good enough to fool the credit card people if this was a hoax. And I knew something else. Kathi and Ivy's dad wasn't the mysterious Robert.

"Thank you so much." I found my car keys in my tote. "I'll get out of your hair now so you can do your tour."

"Just don't put yourself in danger. You know how you are. One minute you're chatting up someone and the next you're locked in a burning house."

"That only happened once." I hadn't really believed the mild-mannered travel agent could have been the murderer, I'd thought it had been the cheating husband.

Brenda wasn't buying my deflection. "Or the time you and Sadie got locked in a gated cave that happened to fill with water during monsoon season."

"Okay, so going out by ourselves probably wasn't smart." I had to admit that idea hadn't been my best.

"Like I said, just be careful. And make sure Greg knows where you are when you go sleuthing. At least that way, he can help get you out of the trouble you get into." Brenda's phone rang. "Sorry, I've got to take this."

I had been dismissed. Brenda's heart was in the right place, but she could make me feel like a rebellious kid just for—I paused my thoughts as I walked back to the car. Just for what? What was I doing? Investigating. And since I was, her warnings to take care made sense. I pushed away my initial anger and instead felt gratitude for my friend's help as well as her concern.

Now I needed to get into Bakerstown, finish my errands, and stop by the caterers to make sure everything was set for Friday's author event. My car's Bluetooth picked up a call from Aunt Jackie a few minutes into my drive.

"Where are you?"

I drove past The Coastal Inn and paused. I'd planned on stopping there too, but I'd forgotten the marketing cookies I took when I was courting a new business to come and join our Business-to-Business meeting. I'd have to buy something in town and stop on my way home. It wasn't Sadie's cheesecake, but bakery cookies would do fine. "I'm going into town. Don't worry, I'd already planned on stopping by the caterers."

"Don't worry about that, I've already called them. Since you're out, stop by Linens and Loots and rent tablecloths and runners for the tables. We need twenty. Then go to the craft store and get large vases, and as many blue marbles as you can find. I'll call your friend Allison for the flowers." Aunt Jackie took a quick breath and I jumped into the empty slot.

"Hold on, I'll call you when I get to Linens and Loots. Are you sure they rent linen?" I'd never been part of the planning for one of these big events so I didn't know much about the whole party scene.

"If they don't, ask who does. I'm sure there's somewhere in Bakerstown we can rent the linens. I was planning on doing these errands myself, but as you know…" She let the sentence trail off, adding to the guilt factor.

Frustrated with the way the conversation was going, I sighed. "Look, I don't mind helping. Oh, and the lost money has been found. Apparently it was an account issue. The check got put into my savings rather than the business account. I really need to set up online access to my personal accounts. If I'd thought to look there, we wouldn't have worried so long."

"Managers lose their jobs over mistakes not even this big. What did the bank examiner say?" Even over the Bluetooth, I could hear the stress in my aunt's voice.

"I didn't talk to a bank examiner, I talked to Claire. The problem is fixed now." Traffic was almost non-existent today, which was a good thing since my aunt's call made me feel like ramming the Jeep into a solid object. Okay, maybe not that drastic; I kind of loved my car.

"I'm sure there's some sort of procedure for this situation. Just because Claire's a friend doesn't mean she should get away with this. What if the money had been put into a stranger's account? Someone without money that watches the balance daily and could have spent it all before we tracked down the problem." Aunt Jackie was getting wound up, again.

"Look, we've got other fish to fry. Can we get back to the errands? Besides linens and vase stuff, do you need anything else from Bakerstown?

I've got to get back as soon as possible." What I didn't say was the reason I needed to return was to find out more about this Robert character. I thought maybe I might have some type of lead in the murder investigation, even if I was just playing at trying to solve the puzzle.

"One more thing before you hang up on me, dear." Aunt Jackie sounded ticked off. Even though I hadn't been planning on hanging up on her. Thinking about it, yes, just not planning to do it. I still feared the woman's iron fist, even if she hadn't disciplined me since I was four and ate all the cookies for the adult dinner party later that night.

"I wasn't planning on hanging up." We might as well get all the cards on the table. If she wanted to play me with the guilt, the least she could do was hear my side of the conversation.

I heard her shrug even if I couldn't see it. "Fine. Whatever you want to tell yourself." She paused for the dramatic effect. "Kathi came into the shop last night after everyone left and ordered a coffee. She said that if the contractors didn't finish soon, she was going to run out of money by the end of next week."

"What would happen with Tea Hee?" I'd been excited when Kathi'd bought the run-down building across the street. I believed in the notion that many hands made light work, even if people just wanted to stand around and watch when the heavy lifting is being done.

"I guess she'd sell the shop and go back home to Texas."

Chapter 17

By the time I returned to South Cove, I'd had five more calls from my aunt, which added six more stops, including the current one where she asked me to drop the supplies off at the shop so she could get a start on making party favors for the guests. I unlocked the back door to the office and was surprised to have Harrold taking the first set of boxes out of my hands. He sat them on a table they'd set up near the walk-in freezer and nodded to the door. "Let me get the rest."

"My personal stuff is in the back seat, all the stuff in the hatchback storage is for the party," I called after him as he hurried out the door. I walked into the shop and swept the mail up from the floor where the postman had dropped them through a slot in the door. Sorting through the envelopes I saw three bills and five pieces of junk mail. I trashed the junk and put the bills on my desk.

Harrold had brought in all the rest of the bags and boxes. He stood going through one of the bags, pulling out white ribbon for chair decorations. "I haven't seen this much craft stuff since Agnes was helping Lille with her wedding planning."

I picked up a bag of blue marbles and tossed them in the air. "I know, it's like craft central in here." Then Harrold's words hit me. "Wait, Lille was married?"

He sat down the roll of ribbon and leaned against the table. "Actually, no. The wedding was called off. The groom got cold feet."

"I've never heard this. Who was she dating? Do I know him?" Lille was a mystery to me and I'd always wondered what made her tick. Thinking of her planning a wedding that never happened made me see her in a more positive light. Man, that had to sting.

"He's dead now, but right after he broke it off with Lille, he married someone you do know." Harrold watched me carefully.

The only person I knew who had a deceased spouse was Sadie. And it couldn't have been her, but as I thought it, I realized it made perfect sense. "Sadie's husband? He was engaged to Lille?"

Harrold nodded. "It about killed the girl when he brought his new bride back to South Cove. And when Nick came along just shy of nine months later, Lille sat on my living room floor and cried for a full day. She was in love."

"Is that why she's so guarded now?" I didn't want to talk bad about Lille, since she and Harrold were still friends.

"I thought you were coming right back up," Aunt Jackie's voice echoed down the stairs as we heard her thump down each step. She paused at the doorway. "Oh, Jill, I didn't realize you were here." Using the furniture as handholds, she moved toward the table.

Harrold grabbed the office chair and put it behind her. "Here, use this to move around."

"Thanks." This time she actually smiled at him as he tried to help her rather than bite his head off. The rest must be helping her control her pain. She considered each of the items out on the table. "These are lovely, Jill. They are just what I would have bought if I'd been able to go shopping myself."

I glanced at the clock. I still had to get ready to present to the council. For this being my day off, it sure felt like I was working. "I've got to get back to the house to be ready for the council meeting. Don't stay up too late."

When I pulled out of the alley, Greg's truck was heading the opposite way down Main Street. He pulled alongside me and rolled down his window. "Hey, I just stopped by the house to let you know I won't be at the council meeting."

"Seriously?" My heart started pounding. I had counted on him being there for moral support. "What's more important than being there for me?" My voice had taken on a squeak.

His eyebrows raised in response to my obvious emotion. "My job? Sorry honey, but you know the drill. Ballistics came back on the bullet they took out of Darryl and even though I don't think she killed the guy, I have to know where Kathi thinks her gun has been."

I felt my eyes widen. "Kathi? She killed Darryl?"

Greg drummed his fingers on the side of the truck. "That's not what I said. Look, all I meant to say was I won't be there tonight but I'm thinking about you."

And with that he drove away. A horn blared behind me and I went home, thinking about what Greg said. Sometimes he fed me information to see what I could do with it. I didn't feel like that was the case with the gun evidence. I think he just slipped. I thought about the blonde who kept her glasses a secret from the world because she was worried about what people might think. No way could she have killed someone, much less a relative.

If I didn't get a move on, I'd be presenting in the tank top and capris I wore into town. I ran upstairs for a quick shower and change. When I was done, I grabbed my laptop and ran through the presentation one more time.

I closed the computer and headed to the door. Pausing at a mirror to check my hair, I figured I looked at least presentable. I knew these were just other business owners, like me, but for some reason, I was nervous for this particular presentation. Mostly since I knew Mayor Baylor would be there, judging every word and gesture I made.

Think of him in his underwear. The old speech saying popped into my head and I grimaced at the visual image that followed, Mayor Baylor, all portly and pink sitting in a chair glaring at me. I decided instead to find some friendly faces in the crowd, like Bill and Amy, and focus my attention there.

I glanced at my watch. In two hours tops, this would be over and I'd be back here in my pajamas, celebrating with a slice of double chocolate cheesecake.

The meeting room at City Hall was crowded when I entered, but I took my laptop up to Amy at the front where Bill and the other council heads sat. She gave me a hug. "You look great. You should do the report for the business group all the time."

I blew out air and shook my head. "I'm a great liaison, I know how to delegate to just the right people. Mary's perfect for this. If she ever plans on coming back now that the baby's here."

Bill turned my way after hearing my comment. "Mary will be back on Thursday. She's excited about the library event. And I'm leaving Saturday morning for my visit with the little tyke."

"Boy or girl?" Amy asked.

We talked about the new grandson for several minutes, until we heard a gavel and Tom Hudson, the council chair, trying to call the meeting to order.

"I didn't give you my slides." I whispered to Amy, feeling sick. If I didn't have the slides to use, I couldn't remember the presentation points Mary wanted me to make.

Amy leaned close and whispered, "Mary already sent them to me. I've got your back."

We found chairs and I found myself sitting next to a woman I didn't know. I looked around the room. Kathi and Greg were absent from the group of business owners and city employees. Pushing Kathi's possible guilt aside, I smiled at the woman next to me. "I don't think we've met. I'm Jill Gardner, owner of Coffee, Books, and More and council business liaison."

She turned toward me and I realized she had to be almost Aunt Jackie's age, even though she dressed in tight jeans and a v-neck top that showed off her ample cleavage. Her lips had a too-red lipstick covering her off-white teeth that made her smile look a little evil. "Tilly Voss. I'm the manager over at The Coastal Inn. My boss told me to come and see if we could get the crime scene tape off one of our rooms. It's kind of bad for our business."

The others were still milling around not following Tom's instructions so I leaned closer. "I'm sorry about the murder. Did you know Darryl well?"

Tilly snorted. "Darryl? Was that his name? He signed in as Joe Cook. I guess it could have been worse, he could have used Smith. Do you know how many Smiths I get a week?"

"Don't you have to show a driver's license or credit card?" Every hotel I'd ever stayed at required some sort of identification. I wondered if it was just in case something went wrong, more than a financial payment issue.

"We're kind of a mostly cash business." The grin reappeared and I tried not to recoil away from the woman. "If they want class, they tend to stay elsewhere."

Now, that I believed. Most of the audience had taken their seats so I needed to hurry if I was going to ask her what I wanted to know. "Darla said that Ivy Corbin visited her cousin with another man often. Did you happen to get a look at the guy? Or his name?" Now I knew I was just wishing for miracles.

"Not really, I mean, I watched them for sure. I figured there was some action going on in the room, if you understand my meaning. One day, I was checking housekeeping in one of the rooms when they walked by. The woman called the big guy Bobby." She looked around the room. "I don't see that police guy here at all. This was a big waste of time."

"He's not coming tonight." The words were out before I had a chance to stop them and Tilly did exactly what I didn't want her to do. She stood up to leave.

"I'm out of here. I've got shows to watch tonight." She grinned at me. "And a six pack that's been calling my name all day."

I thought about following her out and trying to get a better description of this big guy, Bobby, but then Tom announced me and it was time for my talk. I put on my aren't-you-all-charming smile and headed to the front of the room.

Then my autopilot turned on.

Leaving that night, I stopped to say goodbye to Amy. "I'm out of here. If you're ready, do you want to walk together?"

She held up the loose papers. "I'm here until I get this all in order. But the good thing is I get to take off early on Friday to make up for the time. The mayor hates paying overtime."

"Are you coming to the library event or do you and Justin have surfing plans?" Amy's boyfriend had been deep into geocaching a few months ago, but once the waves started up again, he and Amy had been spending most of their free time on the ocean.

"Sorry, we're heading to a beach a little south of here. I don't think I'll be back for Sunday brunch either." Amy nodded to Tom who called a good night greeting as he left the room. "But I'll see you tomorrow and Thursday at the gym. I'm so glad we're taking this class together. I love doing things with you."

I loved having brunch and maybe a girls' night out at Darla's winery, but loving working out? It still wasn't growing on me. I pasted on a smile and nodded though, wanting to let her know I totally agreed, even if it was a total lie. "Yeah, me too."

Amy burst out laughing. "You're such a liar. I know you hate it, but at least you have someone to suffer with you."

We said our goodbyes and I left City Hall to walk home. The night was chilly, but the stars were already out and beautiful. Greg's truck was still parked at the north side of the building where the police station had its own entrance. I still couldn't believe our new resident beauty queen capable of killing someone, especially, her own family.

Then who? I pondered the question as I made my way home and still didn't have an answer by the time I turned back the covers to go to sleep. The mysterious Robert/Bobby was high on my list, but then there was also secretive Ivy who lived like a queen, but acted like a pauper. And what about her claim that Kathi was engaged? And who had beaten up Blake? I'd kind of forgotten about him and wondered if Darla had any word on her band's lead member.

I wrote down a few notes and questions on the pad I kept on my nightstand and then slipped into the covers. Tomorrow would be an early day and with the festival this weekend and the library event on Friday, I hadn't had much of a break from work this week.

I fell asleep thinking of the Mexican beaches and big frozen drinks Greg and I would be enjoying in a few weeks. If he was talking to me after our tiff this afternoon. I pushed away the thought with another one. *Greg loves you.*

The shop was empty from the time I opened in the morning until ten when my first customer arrived, a commuter who had late work hours for the summer. He looked around the empty shop as I poured his large black to go and shrugged. "Everyone stay home today?"

I laughed, putting the lid on the to-go cup. "Seems that way. This is your Monday, isn't it?"

"Actually, I work at home on Monday, Wednesday, and Friday during the summer. I only go in for meetings on Tuesday and Thursday." He took a sip of coffee, apparently not in any hurry to get to his day job. "Did you hear about the murder last week? They really need to shut that rattrap motel down. You know its clients are either hookers or druggies."

"I've heard that." I didn't know why Darryl had chosen The Coastal Inn as his home for the short time he had been here in South Cove. Maybe it was the price, or maybe, like the customer had insinuated, Darryl had enjoyed the extra benefits. If he hadn't been shot in his room with Kathi's gun, would his death be written off as a drug deal gone wrong? Maybe his being related to Kathi and Ivy was just a coincidence. Maybe he had messed with the wrong people.

But for some reason, that explanation felt off.

"So I guess I'll see you Thursday. My wife and I are looking forward to the library event. Anything we can do to support reading in our schools we're more than willing to participate in." He walked out with his coffee and I wondered how much of his conversation I'd totally blanked out on while thinking about Darryl's death. I really needed to stop doing that.

Walk-in traffic stayed slow until Toby arrived for his shift. He put his hand up, "Look, I'm not mad about the bank thing. I should have been more careful with the deposit slips."

"The money has been found. I guess the teller looked up the wrong account number." I looked at him. "Do you remember who helped you that day? Margie?"

"Nope, some new girl. She just kept giggling. Man, she was making mistake after mistake. She tore up the first deposit slip and had to handwrite a new one." Toby put the apron on over his head. "That's when it happened, huh?"

"I guess. I just wish we hadn't worried so much about the money." What I really wanted to say was I wished I hadn't asked him if he'd taken it, but it didn't seem to fit.

Toby's regulars typically arrived a few minutes before he walked in. I saw them parked on the street, refreshing their makeup and staring into the shop windows waiting for Barista Babe. Even though he was off the market again, the women still came to spend their breaks with him. I guess I couldn't blame them, but I didn't really understand why someone would continue to put themselves out there with no chance of success. The dating world was hard enough.

I went to the back and changed into my workout clothes in the employee-only bathroom. Then as I walked through the shop to leave, Toby called out, "Have a great workout. Greg says you're killing it."

If we'd been alone, I would have told him what to do with his words, but the girls in line smiled at him like he'd told me I had just won a marathon. I knew he was giving me grief since I hated the class more than anything I'd ever done, except maybe yoga. I despised that. Amy had dragged me to a month of classes last summer before I'd called uncle. She still attended the early bird class down at the Bakerstown senior center. I'd rather run with Emma.

She'd looked so hard at her leash this morning, I'd thought it would levitate off the hook and float into my hands. When I'd told her tomorrow, she'd stomped off to her kitchen bed and turned her head away from me. Don't tell me animals don't understand what we're saying.

The morning was still cool and besides the cars parked around Coffee, Books, and More, the street was deserted. The lights were already on at Antiques by Thomas and Kyle was sweeping the sidewalk in front of the store.

"Morning Kyle," I called out as I turned the opposite way.

"Morning, Miss Gardner," he called back, a lilt to his voice. He had changed so much from the angry boy that Josh had accepted as an intern last year; now he was a happy young man who loved antiques as much as his portly boss. We'd had four interns that had stayed around town after the work program had ended last year. Kyle, Sasha, Matt, and Mindy, who worked for Marie Jones over at The Glass Slipper. Of course, Matt had turned into more than just an employee for Darla. The two of them had been dating since January.

For being one of the mayor's harebrained ideas, the work program had been successful in at least a few lives.

As I entered the gym, I noticed for the second class in a row, Greg and Tim were noticeably absent. This didn't look good for Kathi. When investigations got hot, Greg was totally focused on his job, working almost 24/7. Well, 24/6, now that he'd implemented No-Guilt-Sunday to bring at least some balance to his life.

Amy waved me over and we started stretching before class. When she thought the instructor was out of earshot, she leaned closer. "Did you hear about Kathi? Can you believe it?"

I tried not to confirm or deny anything Greg told me in confidence but this was Amy. "Seriously, no. When Greg mentioned needing to talk to her I told him it was impossible."

"Well, word is that the DA's ready to charge her. Something about some argument they had before she left Texas. I guess she told him he wasn't her boss and she'd see him dead before he could force her into something she didn't want to do." Amy looked over at the drill sergeant we had hired for a workout instructor and when she saw him looking our way, she shrugged. "Maybe we can do lunch?"

He started walking toward us and I mumbled my response. "Perfect." Then I started in on the 100x5 program he had us start out with. Jumping jacks was the first of the five and it ended with an energetic round of burpees. I never finished the warmup before the real class started. Maybe someday, but I doubted it.

* * * *

At Lille's, Amy filled me in on the gossip she'd heard from Esmeralda. John had indeed decided to charge our newest business owner with the murder of her cousin. He was talking to the judge this afternoon about the specific charges. From what Amy said, manslaughter was off the table, but maybe she'd be able to have a lesser charge if she admitted her guilt and it was a crime of passion.

"What's Kathi saying?"

Amy shrugged. "She's hired an attorney who apparently told her to keep her mouth shut. The lawyer thinks there's not enough evidence for her to even be charged."

"You're the best. How do you hear all this?" I ate a few French fries and decided to focus on the fish instead.

Amy paused before taking a bite of her double cheeseburger. "I deliver the coffee. Most people don't even see me when I'm there."

"Isn't that the truth." Carrie appeared with a pitcher to refill our iced tea. "You wouldn't believe all the stuff I hear just because people think I'm invisible. Heck, sometimes I feel like I am."

"You're not invisible," I said, even though I hadn't seen her walk up.

She eyed my plate. "And you're not eating. What's wrong?"

I looked guilty at the plate. "I hate my workout."

Amy burst out laughing and Carrie joined in. When they were done, I shrugged. "What, it's true."

"Then do something else. Life's too short." Carrie put her hands up in surrender. "You don't have to listen to me. I'm just trying to help."

I watched her walk away and nodded. "Carrie's right. I'm going back to running with Emma. I love doing things together, but can we do something besides the workout class?"

"Like long walks on the beach or geocaching?" Amy held up a hand. "Okay, not that last one. I don't want Justin to get the bug again. I just got him off the habit."

We made an agreement to get together next week in the evening but we didn't make plans on what to do yet. Instead, we agreed we'd both bring a few ideas on things we'd wanted to try or do and then we'd make a schedule for the next month. "So next week, it is a long walk on the beach while we talk, right?"

Amy giggled. "I was kind of being funny, but I think it's a great idea."

Walking out of the restaurant, I felt lighter than I had since Amy and I had fought earlier in the year. We were starting to get past the everyone-be-nice phase and back to the casual friendship I enjoyed.

She turned to go back to work, and I turned the other way, toward my house. When I turned around, a woman blocked my path and from the look on her face, she wanted me dead.

Chapter 18

"Lille," I croaked out, my voice sounding shaky. "You scared me."

Her hands on her hips, she nodded. "Good. You need to be scared. So why are you digging up my past?"

Confusion came over me, then I got it. Harrold must have mentioned our conversation. "I'm not. I mean, Harrold happened to mention the time Agnes and you were making wedding decorations when he saw all the craft stuff I bought for the library event on Friday. I didn't mean to pry, but it shocked me. I didn't realize you had ever…" I stopped talking since Lille's face had turned an even brighter shade of red. It was going to happen. I would be banned from the only place to eat in town. Just as soon as Lille said her next words.

Instead of the you're-out-of-here proclamation, her next words were soft, almost tender. "Look, neither Sadie or Nick know about me and I'd like to keep it that way. He made a choice and he was happy. And so were they until he died. I'd rather they have their own memories."

"I would never tell Sadie." I thought about my declaration and nodded. It was true. This was something in Sadie's late husband's past and had nothing to do with the man she knew. Besides, it wasn't my story to tell. If Lille wanted to keep it quiet, that's the way it would be. "I think it would only hurt her, and she's been hurt enough lately."

Lille nodded, a sad smile on her lips. "She has gone through the ringer lately." She stared out into the western sky. "Nick looks just like his father did at that age. We went to school together, high school sweethearts, I guess. But when he met Sadie, he knew he'd found his soulmate."

"But he was yours." I said the words Lille wouldn't, or maybe couldn't. "So that's why you have been keeping an eye out on Nick."

"And helping him with college." Now the grin was bigger. "Now that is something you can never tell your friend. I know you've sponsored a few people in school yourself with that money the old lady left you. Well, I had my own inheritance, so once he decided on a school, I called the financial aid office and told them I'd do a scholarship for the kid. The good news is they keep me generally informed of his grades and anything extracurricular amazing. I made a certain grade point a condition of the scholarship, so I hear from them each quarter."

I stood there, shocked. This was the last thing I'd thought I'd hear from the bad boy-loving restaurant owner.

Lille took a deep breath. "Harrold didn't even know all that. I felt kind of silly, watching the kid all these years, wondering what our children would have looked like if we'd had any." She looked at me. "So now we share a secret. One you can't even tell Miss Surfer about."

I knew she was talking about Amy and I nodded. "No one would believe me anyway."

Now Lille's grin widened and she nodded. "I know, right? Who would believe that I have a soft side? Especially one for Nick Michaels, my former dish boy."

I watched her walk back into the diner, her step lighter than it had been in years. Telling someone your secret could do that to a person. And now, I helped her carry it.

By the time I reached home, I was drained. I pulled out my laptop and checked my email. Nothing important unless I was interested in getting a Russian bride, a no-credit-needed loan, or to hook up with single men in my area. Not only was I getting junk mail at the shop and my home mailbox, my email inbox was filled with the stuff.

I was about to turn off the laptop and grab the book I'd been reading, when I thought about Robert Marshall. I grabbed my notebook and wrote the name in the page under Kathi Corbin. Then I implemented my ultra-scientific modern investigation technique. I looked him up on Facebook.

Twenty minutes later, I'd found Bobby Marshall, who listed his status as engaged. On Kathi's page, there was no mention of the happy event. Either Kathi hadn't been on Facebook for a while, too busy making wedding plans, or she was ignoring his status. Bobby was from the same little town in Texas and owned the local service station Fill-er-Up. He only listed one organization he was a part of: The Porkers, a local motorcycle club. And when I looked at the pictures of him on his pride and joy Harley, I knew I'd found the guy who'd run down Aunt Jackie.

I dialed Greg's cell and got voice mail. I hung up and called the police station. Esmeralda answered.

"Hey, is Greg there? I need to talk to him." I just hoped she wouldn't ask why, I didn't want to admit to everyone I was sleuthing, just my boyfriend. And this piece of information was more about my aunt than the murder he was investigating.

"He's here, but it's kind of a mad house. They're dealing with some things." Esmeralda paused. "You okay? Do I need to send out one of the boys?"

"No, I'm good. I just needed to talk to him about that motorcycle rider who's been terrorizing South Cove. I think I know who it is." I was about to tell her to have Greg call me when she lowered her voice and started talking.

"Good. We don't need more drama here. I mean, can you believe it? We finally have a suspect in that man's murder and now we have two? Of course, John's pulling his hair out and the fact that the other one turned herself in in some Texas town is making it worse."

"Wait, Ivy said she killed Darryl? Why?" Now I didn't care what Esmeralda thought, I just wanted to know the story.

A chuckle came over the line. "Yeah, I thought you'd react to that. Apparently when John gave Greg the okay to arrest Kathi, a call came in from the sheriff in that town they're from. He said Ivy walked in and told him she'd killed Darryl with Kathi's gun so it would look like Kathi did it."

"And so she ruined the perfect plan by confessing as soon as her sister was arrested?" I sank back into the sofa. "This makes no sense at all."

"Tell me about it." She paused, talking to someone in the lobby. "Sorry, I've got to go. I'll give Greg your message."

Emma sat near my feet, watching me talk on the phone. She had been sleeping in the kitchen so I must have woken her up with my call. "That family is loco crazy." I rubbed her head and gave her a kiss on the nose. "Want to go outside while I make us some dinner?"

She wagged her tail, then followed me into the kitchen. I opened a can of soup and made a quick grilled cheese sandwich for dinner. Sitting at the kitchen table, I stared at the notebook with the clues from Darryl's murder I'd carefully written out. Ivy killing him made as much sense as Kathi. And I didn't know if it was possible anyway with the fact they'd both been at the winery with us that night. Something wasn't adding up, besides Kathi's so-called engagement. I decided I'd stop by my neighbor's shop first thing in the morning. If she was out of jail by then.

* * * *

Greg was waiting for me when I arrived at the store Wednesday morning. He gave me a kiss, then took my keys and opened the shop. I followed him inside.

"What are you doing here?" I flipped on the lights and turned the sign over to OPEN. "Esmeralda made it sound like you'd be stuck at work for months straightening out all the mess."

Greg tossed my keys onto the counter and sat at the barstool. "That's why I'm here. I had to get out of there before I shot someone." He pointed to the delayed timed coffeepot. "You got any of the good stuff ready?"

"We just opened the doors, what do you think?" I went around the counter, washed my hands, and slipped on an apron. Then I poured him a large cup and brought over his favorite creamer for him to use to ruin the lovely dark brew. "Just kidding. I get regulars waiting at the door, so we have a pot set to brew just before we open."

Greg sipped his coffee, then his gaze returned to me. "Wait, what exactly did Esmeralda tell you?"

I shrugged. "More than she should have, I'm sure. So did you charge Kathi or Ivy?"

"Neither." He ran his hand through his hair. "Ivy's being extradited as we speak and should be delivered to the station around five. We're keeping Kathi in holding until I get a chance to talk to Ivy. The sisters are playing some sort of game here and I'm going to find out what it's all about."

"I can't believe either would kill someone. Even someone in their family." I started the second pot, using hazelnut coffee. The smell filled the shop and my stomach growled in appreciation.

"Don't you mean especially someone in their family?" Greg pointed to a lone chocolate cheesecake slice. "Grab me one of those and I'll share it with you."

"With that family, I mean even. I swear I've never met two people who are more different than those two sisters. I can't figure out why Ivy would confess to something she didn't do. Can you?"

"I have my suspicions. Of course, if I'm right, then Kathi's back on the hook for Darryl's murder." He took a bite of the cheesecake. "Neither option smells quite right."

"So did Esmeralda tell you I think I know who the motorcycle guy is? The one that ran Aunt Jackie down?" I took my own fork full of the dessert and decided to call it breakfast.

He wiped his mouth on a napkin. "She actually fell, but I agree, it was the guy's fault."

"Anyway, I think it's Bobby Marshall. He says he's engaged to Kathi. And he's been paying for Ivy's room over at The Castle."

He shook his head. "You are going kind of deep on this one. How did you find this out?"

"It was easy, once I had his name. I used my handy-dandy Facebook investigatory skills." With my morning tasks started, I came around and sat next to him.

"As long as you're not going looking for him, I'm fine with how you're gleaning information." He finished off the cheesecake. "You're not going looking for him, right? And please tell me you're not taking Amy or Sadie. I figure your aunt is out of the picture until her ankle heals."

"I'm not doing any sleuthing this week." *Well, except for talking to Kathi if you ever release her*, I thought to myself. Besides, I had a perfectly good reason to go talk to my neighbor; our joint tea adventure. We needed to talk branding and when she could get me a supply so I could start hawking her new store. My gaze went to the white porch of the little shop across the street. A sign had been erected yesterday, Tea Hee with a tea cup underneath, and the shop looked ready to open.

Greg's cell buzzed and he looked at the incoming text. "I wish I believed you. Anyway, I've got to run. Can I get a refill on the coffee?" He pulled out his wallet, thumbing through the bills.

"Don't worry about that." I pushed the wallet away and returned to the back of the counter to pour his coffee. "Your money's no good here. One of the perks of dating the owner."

Greg put his wallet back into his jeans pocket. "Thanks, but I think your aunt feels differently. I'm not sure, but I have a feeling she charges me double."

I handed him a to-go cup with a sleeve and a lid. "Controlling Aunt Jackie is one of those things I've taken off my to-do list. The woman does what she wants and asks for my blessing afterward. I'm lucky if Sasha or Toby listen to my directions."

"The joy of supervising, I get it. If it makes you feel better, I have the same problem with Toby and Esmeralda." He leaned over the counter and kissed me. "At worst, I'll see you Friday night for this library thing. Tell me it's not formal."

"Here? Formal? Ha. We'll be lucky if beach attire isn't the most common outfit." I ran my hand over his ironed, button-down sheriff shirt. "Just don't come in uniform. I don't want people to think something's wrong."

"I think I can manage a shower and a change." He snorted. "As long as no other Corbin relatives show up and confess to killing poor Darryl.

This feels like one of those mystery books you're always reading where the answer is right there, I just can't see it."

Once Greg left, my Wednesday regulars flowed in. Most were commuters but I had a small stay-at-home mom group that met in the bookstore every Wednesday to talk about anything but kids. Of course, they also talked about the kids. Apparently babies were welcome up until the time they started walking, then the group rule was they needed to stay home with a babysitter. The group had grown from two local moms to six and a stay-at-home dad. The conversation was always fun and they loved their coffee and treats. Bonus for me, it made a typically slow morning interesting.

I'd just gotten them settled when the door opened and Kyle came in carrying a deposit bag.

"Hey, I planned on stopping by before I left for the bank today." Okay, so I'd forgotten to do both our deposit and Josh's yesterday.

Kyle handed me the bag. "I just want to make sure you get this. Mr. Thomas is fanatical about making regular deposits. He says it keeps the lowlifes from thinking you're an easy target and robbing the store."

I didn't think anyone watched the store that closely to know if Josh had made a deposit in the last day or so, but I wasn't going to argue. Kyle took everything Josh said as retail gospel and since he had to work for the guy, I wouldn't ruin his crazy training methods. "I appreciate you stopping by with this. I'll drop the deposit slip off on my way home."

He stood there, not moving, his gaze on the bookshelves.

"You can go in and browse if you want. You won't disturb the group." I figured he was feeling a little shy around the chatty group.

He shook his head and pulled out a slip of paper. "I don't see a real estate section over there. Can you order me these books? I could get them online, but I'd rather support you. Mr. Thomas is a big supporter of small businesses. He thinks online shopping is going to put us all out of business."

I nodded. "In the book business, he might be right, sooner than later." I looked over the list, which mostly seemed to be books about staging your home for the quick sale. "Are you thinking about getting into real estate?"

"What?" He shook his head. "No, I love working with antiques."

I watched him leave and opened my laptop to order the five books. I didn't understand his interest, but the kid was a little different. Which I liked. And who was I to question a book order?

Toby came in just as I was finishing cleaning up from the moms and dad group. I put the cups in the sink and watched him get ready for his shift. "I wasn't sure I'd see you. I hear the station is crazy busy."

He dried his hands and put on an apron. "Greg's crazy busy. I went in earlier to help out with some driving, but mostly he's stuck in the war room trying to figure out which sister to charge." He grinned. "I can tell you this since he said he already did. Boy, did Esmeralda get a talking to this morning when he came back with his coffee."

"I didn't mean to get her in trouble." I cringed a bit. "Is she upset?"

Toby laughed. "At you? No. She said you needed to know the information and if she had to do it again she would. They stood staring at each other until finally John broke it up. I've never seen either one of them stand their ground so intensely."

"Maybe I should take over a cheesecake to smooth the waters." I pondered what we had in stock, considering the event on Friday.

"I wouldn't go near the station until this is settled. It's bad juju over there. Everyone's in a tizzy." He shook his head. "That level of stress is why I love working here. The worst thing that can happen here is a spilled latte."

I got the deposits ready and left for the bank, thinking about Toby's last statement. Of course, he didn't know about the lost money or staffing issues. Okay, maybe he knew about the staffing problem since he had volunteered to take on one of Aunt Jackie's shifts while she was out, but he'd been turned down flat. My aunt had told him she was working tonight and that's all the talking we would do about it. And he knew about the lost money. Boy, working at the police station must be really stressful.

Of course, I knew Harrold would be here to help Aunt Jackie, which eased my mind. And if they decided go through with this marriage thing, I guess that wouldn't be a bad idea. He had a store here and roots, and he seemed like a good guy.

Claire was working with a customer at the teller window when I entered. She waved me over to her line as she finished with the woman ahead of me. "Hey, we missed you yesterday."

"I forgot. Besides, the Tuesday deposit is light since I do one on Monday that covers the weekend." Two people had commented on my lack of a regular deposit practice today. I figured I'd get a call from Aunt Jackie next when she started updating the accounting.

"Not a problem, I just worry when I don't see my regular customers." She quickly keyed in the two deposits. When she handed me back Josh's slip she tapped it before she pushed it toward me. "When is our big guy coming home? I miss his grumpy butt."

I snorted. "I think by Friday." I thought back to the conversation where he'd told me he needed a favor. Had he said a week? Or was it two? I couldn't remember. "Anyway, Kyle's doing a great job with the shop. He's on top of things over there."

Claire nodded, looking past me at a carefully dressed woman who had just entered the bank. "If you hear from him, tell him I'm thinking about him." She nodded to Margie and put a sign CLOSED sign on her window. "Looks like my first interview is here. I haven't heard back from your friend Ivy. Is she still looking for a placement?"

I thought Ivy might have a long-term placement, but I just shrugged. "Not sure. I think she took a quick trip back to Texas."

"Well, if you see her, I'm trying to hire two tellers as soon as possible. And I'd like to hire locals. They tend to be more invested in South Cove's success. Got to go." Claire smiled at the woman as she walked up to her, holding out a hand to introduce herself. I nodded at the pair as I walked past to the door, but they were too involved in the interviewing ritual to see me even walk by.

The only thing left on my list was to drop off Kyle's deposit slip and head home. Josh's slip, I corrected myself.

A chill ran down my spine. Where was Josh and why hadn't anyone heard from him?

Chapter 19

I'd promised Amy I'd finish up the week of classes, so that Thursday I put my workout clothes in my tote, gave Emma a new dog bone to make up for not taking her running, and headed off to open the shop. I wondered if giving Emma a food-based treat to solve her sadness was for her benefit or my own. People say dogs tended to take on the personality of their owners. Was I teaching my dog to be an emotional eater?

I powered through my morning tasks, and after the commuter traffic slowed, pulled out a book off the advance reader's pile my bookseller had dropped off and got lost in Regency England chasing a murderer. When the bell chimed over the door, I assumed it was Sasha coming in for her shift. "Hey," I called to her.

"Miss Gardner?" A definitely not-Sasha male voice brought me out of my book. Kyle stood in front of the sofa, holding out the bank bag.

I sat the book on the coffee table and stood, taking the bag from him. "Sorry Kyle, I thought you were someone else."

"My ma used to read like that. Sometimes it took me giving her arm a little shake to pull her out of the story. I worried her house would burn down around her and until she smelled the smoke or felt the heat from the flames, she wouldn't notice." He smiled a little sadly.

"Readers are an interesting breed." I didn't want to pry about his mother since it appeared something had happened. Or maybe she just didn't read anymore.

"Well, anyway, I better get the shop opened. See you in a few." He turned toward the door.

"I ordered those books for you. They should be here early next week," I called after him. He raised his hand, indicating he'd heard me and I heard a muffled thanks as he walked out the door.

Sasha came in as he held the door for her. As she paused by me, she picked up the book on the table. "I read this last week. It's wonderful."

"Got me through an extremely slow shift." I took the book from her to put in my tote for later that afternoon. A thought came to me. "Do you need help setting up for the event tomorrow?"

Sasha followed me to the coffee bar where she started her setup. "I don't think so. Toby's handling the shop until six when we're closing so I'm sure Jackie would like you to be at the library auditorium about three. Then we can finish the setup and get back home to change before we're needed back at six. I've been meaning to ask you, though; can I change at your house? I don't really want to drive back and forth to Bakerstown tomorrow."

"Not a problem. I can just take you with me when I go to get ready. Greg will drive us up, or if he's working, we can take my Jeep."

"Sounds like a plan." Sasha greeted the group of women who were standing by the cash register. "Toby's running late, what can I get for you?"

The women looked at each other and then proceeded to order. When they'd all gone to wait at a table for their drinks and the missing Toby, I moved closer to Sasha where she was making a latte and whispered in her ear, "Uhm, Toby's not scheduled."

Sasha didn't look at me, just kept foaming the milk. "If I'd told them that, they would have left and driven back to school without buying anything. This way, when they ask again, I'll tell them that he's tied up and will be back tomorrow."

"You realize you just lied to a customer." I had to admit, though, her logic was solid. The group of five women would have left. I saw them only on days Toby was scheduled to work.

"Not exactly a lie. He said he might pop in during my shift for coffee and to talk if it's slow." She grinned as she put the last piece of cheesecake on a plate and double-checked the tray. "What can I do, I don't bring in the customers like Barista Babe. I just don't want to run them off."

I followed her out to the table and made my exit. Let Amy and the boys do the 100x5 warm up. I didn't want to do it anymore, even if I could trim my waist by an inch over three months, which had been his promise to get me to come twice a week.

At the bank, Claire was in her office interviewing, but Margie didn't have anyone at her window so I sailed through that chore in minutes.

Finally, I made it to the gym and waved at Amy as I made my way to the ladies' locker room to change.

I heard voices out in the gym and hurried to get dressed. Adjusting my tank as I walked out to the gym, Amy greeted me at the door. "You're not going to believe who just joined the class."

I looked up and saw Josh talking to the trainer. When he saw me, he glared, then turned back to listen to the trainer.

I didn't start my warm up. Instead I went over to where the two men were standing. "You're back." I eyed Josh closely. Clearly, something was different. His face seemed thinner and the off-brand track suit he'd worn when he'd been walking with Aunt Jackie looked a little looser. "Did you lose weight?"

He threw his shoulders back and I saw what was almost a smile creep on to his lips. "Fifteen pounds."

"And you'll lose more if you stay on my program." The trainer glared at me. "Don't you have 100x5s to do?"

"I wanted to tell you that this is my last class." My body felt light as I smiled at the guy. As I left the pair, I nodded to Josh. "You look good."

I went back to where Amy had already started working on her warm up and started the jumping jacks. I couldn't talk and count at the same time, so it wasn't until I was done and we were running laps that she finally asked me what Josh had said.

Josh was gone by the time we'd finished. I guess he'd had a private session with the trainer from hell before class. As I walked toward home, I realized I still needed to drop off the bank bag and deposit slip. Thank goodness this favor was over. I still wondered where Josh had gone, but at least he'd turned up safe and sound.

He was standing at the counter when I walked in. He'd already changed into his funeral director-style black suit and white shirt, but his face was still beet red. He grimaced as he saw me walk in. "Miss Gardner."

"Don't blow a gasket. I just came by to drop off the bank stuff." I handed over the bag and slip.

He stared at the amount keyed onto the slip then hit a key on the cash register causing the drawer to come open. "Thank you for your assistance last week."

I waited, but apparently that was all I was going to get. If I wanted to know more, I needed to ask. "Kyle did a great job while you were gone. He's very sharp."

"He's coming along," Josh muttered, like Kyle was a wild dog Josh was training.

Finally, I couldn't stand it anymore. "So where did you go? No one heard from you. I was beginning to worry."

He stared at me and for a minute, I didn't think he was going to answer, just demand I leave his shop and him alone. Instead, he sighed. "I went to a fat farm."

"Those things are real?" My mouth gaped open as I looked at the now smaller Josh.

"Close your mouth, you'll attract flies." He looked down at his ledger. "Yes, they're real. David is one of their trainers and he told me about the program last week. He thought doing a quick and fast boot camp that had a doctor onsite where they could monitor me would be the best way to start."

"Wow. That's amazing." I knew my aunt had worried about Josh's weight affecting his health, but I hadn't thought Josh had taken the doctors' warnings very seriously.

"Jackie told me I should take care of myself, and for once in my life, I listened." He raised his eyebrows. "Anything else you want to know? My shoe size? Where I was born? My Social Security number?"

"No, I mean, I'm just happy you're okay. More than okay." I turned toward the door but Kyle exploded out of one of the back hallways.

"It's ready. I had to hurry up 'cause I didn't expect you until tomorrow, but come back, it's ready now." He waved at Josh to follow him into the back.

"What have you done?" A panicked look covered Josh's face and he turned to me. "He hasn't been using again, has he?"

I shook my head. "No. I mean, I don't know for sure, but I don't think so."

We followed Kyle into the first showing room. When I'd walk through last year looking for furniture for my guest room, the place had been stuffed with boxes and furniture. Now, it looked like a furniture store, staged in different setting arrangements with trinkets and books on the end tables.

"Kyle?" Josh wheezed. I turned to look at him and the man looked like he was about to faint. Both Kyle and I rushed to his side and lowered him onto one of the couches.

"It's called staging. I've been reading about it on that antique dealers website I told you about. Dealers say once they've changed up their displays, their sales skyrocketed. I've started on a dining room setting in the next room, but it still needs a lot of work." Kyle adjusted the stained glass lamp on the table next to Josh.

Josh looked around the room. "I can't believe it."

Both Kyle and I waited for the next shoe to drop. I figured Kyle might just get fired for messing with Josh's system. We watched as Josh started to speak and my heart dropped for the kid.

"Thank you. It's wonderful." Josh coughed into his hands, clearly overwhelmed with emotion.

My eyes widened as I listened to Josh's words. I don't think I'd ever heard him say a kind word to anyone except Aunt Jackie in the entire time I'd known him.

The room was thick with emotion and I used the awkward silence to make my break. "Looks really good, Kyle. Well, I've got to go."

I don't think I ran out of the shop, but I probably could have described my pace as a power walk. I didn't get far before the giggles came over me. Josh had a heart after all. As I composed myself, I saw Kathi going into the front door of Tea Hee.

Time to figure out what's going on. I crossed the street and made my way onto her wooden porch, just large enough for two rockers, which I'd assumed she'd add when the shop opened. A touch of Southern hospitality for South Cove.

Knocking on the door, I tried the knob and it swung open. "Kathi, are you in here?"

"Around back," she called, and I walked through the almost finished shop, pausing to look at a tea cup and pot set with roses around the edges. The sign said the pattern was Old Country Rose and I fell in love with the idea of a set right there and then. Looked like Kathi would have at least one customer as soon as she opened. I could totally see people impulse-buying the china and having it shipped back to their homes. The room reminded me of a country kitchen, with each wall with a different type of finishing to bring out a mood. Country kitchen, classical china, and even modern with its clean lines and cool colors, they all had a place in the shop.

I heard a noise and saw Kathi leaning against the doorframe to the back storage area. She smiled. "I thought you got lost."

I slowly turned in a circle. "I did. Lost in this shop. You've really done a great job. It's magical."

She looked around at the store and sighed. "I know." Then she burst into tears.

I hurried over and grabbed tissues off the counter next to an old-fashioned cash register. "Don't cry. It will all work out. You'll open and people with fall in love with this shop."

"You don't understand. I can't open." Kathi sank into a bench that lined the wall. I sat next to her, holding the tissue box.

"You have to open. It's a great concept and just what South Cove needs." I held out the tissue box. "Believe me, I was scared too. What I knew about running a business could fill a single sheet. But I learned."

"I know how to run a business. Uncle taught me well." She looked around. "The problem is if I open, Ivy goes to jail. He'll see to that."

"Greg?" Now I was totally confused.

Kathi looked at me and even with her tear-stained face and swollen eyes, she was beautiful. I tended to look like those DUI mug shots they post on Facebook when I cried. "Your Greg is such a lovely man. Kind and thoughtful. You're a lucky girl."

"Thanks, but who won't let you open the shop?" I wasn't following her conversation. Maybe it was her father, maybe she had to go home and take care of him if Ivy was going to jail, but that didn't make sense either.

A shadow fell over us and my heart sank.

"I won't let her. No wife of mine is going to sell trinkets to rich snobs spending their money on trash." The man's voice was calm, but I could hear the tinge of madness in his tone.

I looked up and there was the motorcycle rider who had caused so much havoc over the last few days. I looked him square in the eye and said, "So you must be Bobby Marshall."

Chapter 20

A slow grin came over his face. "Aren't you the smart one?" He poked Kathi with the revolver he held in his right hand. "Ain't she just a rocket scientist? Or have you been talking out of school again?"

Kathi didn't respond, even when he placed the gun under her chin and lifted her head.

"Answer me." His voice was a little louder now, and firmer, like he was talking to a wayward child.

"She didn't tell me anything about being engaged or about you." I put my hand over Kathi's, hoping to comfort her. It was ice cold.

He dropped the gun and focused on me. "She should have told people about us, especially that music man. He might not be in the hospital right now if she had."

"So you beat up Blake?" That was obvious, now. Who else besides the crazy man who thought Kathi was his property would have beaten the guy up and left all the expensive equipment, not to mention over five hundred dollars in Blake's wallet. That was a piece of information Esmeralda had let slip a few days ago when I called to see if Greg was coming over for dinner.

Today, I had no plans, no one to miss me until Toby came to relieve me at the shop tomorrow at noon. I could be dead behind one of Kathi's beautiful table settings for days before they thought to look just across the street. My only hope was to keep him talking while I thought of something.

"Is that what the worm's name is? Blake?" He pushed Kathi's hair back with the gun. "Honey, you never did have good taste in men. Present company excepted."

"We never dated." Kathi's words came out strong, surprising me. Maybe she was keying into my thought wave to keep him talking.

Bobby just shook his head. Then he turned to me. "Where are your folks from? Around here?"

I nodded, wondering where he was going with this question. "Sacramento."

He squatted down, putting his face closer to us and taking Kathi's other hand in his. "You may not understand this then. You all out here might not be Yankees, but you sure act like them sometimes."

"I think I can manage." I puffed out bravado I didn't feel.

He chuckled. "I do love your spunk." He slapped Kathi's leg. "Ain't she a spunky one, honey?"

Kathi didn't respond, but he didn't seem to notice. He turned to me. "In the south, we have traditions. And when I was born, my mama knew I would be a great man. So she went hunting for a suitable bride. When Kathi was born to her folks, my mama made a deal and we were betrothed."

"As babies? How can you expect her to even honor that? Kathi has a choice in who she'll marry. Haven't you heard of a little thing called love? Not to mention free will?" I couldn't believe this was the reason I was probably not going to see tomorrow. An arranged marriage.

"Now, see, I knew you wouldn't understand. You just don't understand tradition." He looked around the shop waving his gun from one table to the next. "Now, Kathi, she understands tradition. Look at how beautiful these tea parties are. She'll be an amazing mother, especially if we're lucky enough to get at least one little girl."

He had a dreamy look on his face and I wondered if he was seeing their little family in his mind. Kathi, baby, and crazy daddy.

"You won't have any future if you don't let me go." I needed to state the obvious, even if it was going to tick him off.

He stared at me. "See, you're an outlier. I wasn't expecting to have to deal with a nosy neighbor, at least not here. Back home, sure. But here, you all are too self-absorbed to notice anyone but yourself." He paused and turned his attention to Kathi. "What do you think, darling? Kill her, tie her up and leave her here, or should we take her with us? I'm pretty sure we could have some fun with her, don't you think?"

My blood ran cold as I realized what he was saying. Now I was thinking my best chance was to be tied up and left here. Someone would come, eventually. The other two alternatives only ended one way: in my own pine box. While I was considering the alternatives, a noise sounded from the back. Bobby turned the gun toward the open doorway, putting his finger on his lips.

"Kathi? Are you in here? I need to talk to you." Blake's voice echoed through the empty room and as I watched the wheels turn in Bobby's head, even I knew where this was going.

Kathi must have seen the writing on the wall as well because she screamed at the top of her lungs. "Get out of here, Blake! Go to the police station and stay there."

Bobby backhanded her, his hand a fast flash. "Shut up. If you talk again, I'll shoot her and then your boyfriend." He stood and inched toward the doorway. Another bang sounded closer, not farther away. I saw the fear in Kathi's eyes.

"Don't move," Bobby demanded. Then he went into the storage room.

I grabbed Kathi's hand and pulled. She tried to twist away. "He said not to move." Her words hissed out of her.

"He's crazy and we're not staying here." I pulled her to her feet and we ran to the front door. A shot rang out and Kathi tried to turn back.

"Blake," she cried, but the fight had gone out of her and I dragged her out into the open air. Glancing around I knew we'd never make the police station before Bobby caught us. Knowing that Bobby must know I ran the coffee shop, I aimed for Antiques by Thomas and flew into the building shutting the door after us. Josh stared at me, but I shook my head. "Call 9-1-1 now." I pulled Kathi into the next room. With the new setup, there was nowhere to hide. I moved to the next.

"Where are we going?" She kept her voice low, but I knew she didn't think this would work.

I listened for the door to open and Bobby to come roaring in, but all I heard was Josh quietly asking for police involvement and listing off his address. Then I heard the click of the phone. Josh had hung up.

"Crap," I whispered as I pulled us behind a table and lowered to the ground. I reached for my cell and realized I'd left it and my tote in Kathi's shop. I looked at Kathi, but she didn't have pockets in the flower dress that hugged her curves.

Kathi looked at me like I was crazy. "What the hell?"

But as the bell chimed and the door slammed against the wall, her face paled.

"What can I help you find today?" Josh asked, his sales voice sounding calm and cool.

"Where are they?" Bobby roared.

I closed my eyes for a second, wondering if I'd just gotten my portly neighbor killed as well as trapped Kathi and I under a table. She might live long enough to be dragged back to Texas, but this would be my last resting place.

"I can't help you if you don't tell me what you're looking for. Is it a dining set? Or maybe something unusual for your man cave?" Josh sounded reasonable, just wanting to help out his new customer.

Then the bell over the door rang.

"Hey boss. Sorry it took so long, but they messed up your salad by putting the dressing on top and I made them redo it. You should have seen how much they poured on."

"Get out of here, now. Run, Kyle. Run!"

Great, now Josh had blown his cover and Bobby knew he'd chosen the right store.

The door chimed again and I hoped that was an indicator that Kyle was out of harm's way.

"That wasn't too smart, old man." Bobby's voice was as calm as if he'd just told Josh he needed to replace his shirt as he'd dribbled coffee on the front. Not really caring if the other person followed his advice or not. "Now, where are the women before I shoot off one of those fat toes of yours?"

Hold fast, Josh, don't give us up. My mental mantra went out into the universe, over and over.

"Look, sir, I don't know what you're talking about. I'm just an antique dealer." Josh was still trying and I blessed him for it.

"Wrong answer, fat man."

I heard the click of the safety, then felt Kathi move beside me. She stood up and yelled, "Stop this. I'll go with you. Just leave everyone else alone."

I pulled on her leg trying to get her to hide, but she looked down at me and shook her head. "I might not be a real South Cove resident, but I won't let anyone else die for me. I'll already carry Blake's death on my heart forever."

"Darling, is that you? Now come out here like a good girl so we can blow this place," Bobby called out to her.

My skin chilled. There was no way this guy was ever going to give up on Kathi. On what he believed was his property. "You don't know he's dead." I tried to reason with her.

She was already walking around the furniture to go meet the crazy man. "I know Bobby, he doesn't miss."

Before she could get much further than the first doorway, a crash sounded in the lobby.

"Drop your gun and put your hands up." Greg's voice had never sounded so good, but then I heard a shot crack through the building. When a dull thud followed, my heart sank. Now I jumped up and followed Kathi's path.

What if Greg had been shot? I was walking into a bad situation, but I couldn't just cower there anymore. I needed to know what that shot had meant. I bumped into Kathi who stood frozen at the doorway to the lobby.

Greg was kneeling over Bobby who had his hands cuffed behind him, bleeding on Josh's antique rug. Toby was on his walkie-talkie calling for an ambulance, and Josh was slumped in a chair behind the counter, shaken but alive.

I squeezed out a little *oh*, and then sank into a dining room chair that was positioned next to the door. Kathi ran to Toby. "Blake, he's been shot. He's in my shop."

At that moment, Blake walked in, and except for the bruise and cuts he'd gotten days before, looked perfectly alive. "Actually, I'm fine. Your ex-boyfriend may be a good marksman, but he's kind of stupid. We played hide and seek in that storeroom of yours forever before he gave up. I'd hoped it would give you some time to…" He didn't get the last words out before Kathi molded her body to his.

"I was so scared he'd killed you." She sobbed into his shirt.

Blake stroked her hair. "Honey, now that I've found you, no one is going to keep us apart."

Greg left Bobby and came over to me. He looked me over and asked one question: "Are you all right?" When I nodded, he pulled me into a tight squeeze. "We didn't know you two were in here. I may have waited for the hostage investigators except when he started into the back, I knew we had one chance."

"Kathi called to him. She was going to give up, to go with him to save Josh." I put my hands on his face. "I didn't know who got the shot off first."

His mouth turned up into a small grin. "Sweetheart, that's one situation where you should always bet on me."

"Is he dead?" I glanced around Greg to the man who lay in the middle of the lobby, Toby standing over him.

"I don't think so. The paramedics will be here in a minute and they can deal with the shot. I'm pretty sure I just wounded him. That's why I put on the cuffs." He patted my leg. "I've got to deal with this. Can I trust you to stay put and not get into any more trouble?"

"Of course. I'm not stupid."

This time Greg didn't just smile, he laughed.

Chapter 21

I'd been told to stay home and not worry about setting up the event, so when Sasha came on Friday to change into her evening attire and pick me up, I peppered her with questions. Finally, she held up one hand, stopping the barrage.

"You'll see everything when we get there. Just be patient." And then she took her bag upstairs to my room to shower and change.

I was already in my little blue dress with actual heels and a diamond necklace my grandmother had left me. It wasn't big, but it shined like its larger-carat brothers. Emma sat on the rug by the couch, thumping her tail. I took my coffee cup into the kitchen and dumped the contents. I'd been mainlining the stuff all day and even I felt the jitters. I took out the water pitcher and poured a glass. Emma whined at the door and I let her out. I leaned against the doorframe and stared at Toby's cottage. He hadn't stopped in when he came home from the station to change into his barista clothes. I think he didn't want me to grill him for information.

I heard the front door open and Greg call out my name.

"In the kitchen." I turned around, watching the entry.

When he walked in, he whistled. "Man, do you clean up nice." He came over, took me in his arms, and kissed me, long, slow, and proper. When we came up for air, he pushed a wayward tentacle of hair out of my eyes and said, "Do we have to go to this thing?"

"Sasha's upstairs changing in my room."

He sighed and let me go. "I guess that's my answer."

"So what happened to Bobby? No one will tell me anything." Well, I hadn't gone as far as calling Bakerstown Memorial, but I had called the station.

Greg went to the fridge and poured his own glass of water. He sat down at the table and took a sip before answering. "He made it out of surgery. So we'll see. I guess the bullet hit a lung and that's why he went down so fast. I thought I'd killed him."

"You saved Josh, Kathi, and me. If you had, no one would have blamed you." I put my hand on his.

"It's a nightmare no police officer wants. I came back to South Cove so I wouldn't have to make these decisions. When to negotiate, when to call in SWAT, when to charge in guns blazing. I'm sure the investigators would have told me I made the wrong choice, if things had gone south. Now that they turned out okay, I'm some sort of hero." He leaned against the back of the chair. "I just knew you were in that building. I could feel it."

"What, like I'm in the middle of all the trouble in South Cove?"

He just looked at me.

"Fine, whatever. So did Bobby kill Darryl? Why?" I wanted all the loose ends tied up before Greg remembered he wasn't supposed to be telling me this stuff.

"Darryl told him that he'd talked to Kathi and she didn't want to go back. I guess he had a bro moment, trying to get Bobby to move on." Greg shook his head. "Ivy said he just shot him, right in front of her. Then he turned and told her that she better be more convincing with her sister."

"Poor Ivy. So she thought if she convinced Kathi to go back with Bobby that he'd let her live?" I sipped my water. "What kind of life would that have been for either of the women?"

Greg shrugged. "I guess their father's not very with it and Bobby's been footing the bill for the nursing care he needs. Ivy felt they had no choice."

"And that's why she confessed. So Kathi would be available for Bobby's perfect life plan."

"That about covers it. I've got hours of interview tapes to go through in the next week to prepare the charges against Bobby, if he lives." Greg rubbed his face and covered a yawn.

"And yet, you're here for me and the library event. I appreciate it." I paused. "Wait, how did Bobby have Kathi's gun?"

"Ivy thinks he took it the day after Kathi left for California. He was in her room a long time." Greg looked at his watch. "Should we hurry Sasha along? I'd hate to be late for this shindig."

"I'm ready," Sasha called out behind him. She'd swept her hair back with jeweled barrettes, and wore a red slip dress that hugged her curves.

"Hot, you're just hot." Greg leaned over the edge of the chair. "Someone's in trouble with you looking like that."

A bright smile filled Sasha's face. "We can only hope so."

I let Emma in the house and we left for the event. "I know I said this before," I whispered as we followed Sasha out to my Jeep. "But I appreciate you coming tonight."

Greg laughed as he opened the doors for Sasha and me. "I'm afraid to leave you alone even at a book party. Trouble follows you. It's just a fact of life."

* * * *

"What do you mean, I'm doing the introduction?" Sasha stared at the paper in her hands. She shoved it towards Aunt Jackie. "You take this, you're better at public speaking."

Aunt Jackie gently pushed her hand away. "No, dear, this is your brainchild and you need to get used to speaking in public. I believe you'll go far once you graduate, so think of this as your first step in the spotlight."

Sensing she was losing the battle there, Sasha turned to me. "You're the shop owner. *You* do the introductions."

"You'll do fine." I took her hand and led her toward the stage. "All you have to do is thank everyone for coming, the school and library board for co-sponsoring, and if you can throw Coffee, Books, and More in there, that would be lovely."

Sasha took the stairs to the stage and stood in the wings. I blocked the exit so she couldn't turn around and run, or if she did, she'd have to go through me. Aunt Jackie and I nodded encouragement and when she walked onto the stage, the crowd politely clapped.

"You think she'll throw up or faint first?" I didn't look at Aunt Jackie as we placed our bets.

"I'll put ten on the fainting. The girl doesn't like being sick and can't even make herself throw up." I could see Aunt Jackie's grin out of the corner of my eye. "It is good for her."

"I don't think you will convince her of that." I watched as a pair of women walked up to us.

"Looks like you're on." One woman dusted the blazer of the other with her hand. "Let me look at your teeth. I don't want today's salad to be all they talk about."

"Cat Latimer?" I held out a hand. "I'm Jill Gardner. We're so happy you could come tonight."

"Well, I said I'd do anything to support a library, and I guess this is *anything*." The taller of the two smiled at me, softening the words. She held out her hand. "Cat Latimer, at your service. Actually, I hate all appearances. What happened to the days of the hermit writer? Just throw me food and water and I'd do fine in the middle of a forest."

"Then I'm doubly glad you chose to come to our event." I nodded to the now-quiet audience. "I believe they're waiting for you." The crowd had started chanting and out on the stage Sasha looked like she was frozen in place.

Her friend nudged her and Cat nodded. "What I meant to say was thank you for putting this together. I appreciate your hard work and inviting me."

I pointed to Sasha who now was making hand gestures to get the author to switch places with her. "That's the girl you should thank. She fought to invite you because she and the book club love your stories so much."

Cat nodded and strolled out to the podium. When she arrived, she gave Sasha a big hug and then still holding her arm, dragged her back to the microphone. "I understand this woman is the main reason I'm speaking tonight, so join me in thanking her for putting this all together."

Tears came to my eyes as I watched the room stand and cheer for Sasha. She'd remember this night forever.

Chapter 22

Sasha bounced into the shop Saturday morning, still grinning from ear to ear. "So I just dropped Cat off at the airport and guess what?"

I smiled at Aunt Jackie who had come down from the apartment to talk about our bookstore schedule for the next few months. We were almost through the holidays, but I was glad Sasha had arrived early so we could get her input. "Come over here and look at the planning schedule."

She bounced across the empty shop and then plopped next to me on the couch. "I will, but guess what Cat said?"

"You might as well let her talk, you know we aren't going to get anything done until she does." Aunt Jackie sat the paper calendar down on the coffee table and waved at the girl. "So go ahead, tell us what Cat, your new best friend, the author, said."

Sasha ducked her head. "She's not my new best friend." Then her head popped up. "But she's invited me to come visit during one of her writer retreats. All I have to do is get myself to Colorado and she'll foot the rest of the bill. She said I could even do a session with the group, giving them a bookseller's opinion. Me, a bookseller!"

"You have experience setting up not one but two successful book clubs, why wouldn't she want you to come speak to her groups?" I patted her leg. "You just tell me when you want to go and we'll take you off the schedule."

"We'll pay for the flight too," Aunt Jackie said.

Sasha and I both looked at her, stunned.

"It's a marketing cost. She's going as our representative, we'll handle the costs." She stood and hobbled to the coffee bar with her cup. She was healing well, but still used a cane to steady herself as her ankle healed.

"That's too much," Sasha protested, looking to me for support.

I shook my head. "Honestly, Aunt Jackie's right. We'll make up some postcards to send with you. Maybe something about 'We order hard-to-find books and ship directly to you'? That way we wouldn't only reach people who were planning on visiting South Cove."

The bell over the door chimed. Kathi Corbin walked in with her sister, Ivy, and a basket. She appraised the three of us sitting on the couch. "Sorry, did we interrupt a meeting?"

"Nope, we're just talking about our marketing schedule for the next few months. What's up?" I stood from the couch to go hug Kathi. "Glad to see you're okay."

"Thanks to you. I froze in the shop when Bobby had my gun. I always hated that thing, but Daddy insisted I take it and learn how to shoot." She looked at Ivy, "How old was I, twelve?"

Ivy shrugged. "Thirteen, but he gave me mine when I turned nine. I guess he thought you had too much on your plate with all the pageants and stuff." She smiled shyly at me. "Thank you for saving my sister. I didn't know what we were going to do, except follow Bobby's orders."

"I didn't really save either of us, I just knew enough to run. Although I didn't think he'd follow us to Josh's store. I assumed he might go looking for us here in the coffee shop but I hoped we would be able to get Greg here before he even left the tea shop." I looked over at Aunt Jackie and Sasha. We might talk a big game, but in the end, gun trumps bravado any day. "So Ivy, are you staying around now?"

She shook her head. "Nope, it's time for me to head back to Daddy. He's been with a caregiver for a couple weeks now and I'm heading home to tell her she's out of a job. It's sad when the money tree shrivels up and dies."

"You'll be okay. I'll send money as soon as I can. We have to work together now that it's just the three of us." Kathi patted her sister on the back. For the first time, I saw the affection and mutual respect the two sisters held for each other. When Ivy nodded, Kathi turned to me. "I wanted to drop this off to you." She handed me the basket. It was filled with Tea Hee's special blend and a cute teapot and set of four cups. "I'm hoping you're still willing to add the blend to your menu."

"Of course." I took the basket and set it down beside me. "I'm glad you're still opening your store. We needed fresh blood in the Business-to-Business meeting."

"Blame your boyfriend for that. He's the one who took down Bobby and made it safe for me to stay here. I was planning on starting over again but Greg says Bobby should be in jail for a long time, if not forever." She looked at her watch. "We've got to go. Ivy's got a plane to catch in a few hours and we haven't even cleaned her room out at The Castle."

"It was really nice to meet you, Ivy. I hope you come visiting again, real soon." I was able to say it with a completely straight face.

"Thanks, I love it here. I'll be back soon." Ivy waved at the other two women. "See you all later."

The two women left the coffee shop and I returned to the couch where Aunt Jackie and Sasha were sitting. Sasha dug in the basket and took out the teapot and cups. "Seems like you're getting pretty chummy with the beauty queen."

"Our new business owner, not a former beauty queen," Aunt Jackie chided. "Besides, a woman can't help being beautiful. It's a curse one has to live with one's entire life. You don't realize how tiring it can be."

I started chuckling first, then Sasha joined me.

Aunt Jackie looked at the two of us like we were nuts. "I think the stress has gotten to you both." She sniffed and picked up the laptop. A few minutes later, she grabbed the calendar. "We need to change up our December plans."

"Wait, why? I like the idea of doing a book drive for the Bakerstown Boys and Girls club. And we have to participate in whatever Darla has up her sleeve for South Cove, so that's going to keep us pretty busy." I pointed to the already colored lines we'd used to indicate when a project or a signing was occurring. "See, filled."

"We need at least one weekend for this. I guess from his email, we could host it in early January." Jackie turned the page and looked at our January schedule.

"Host what? Or who?" I looked at Sasha, who shrugged, saying she didn't know what the heck was going on either.

"Nathan Pike just emailed us and wants to do a signing while he's here writing his next book. I guess he's already talked to the mayor about getting a month of exclusive access to Greg and the police force here. He wants to make his book more realistic for the smaller town he's writing this time."

"The mystery author Nathan Pike?" He'd been our Cloaked in Mystery author over a year ago and his books were still selling well out of the store. Then her words hit me. "Wait, Greg doesn't know about this, does he?"

It was Aunt Jackie's turn to shrug. "It's not like you have to tell him. Let his boss, the mayor, break the news."

"Whoever does it, Greg's not going to be happy. The last time he did a ride-along, the guy almost shot Greg with his own gun." I thought about our upcoming trip. "Maybe Nathan will change his mind between now and January. It could happen."

Sasha giggled. "And pigs can fly."

I closed up the planning calendar and gathered my stuff to head home. Emma and I had some porch sitting to do and Greg would be over for dinner. And I wasn't going to ruin that with a possible issue over six months away.

"We'll see you tomorrow." I headed out the door and pondered the meaning of family again. My immediate family seemed to be growing day by day. I thought that might just be all right.

The family you build is much stronger than your birth family. Or at least that was my mantra for today. I might just paint it on a rock for my garden.

The sun beat on my face and the wind brought over a slight salty ocean breeze. Life was good today.

About the Author

Lynn Cahoon is the author of the *New York Times* and *USA Today* bestselling Tourist Trap cozy mystery series. *Guidebook to Murder*, book 1 of the series, won the Reader's Crown for Mystery Fiction in 2015. She's also the author of the soon to be released, Cat Latimer series, with the first book, *A Story to Kill*, releasing in mass market paperback September 2016. She lives in a small town like the ones she loves to write about with her husband and two fur babies.

Sign up for her newsletter at www.lynncahoon.com

A Story to Kill

Keep reading for a sneak peek at the first book in Lynn Cahoon's new series
Available September 2016
From Kensington Books

And be sure to keep an eye out for more books in the Tourist Trap series!

Available from Lyrical Underground

Chapter 1

When Thomas Wolfe said you can't go home again, Cat Latimer wondered if he knew he was full of crap. She stood at the turret window looking out on her backyard in Aspen Hills, Colorado. During her marriage, she'd made this circular room into her office. The wall-to-ceiling built-in bookshelves were now bare, waiting to be refilled with the rare and not-so-rare books she'd collected during her two years as an English professor over at Covington College. She brushed her fingers over the cool window glass, not quite believing she was back.

"So you're just standing around, staring out the window? You realize we'll have guests arriving in less than two weeks." Shauna walked into the room and put her arm around Cat. "You aren't thinking about Michael, are you?"

Shauna Mary Clodagh had been her best friend since the minute she met the tiny, redheaded bartender at the local pub near the apartment she'd rented in Los Angeles. It hadn't been the best job, but Cat had jumped at the first teaching position that took her away from Aspen Hills.

Into the frying pan, her mother would have said. But she didn't regret her years in California. She'd learned how to surf, or at least how not to drown. She hoped that skill would keep her above water now.

"I love this office. I always wanted to write here. Not grade papers, not work on lesson plans, just write the stories in my head."

"Now you can. But first, I need to talk to you about the breakfast menus. I've baked a few batches of different muffins and breads to try. Oh, and the handyman called back and he'll be here first thing tomorrow morning." Shauna looked out the window. "You really lucked out on this deal. Good thing Michael was too busy dating all those co-eds to remarry or change his will."

"Brutal. Good thing you're my friend." Cat picked up a notebook and a pen. "Let's go walk through the guest rooms on the second floor and make a list of what needs to be finished so the guy can get right to work."

As she shut the door to the office, she thought about Shauna's words. Why *hadn't* Michael left the house and his estate to someone in his family? She vaguely remembered him talking about a cousin somewhere in eastern Washington. She sighed. There was no use trying to figure out what Michael had been thinking, the house was hers again.

This time, *she* would make her own decisions.

* * * *

Aspen Hills' largest employer and claim to fame was Covington College. The small liberal arts school was located just a few blocks away from 700 Warm Springs, her new-slash-old home. Cat made her way to the Abigail Smith building, home of the English Department and her former employer.

Behind the front desk was a large trophy case with a lighted sealed section for the Covington English Department Cup. Each year, the professors voted on the student with the most potential to make his or her mark in their career. When Cat had been a professor, she'd taken the voting seriously, nominating several of her exceptional students. One, a budding poet, got shortlisted, but mostly, she noticed the final nominations looked like a popularity contest rather than true talent. She squinted to see who had won the cup this year and paused. Sara Laine. She pulled out the list Shauna had given her. Yep, it was the same. She had a cup winner attending her retreat.

A student sat at the reception desk, reading. She looked up as Cat stopped at the desk.

"You need help?" She put her finger on the line to mark her place and waited for Cat's response.

"I've got an appointment with Dean Vargas. Can I just go to his office?" Cat nodded down the hall. Some things never changed, especially the fact that the dean of the department always had the biggest office.

"Whatever." The girl went back to her reading. Work-study jobs on campus tended to be more 'make work' positions, so Cat didn't blame the girl for being bored out of her skull.

Knocking on the door, a muffled voice answered, "Come in, it's not locked."

She peeked around the door, making sure the man was alone. Michael wasn't the only professor with a history of enjoying time with the female students. "Dean Vargas? Do you have a minute?"

"Well, if it isn't the prodigal daughter come home. So good to see you, Catherine." Dean Vargas stood and stepped around his desk. He looked the same as he had when she'd put in her resignation letter two years ago. Hair gently graying, he stood tall and trim. She'd never been able to pin point his exact age and several times when she was teaching *The Picture of Dorian Gray*, Dean Vargas's image had come to mind. "So how are sales of that *Tales of a Teenage Vampire* book going?"

Cat thought about correcting him on the title, but knew he wouldn't remember anyway. "Very well, thank you for asking. The book is getting great reviews from the major players." She pulled out a list of next week's retreat guests from her tote and handed it to him. "I'm glad we could settle on the contract terms for the retreat customers. My first group is arriving next week. These are the five people who will need library passes."

Dean Vargas took the list and without looking at it, set it in a tray on his desk. "I'm happy we could be of assistance. I understand Professor Turner is doing a short presentation on the Hemingway papers as part of the retreat."

"He is. Hemingway is just such a large part of the American writer mystique, I'm sure all of my guests will enjoy his session." Cat looked around the office. On a side table, a pile of the university's latest literary journal set on display. "I've loved the last few editions of *The Cove*. I miss working with the journal staff."

"The new professor we hired to replace you is enjoying the task just as much as you did." He paused at the desk before returning to sit in his chair, choosing an appropriate look of concern or gravity for his facial expression. "We were shocked to hear about Michael's passing. He was a vital part of this college. The Economics Department is finding it very hard to replace him with a candidate of his stature."

Cat didn't know the etiquette regarding accepting condolences about a divorced, deceased spouse, but she decided it didn't do anyone any good to be rude or point out the obvious. "Michael will be missed by many people." She wondered if Dean Vargas had guessed her husband's extracurricular activities had been the reason behind the split, but decided to take the high road anyway. She adjusted her tote. "Anyway, lots to do. Thank you again."

Dean Vargas nodded and focused on his monitor. "You are most welcome. However, in the future, there's no need for you to bring this over in person. Just drop the list off in the mail. Good-day, Catherine."

Dismissed from his Excellency's presence, she hurried out of the building, hoping not to meet anyone else from her past. Dean Vargas had been a jerk to work for back then and he was still a jerk today. Hell, he probably was born a jerk. With that thought lifting her spirits, she strolled through the commons to the street. Walking back to the house, she soaked in the warm, autumn sunlight. Indian summer, her mother would have called the warm October day. School had been in session for a few weeks, so students were hanging around the grounds as she walked by, enjoying the summer's last hurrah of warmth.

A police car pulled up next to her. Two short blasts of the siren made her jump, and brought her back to reality. The passenger window eased down and an officer leaned across toward her. "You know there's no loitering in town. I may have to arrest you."

"I'd like to see you explain that at the family reunion next summer." She squatted down by the car, her arms resting on the open window. "How are you, Uncle Pete? I was planning on stopping by the house as soon as I got settled."

"Old and crotchety, just like always. How're the house renovations going? You going to be up and ready for that group coming in next week?" He took off his baseball cap and rubbed his head with his free hand. "If you need me, I can come over and help this weekend. I'm knee-deep in paperwork from the college opening, but I could spare a few hours."

Cat shook her head. "You don't worry about it. Shauna has found a handyman who works at a reasonable rate." She checked her watch. "In fact, he should be there right now."

Her uncle frowned. "The only handyman around these parts is—" The radio in his car blared and he paused, turning his attention to the dash.

"Chief? They need you over at campus security. Some kid brought his stash of pot. I guess he didn't realize he had to be 21." The dispatcher sounded like she was in another town, on the other side of the mountain, and in a well.

"Sounds like you're busy, I'll let you go." Cat tapped the car. "You stop in for coffee and a treat some morning. I'd love for you to meet Shauna."

Her uncle peered at her for a second before the radio blared again.

"Chief?"

He pulled out the microphone. "I heard you." Putting it back on the holder, he smiled. "I'll drop by soon. We might have something to talk about."

Chief Pete Edmond gunned the engine in his black Dodge Charger and pulled away from the curb.

Cat watched him as the car made its way up the road to the Administration Building. "The guy gets weirder every year." She loved her uncle, but sometimes—like now—he could be cryptic about the silliest things. She returned to her stroll and was walking up the stone path to her front porch when someone barreled through the front door and down the porch steps, a sheet of plywood in his large rough hands.

Jumping off the sidewalk to avoid being smashed by the wood or its carrier, she waited for the guy to slap the sheet on the saw horses set up in the middle of her front lawn. This must be the repair person Shauna hired. Something about the guy, and his short brown hair seemed familiar. In tighter than normal jeans and a faded T-shirt, at least he was easy on the eyes from the back.

"You need to watch where you're going with that," she muttered and turned toward the front door. Her day had been filled with bulldozing men, but this was the first one who actually could have run her over.

"Kitty Cat? Is that you?"

Crap. Cat stood frozen to the ground, not wanting to turn around. There was only one person who called her by that nickname. No one had dared since she beat up most of the fifth grade class and put them straight that she was not a feline. Seth Howard had just laughed when she'd wrestled him to the ground. When he'd flipped her over, trapping her instead, he'd whispered in her ear, "you'll always be Kitty Cat to me." Then he'd let her up and shrugged for the class to see.

Slowly she turned around, banishing the memory from her mind and bringing her back to the here and now. "Seth? You're the handyman?"

He laughed that easy laugh she remembered from too many weekend trips with the gang, camping, fishing, and drinking around the campfire. He had been her first and last boyfriend before she met Michael. The two men couldn't have been more different. Seth was Colorado born and raised. He could fish, hunt, and build a small shack in the woods to live off the land. Michael preferred his fish gently poached and served with a little Riesling. Or had.

"I didn't realize you were back in town." He reached out and touched her brown hair, cut short into a pixie. "You look good, I like the new 'do."

She should have melted on the spot, but there was just enough ice left in her veins to cause her to nod like one of those Hawaiian dolls Uncle Pete had on his old truck's dashboard. She licked her lips, suddenly feeling her mouth dry up like the Salt Lake Desert. She should start carrying bottled water when she walked. Yeah, that was the problem, her drinking habits. She gave in, trying not to be rude. "Thanks. You look good yourself."

"You buy this?" He nodded to the weathered blue Victorian behind her.

Cat squirmed a little. Seth hadn't approved of her dating Michael. And when they got married in the little church on campus, he'd snuck in the back, standing in front of the closed doors, his hands crossed in front of him as the vows were read. Then he disappeared. A total Benjamin Braddock moment, only Seth hadn't said a word. This was the first time she'd seen him since her wedding day. "Actually, Michael left it to me." She paused. "He died earlier this year."

Seth nodded and walked closer, putting a hand on her arm. "I'm sorry to hear that. But weren't you divorced?"

So he had kept up on the gossip about me. For some reason, this made her gut tighten, just a bit. "Three years now. Believe me, I never thought he'd keep me in the will. I hadn't even talked to him since the day the papers were signed."

He searched her face, looking for something, what, she didn't know. He lowered his voice when he responded. "I am sorry."

She wondered exactly what he was sorry about, but didn't want to ask. They'd gone their separate ways and now she was back and single. That didn't mean that he was available. For all she knew, he had a wife and six kids stashed somewhere in the woods. She dropped her gaze to his hand still on her arm. His left hand with no ring. He noticed her look and dropped his arm back to his side.

"About the house. Shauna tells me you're opening some kind of hotel?" He took a step back, increasing the distance between them.

Cat wanted to step forward, close the space back up. Hell, if she was honest with herself, she wanted to step into his arms, kiss him, and drag him up to her bedroom. But no ring didn't mean no attachments. She'd learned that early in her LA dating years. Besides, how cliché was it to fall back in bed with your high school love? She banished the thoughts of what they could be doing and turned toward the house so she wouldn't have to look into those dark brown eyes.

"Actually, I'm opening a writer's retreat. People come for a week, we feed them breakfast and a few dinners, set up time for them in the college library and a couple seminars, but mostly, they are on their own to write." She regarded him. He didn't seem bored with the conversation topic yet. "I'm an author now."

Seth nodded. "Sounds about right. You always were good with stories." He nodded to the wood. "You've got some flooring that needs replaced in most of the second floor bedrooms. I should be able to get that done today and I can paint tomorrow."

She stared at him, wondering if there was something more to his comment about "stories." "Sounds good. Let me know if you need anything."

Then she turned and ran into her house, up the three flights of stairs and into her office, shutting the door behind her. When she'd caught her breath, she stood at the end window and watched him work, willing him not to look up so she wouldn't get caught.

A knock came at the door. "Cat, you want some lunch?" Shauna rarely came into the office if the door was closed, assuming Cat was writing, unless she was dropping off coffee or food.

Which she should be doing, rather than watch the way Seth's muscles rippled in the sun, especially after he surrendered to the heat and stripped off the t-shirt to the tank underneath. "I'm not hungry right now," she called back.

Well, she was hungry, just not for the soup and sandwich Shauna had prepared.

Guidebook to Murder

In the gentle coastal town of South Cove, California, all Jill Gardner wants is to keep her store—Coffee, Books, and More—open and running. So why is she caught up in the business of murder?

When Jill's elderly friend, Miss Emily, calls in a fit of pique, she already knows the city council is trying to force Emily to sell her dilapidated old house. But Emily's gumption goes for naught when she dies unexpectedly and leaves the house to Jill—along with all of her problems…*and* her enemies. Convinced her friend was murdered, Jill is finding the list of suspects longer than the list of repairs needed on the house. But Jill is determined to uncover the culprit—especially if it gets her closer to South Cove's finest, Detective Greg King. Problem is, the killer knows she's on the case—and is determined to close the book on Jill *permanently* . . .

Mission to Murder

In the California coastal town of South Cove, history is one of its many tourist attractions—until it becomes deadly . . .

Jill Gardner, proprietor of Coffee, Books, and More, has discovered that the old stone wall on her property might be a centuries-old mission worthy of being declared a landmark. But Craig Morgan, the obnoxious owner of South Cove's most popular tourist spot, The Castle, makes it his business to contest her claim. When Morgan is found murdered at The Castle shortly after a heated argument with Jill, even her detective boyfriend has to ask her for an alibi. Jill decides she must find the real murderer to clear her name. But when the killer comes for her, she'll need to jump from historic preservation to self-preservation . . .

If the Shoe Kills

The tourist town of South Cove, California, is a lovely place to spend the holidays. But this year, shop owner Jill Gardner discovers there's no place like home for homicide . . .

As owner of Coffee, Books, and More, Jill Gardner looks forward to the hustle and bustle of holiday shoppers. But when the mayor ropes her into being liaison for a new work program, 'tis the season to be wary. Local businesses are afraid the interns will be delinquents, punks, or worse. For Jill, nothing's worse than Ted Hendricks—the jerk who runs the program. After a few run-ins, Jill's ready to kill the guy. That, however, turns out to be unnecessary when she finds Ted in his car—dead as a doornail. Detective Greg King assumes it's a suicide; Jill thinks it's murder. And if the holidays weren't stressful enough, a spoiled blonde wants to sue the city for breaking her heel. Jill has to act fast to solve this mess—before the other shoe drops . . .

Dressed to Kill

Jill Gardner is not particularly thrilled to be portraying a twenties flapper for the dinner theater murder mystery. Though it *is* for charity . . .

Of course everyone is expecting a "dead" body at the dress rehearsal… but this one isn't acting! It turns out the main suspect is the late actor's conniving girlfriend Sherry…who also happens to be the ex-wife of Jill's main squeeze. Sherry is definitely a master manipulator…but is she a killer? Jill may discover the truth only when the curtain comes up on the final act…and by then, it may be far too late.

Killer Run

Jill has somehow been talked into sponsoring a 5k race along the beautiful California coast. The race is a fundraiser for the local preservation society—but not everyone is feeling so charitable . . .

The day of the race, everyone hits the ground running. . .until a local business owner stumbles over a very stationary body. The deceased is the vicious wife of the husband-and-wife team hired to promote the event—and the husband turns to Jill for help in clearing his name. But did he do it? Jill will have to be *very* careful, because this killer is ready to put her out of the running . . .forever!

Murder On Wheels

The food truck craze has reached the charming coastal town of South Cove, California, but before Jill Gardner can sample the eats, she has to shift gears and put the brakes on a killer . . .

Now that Kacey Austin has got her new gluten-free dessert truck up and running, there's no curbing her enthusiasm—not even when someone vandalizes the vehicle and steals her recipes. But when Kacey turns up dead on the beach and Jill's best friend Sadie becomes the prime suspect, Jill needs to step on it to serve the real killer some just desserts.

Printed in the United States
by Baker & Taylor Publisher Services